Also by Natasha D. Frazier

Devotionals

The Life Your Spirit Craves

Not Without You

Not Without You Prayer Journal

The Life Your Spirit Craves for Mommies

Pursuit

Fiction

Love, Lies & Consequences

Through Thick & Thin: Love, Lies & Consequences Book 2

Shattered Vows: Love, Lies & Consequences Book 3

Out of the Shadows: Love, Lies & Consequences Book 4

Kairos: The Perfect Time for Love

Fate (The Perfect Time for Love series)

With Every Breath (The McCall Family Series, book 1)

With Every Step (The McCall Family Series, book 2)

With Every Moment (The McCall Family Series, book 3)

The Reunion (Langston Sisters, book 1)

The Wrong Seat (Langston Sisters, book 2)

The Missing Link (Langston Sisters, book 3)

Batch of Love

Non-Fiction
How Long Are You Going to Wait?

Acknowledgements

20 books?! Wow!

None of this would be possible if my Heavenly Father didn't give me the capacity and provision to do the thing that I love—write. So, thank You, Lord.

My husband, Eddie, and my children Eden, Ethan, and Emilyn—thank you for your love and support. I couldn't do any of this without you all sacrificing a moment or two with me every now and then.

Chandra—Thank you for your editing expertise. This story wouldn't be as amazing without you.

Special thank you to my sisters, Tiera, Toccara, and Shenitra, who have prayed with me, for me, and encouraged me in my journey.

Page 35—Thank you for making me better. I appreciate every ounce of feedback.

Mom and Dad—I wouldn't be here if it weren't for you. And as always, thank you for encouraging me to "go for the trophy." Courtney, Amber, Aunt Rosie, and Quita —thank you for your continued love and support.

My CBLR family—Thank you for your support, readership, and love. I appreciate each of you.

Ladies of LitJava – Thank you for your love and support. Hugs and Kisses to you.

Sherrele and The Book Readers Venue, LLC – From the moment we met, you have supported me. Thank you!

Dearest reader—Thank you for supporting me by reading, reviewing, and sharing my books with others. (Please don't stop.) I promise you're all I think about as I write every story. Laugh and swoon as you take this journey with Lisa and Jayden. Enjoy!

Natasha

LOVE BETWEEN THE PAGES

At Last series

Natasha D. Frazier

Chapter One

Lisa Atkinson stood in the parking lot of Between the Lines bookstore, crushed gravel under her feet, and breathed it all in.

New air.

New goals.

New direction in life.

She inhaled the endless possibilities and exhaled small prayers of gratitude. Excitement and nervousness racked through her as she locked her car and trekked around to the front entrance. Her mom retired and passed down the keys to the kingdom, which was outfitted as a charming purple brick building with a white wraparound porch sitting on the corner of Main Street in Katy, Texas. Between the Lines.

Her dream of owning her own bookstore was now a reality. Good-bye life as an employee. Hello, woman-in-charge.

For the past two years, she'd worked part-time at the bookstore and full-time as a human resources consultant. She would miss the flexibility of her consulting role, but nothing could outweigh the euphoria of taking over the bookstore and calling all the shots.

She jammed the key into the knob with trembling fingers. Twisting the door open, her favorite smell—paperback books—greeted her. She flicked on the light switch by the door and strolled inside, noticing an extraordinary amount of dust she hadn't observed when she'd come in last week to work her shift.

Her new first task of the day would now be dusting, shifting ahead of reviewing the bookstore's accounting records. There was something about a fresh space that made her more productive and aligned with her new beginning. Lisa stuffed her cell phone in her back pocket and tucked her purse away in the storage closet. Before she closed the door, she grabbed the Bluetooth speaker and a green microfiber duster to set her workday in motion.

Lisa trudged through the romance section—her favorite genre—to the front of the store. She set up the speaker; found her favorite radio station, which played love songs all day; connected her phone to the Bluetooth speaker; and moved to the children's section.

She took her time gliding the duster across the bookshelves. The morning would be slow anyway, given they didn't open until noon on Mondays, so there was no rush. Lisa only wanted to give herself time to get things in order—time alone with her thoughts and vision for the store. No doubt they'd need to have a grand reopening soon—something to reintroduce the store to the community, show customer appreciation, and to establish herself as the new business owner. And maybe a new coat of paint, furniture, and lighting. But baby steps. One thing at a time.

Lisa danced and sang her way through the aisles of bookshelves, often using the duster as her microphone, especially when the radio station played old nineties R&B music like Dru Hill, Mariah Carey, and Whitney Houston. Two hours later, she put the duster away and flipped the closed sign to open before she took up residence behind her desk with her laptop. Although she still had several hours until official business hours, she didn't mind a customer interruption when dealing with spreadsheets.

Only the Lord could help her when doing anything with spreadsheets, so she switched the music to contemporary gospel. Lisa would swear that her eyes would cross anytime she had to look at numbers for too long. She hoped the task wouldn't take more than an hour, maybe two. All she needed to do was review her mom's income and expenses file and ensure the bills were paid, which they should be because she often took care of paying the utility bills online. And thankfully, her family owned the building, so paying a mortgage wasn't an issue.

Whew.

Business may have been a little tougher over the past couple of years if that were the case.

"Ding-dong," a male voice called from the door.

Lisa's head shot up to see her best friend, Jayden Reynolds' six-foot two-inch frame ducking into the front door. He wore one of his tailored black suits, a crisp white button-down shirt, and a red tie. He held a pink Ginger's Goodies bag and a cup of coffee. She smiled and waved him in.

"Hey there. Why aren't you at work?"

Jayden wrapped his arms around her and squeezed where she sunk into the safety of his embrace. A waft of his made-for-him cologne teased her senses. He'd worn the same brand for the last ten years—masculine, but not overpowering. Woody but fresh. It reminded her of his strength and compassion. Yep, the scent was created for him. "Thought you could use something sweet to start your day, boss."

"You know I won't turn down anything sweet, especially from my best girl."

Lisa stepped out of Jayden's embrace and opened the bag. A note from her best friend, Ginger Evans, was tucked inside among the treats.

You are exactly what Between the Lines and the Katy community needs. I'm so proud of you and can't wait to catch up with you later.

XOXO,

Ginger

Lisa led Jayden to one of the bookstore's sitting areas. "Since you're here, you may as well enjoy one of these scones with me."

Instead of taking a seat across from her in one of the chairs as she expected, Jayden sat next to her on the two-seater sofa, what she'd grown up knowing as a love seat. One of his knees touched hers, and her heart skipped a beat, which was unusual. With their mothers being best friends and them attending the same church all their lives, she'd been next to Jayden more times than she could count. So why a simple, unintended touch affected her now was beyond her imagination.

Their gazes locked.

Jayden had this look in his eyes—an expression he'd never given her before. Something transpired between them. Was she imagining it? Her breath hitched in her chest, and she released it slow enough that she hoped it would be unnoticeable by him. Too many romance novels maybe?

"Sure. I'll take one." Jayden flipped his tie over his shoulder and took a bite of the blueberry scone.

Lisa chewed. "While I have you here, did your mom talk to you about doing the bookstore's taxes this year? Melvin resigned, and my mom hasn't contracted anyone else." Melvin had been her mom's accountant and tax preparer for the last thirty-five years. As her mom's friend, his work had been mostly pro bono. He stated that he'd done the tasks as a favor since they weren't too time consuming.

"Yeah. She did. Consider it done."

"You sure it won't be too much for you? I know they keep you busy down at that accounting firm, which is why I'm surprised you're here now."

"Being a senior manager comes with certain advantages. I don't necessarily have a set time to be at work. Not sure it matters since I'll be there about ten hours anyway. Besides, there was no way I could not come by and wish you well today."

Jayden squeezed her shoulder, and her eyes roamed to his hand. The heat increased under his touch. *Okay. This is crazy.*

"I appreciate it, especially since I'll be in here all by my lonesome this morning. Your mom will be here to help out tomorrow though, so I'm looking forward to the company."

"How about I come by with lunch or an early dinner to break up the loneliness?"

"You know I won't turn down food too fast, so you've got yourself a lunch buddy."

Jayden chuckled. "Yep. How do you think I've managed to stay on your good side all these years? I've earned at least an associate's degree in Lisa Atkinson."

Lisa nearly choked on her scone from the laughter bubbling in her throat. "I haven't issued you a diploma just yet. How do you suppose you've made it to college?"

"I've been studying you my entire life. Test me."

His near-perfect smile, thanks to three years of braces back in grade school, didn't waver. But the intensity of his eyes changed, with his eyelids narrowing, and his voice dropping an octave. Lisa detected a level of seriousness she didn't know what to do with, so she did what any good friend would do: Changed the subject.

Lisa pushed a strand of hair behind her ear and diverted her attention to the last blueberry scone inside of the pink Ginger's

Goodies bag. "Speaking of tests, how are things looking with you becoming partner?"

Jayden shook his head, and the light in his eyes dimmed. "Not really sure, but I should know more today. Lately, the reward for my hard work has been more work. We'll see if that changes once I've had my meeting with the partners later this morning."

Lisa placed the treat bag on the table and took one of Jayden's hands in hers. "They must not know the man sitting next to me. You've been working toward partner since you started at the firm. If anyone deserves this promotion, it's you. Maybe I should be the one bringing you lunch today."

Jayden was the definition of passion and dedication. Late hours. Working weekends. Picking up his coworkers' slack. Missing birthday parties and trips. Taking very little time off.

He shrugged and squeezed her hand. "I can use the time away from the office, so coming to see you is just what I need."

Lisa couldn't put her finger on it, but something about Jayden was different today. Very different. From the way he greeted her—his hug lingered a few seconds longer than usual—to the way he touched and looked at her. As his friend since they were in diapers, shouldn't she be able to discern if something was wrong? Since he'd proclaimed to have an associate's degree in her, he'd likely pick up on the fact that something beneath the surface troubled her. So why hadn't she noticed what was going on with him before now?

They finished up their pastries with promises to see each other later. Lisa put their trash away and walked Jayden to the door where he squeezed her in a bear hug before leaving. She stood in the doorway until his truck disappeared from view.

Back to her solitude and spreadsheet, Lisa reclaimed her seat in front of her laptop. Maybe the break was what she needed because the numbers no longer caused her head to spin. She pecked away, checking formulas and going through the budget. The numbers weren't bad. Sales were not quite where she wanted to see them, but they were still profitable. Barely. Lisa remained hopeful that the grand reopening could be just the push they needed to remind the community Between the Lines was there and ready to feed their book-loving souls.

Two hard taps sounded at the door, and her heart fluttered. She glanced around the store. Had Jayden left something? When no one entered, she strolled to the door. A young man dressed in a baseball cap and a blue shirt with matching shorts stood there with an envelope in his hand.

"Are you the owner, ma'am?"

Lisa stood a little taller and grinned. "Yes, I am. What can I do for you?"

"Please sign here." He handed her a pen and tapped the sheet on his clipboard. After she signed, he handed her the envelope. "Have a good day."

"You, too."

Lisa eased back inside the bookstore, ripped open the envelope, and removed the contents. A smaller envelope with a message stamped in red ink. *Past-due taxes. 60 days until foreclosure proceedings.*

∞

Jayden Reynolds cruised along Katy Freeway. The stop to see his close friend, Lisa Atkinson, proved to be successful on two fronts—lighter traffic making the drive downtown easier and less stressful and the opportunity to see her beautiful face. That woman had his heart singing long before he'd even understood what was happening, yet he concealed his feelings, deciding early on that having her as a friend was better than not having her in his life at all. And for many years, he didn't have much of a choice anyway. With their mothers being best friends, he spent time with her several days a week every week. When they were young, their families vacationed together. They went to the same college—she majored in liberal arts while he studied accounting. Though he was passionate about reading and writing, accounting was the logical and practical choice—a surefire way to make money.

And he did.

Plenty of it.

He navigated his truck into the parking garage, grabbed his leather portfolio case, and climbed out. Jayden strolled into the offices of Dallas & Smith, LLP, one of the largest accounting firms in the Houston Metro Area, housed in a sixty-two-floor building. He smiled and greeted some of the same familiar faces he'd seen over the past seventeen years. The turnover rate at their firm—well, most public accounting firms—was high with the average accountant leaving after four years. Enough time to advance to a senior associate and garner what employers in the private sector would call a well-rounded experience.

But that wasn't Jayden's story.

He pushed the call button and waited for the elevator.

"Jayden, morning. How's it going?" Joe Beecham, one of Dallas & Smith's senior partners and Jayden's friend and mentor, called to him.

"I'm good. How's the wife and Junior?"

The elevator arrived, and they stepped on. Jayden hit the button for the forty-fifth floor.

"Pam and Junior are good. He keeps her busy with all the activities he's plugged in. I find it hard to keep up with most days, but she has it under control." He waited a beat before adding, "Oh, and good work landing the new account with Limestone. Your name is buzzing around the office."

Joe winked, and Jayden assumed that meant his fate was sealed when it came to becoming partner. As hard as he worked for the opportunity, there should be a part of him that wanted to shout, but instead, the air in the elevator grew thick, and he had to inhale deeper to breathe properly.

"You alright, man?"

Jayden coughed and nodded. "Yeah, I'm good. Just need a little water."

When the elevator doors retracted, Jayden stepped off first. He normally stopped by the breakroom to grab a cup of coffee before making it to his desk to set up his laptop, but today he didn't make the pit stop. Jayden strode through the narrow halls where the walls were painted light blue. He greeted tax associates and managers who sat in open cubicles on his way to his corner office. The floor-to-ceiling glass offices were reserved for senior managers and partners. When he entered his, he plopped in his leather chair, loosened his tie, and palmed his face. Thankfully, no cubicles were positioned directly in front of his office, so even with the glass panels, he had a little privacy.

Get your head in the game, Jayden.

Jayden started his laptop. Checked emails. His phone vibrated, and he whipped it out of his pocket to check the message. An email regarding his manuscript submission—one he'd long forgotten. During the pandemic, he'd used the extra time to write his first book—something he'd promised himself he would do one day. Edited and polished, he'd spent a couple of years shopping it around—for kicks is what he told himself. Just to see what would happen. Nothing too serious because he had his accounting career— a career he busted his butt at since he earned his Certified Public Accountant's license. And good thing he wasn't too serious because he'd received more rejections than he ever had in his entire life. This email was probably another one, so he didn't bother opening it. He'd already self-published the book under a pseudonym two months ago.

For the next ten hours, he'd focus on today's tasks, the thought of which didn't sound thrilling. A stretch from how he felt about work in the not-so-distant past.

Was he spiraling out of control? At forty years old, was he having an early midlife crisis?

Nothing felt *right*.

Except for the few minutes he'd spent with Lisa that morning.

Jayden bowed his head and whispered a prayer. He didn't understand where all of these strange feelings were coming from, but he didn't need the distractions today. Not when he had his meeting slash interview with the partners in the next hour. And that was only a formality. Their minds were already made up, so he doubted there was anything that could be done or said to change them.

He needed that cup of coffee after all. Jayden pushed out of his seat and made his trip to the break room. As the hot liquid flowed into his mug, thoughts of the last seventeen years flooded his mind. He'd stood in this same spot over the years. His career advanced quickly. Jayden was what they would consider on the fast track, advancing from level to level within two to three years. At one point, he loved the challenge, thrived off it, and from time to time, even bragged about how late he stayed in the office to finish a project.

But he wasn't that person anymore, and he couldn't be sure when all of that changed.

Was it fear of the unknown regarding life at the partner level?

The coffee brewer shut off. Jayden added his customary French vanilla creamer and half packet of sugar. Matthew, a senior partner, walked past the breakroom and waved hello, and Jayden's thoughts exploded like an egg heated in the microwave too long. Matthew was twice divorced. Joe seemed to have a loving family, but even he acknowledged that he was hardly there for them. The other partners in his function—federal tax—were all divorced or into their second or third marriages. Jayden's relationships hadn't lasted long enough for him to even consider holy matrimony, but he knew for sure he didn't want his marriage—whenever that happened—to mirror what he'd witnessed in the firm.

"Jayden," Matthew called to him, walking into the breakroom to make his own cup of coffee. Jayden referred to him as the Polo partner. It seemed that was the only type of shirt the man owned. Even when he wore a suit, instead of a crisp button-down shirt, Matthew sported a Polo. No one ever questioned him about it either, so perhaps that came along with being the boss. "Ready for the big meeting?"

"As ready as I'll ever be."

"Good to know." Matthew gave him two slaps on the back. "Looking forward to having you join us."

Jayden's belly seized in a knot. Was today *the day*? "Been a long time coming."

Matthew removed his coffee mug from the brewer stand, blew over the top, took a sip, then offered a wide smile. "And much deserved."

Jayden nodded and lifted his mug in salute. "Thanks, Matthew."

Matthew's unofficial word about his entrance into the partnership should have brought on a level of excitement with him finally reaching this pinnacle in his career, but all he sensed was a level of dread—dread that came knocking on his door at one of the worst moments of his career.

Chapter Two

Like a piece of chewed gum attached to the bottom of her shoe, Lisa had been stuck in her seat for the last hour staring at the letter from the Fort Bend County Tax Assessor's office. She'd read and re-read, then read it again. How could this be happening? What she should have done was call her parents; Melvin Mason, their previous accountant who handled such matters; or Jayden. He'd know how to handle the situation. Or even her best friend Ginger who owned a bakery business.

But confusion stilled her.

Anxiety trapped the air in her chest.

And fear paralyzed her limbs.

Sixty days?

Nearly twenty thousand dollars for three years of past-due taxes, penalties, and interest?

"Just breathe, Lisa."

Coaching herself out of paralysis, she then prayed. *Lord, I haven't even been running the store for an entire day by myself. You know I wasn't expecting this, but I'm going to trust You to help me fix this, in Jesus' name. Amen.*

Now she needed a plan. She could assert that this wasn't her problem as the new owner and to do so would be to put stress on her mother. That was not something Lisa would want to put her mom through. Besides, the business owed the taxes.

Her business.

Her problem.

A problem that she could handle.

Lisa took several more calming, meditative breaths and read the letter again. After, she scrubbed through past bank statements for proof of payments to the tax office. There was no way Melvin would allow a bill as important as property taxes to go unpaid and not say anything to her Mom about it. And if memory served her correctly, she'd written a check for the last property tax bill. Didn't she? Talking to her mom might clear this up quickly, but Lisa didn't want to say anything until she couldn't find receipts or cashed checks.

None of this made sense.

The door chimed, and Lisa whipped her head up from the computer. She couldn't take another surprise today—unless it was Jayden. His presence often calmed her, and he always knew what to say to make things better.

Instead, Wanda Reynolds, Jayden's mother, sashayed into the building. She'd known her for as long as she had memories and had always referred to her as an aunt. A retired school librarian, she spent her time helping out at Between the Lines, mostly to spend time with Lisa's mom, Barbara, her best friend. It surprised Lisa that

Aunt Wanda agreed to stick around after her mom handed the store over to her.

Should she mention the tax situation? Nope. That'd be like talking to her mom about it, which she wasn't ready to do.

A multicolored print headband was wrapped around her hair to tame her curls. It also matched the maxi skirt she wore. Her wide smile—one that reminded Lisa of Jayden's—adorned her face. She advanced toward Lisa squealing with outstretched hands like it had been years since they'd last laid eyes on each other, instead of yesterday morning at church. Standing and rounding the counter, Lisa sunk into the comfort of Aunt Wanda's arms, like a child to her mother. Lisa refused to sulk though. Because she'd been around Aunt Wanda most of her life, Aunt Wanda could smell when something was off.

Lisa stepped out of her embrace and returned to her seat. "Aunt Wanda, I wasn't expecting you until tomorrow, like we agreed." Lisa had always affectionately referred to her as an aunt. She was the closest person her mom had to a sister.

Aunt Wanda waved her off, sashayed behind the counter, and sat on the stool next to Lisa. "You know me better than that. Besides, there's only so much to do inside that house. I had to fight the urge to beat you here this morning."

They shared a laugh.

"Well, I'm glad you're here. Although I enjoy the quiet, it's nice to have another body around here."

Aunt Wanda cocked her head to the side. "And why do you think I'm here? I've seen enough of my house. Done all the redecorating and rearranging I could do. I'm over it. What've you done around here so far, and what can I help with? Put me to work, dear."

Lisa was tickled, but knew Aunt Wanda was as serious as that letter from the tax assessor's office. "I've done a little dusting, saw Jayden, and now I'm going through the books and budget. Nothing much else. Want to build a display for the new releases?"

Already back on her feet and waving her hands in true dramatic Wanda fashion, she said, "Got it."

I hope I have that kind of energy when I'm in my mid-sixties.

Aunt Wanda half-strolled, half-danced to the storage room and rumbled through it for several minutes. She returned wheeling a box of books and stands and décor used to highlight new releases and stopped beside the empty table at the front of the store.

Lisa probably should focus on the tax issue, but she needed to clear her mind and turn her attention to something that made her happy: books. The entire reason she'd chosen this work in the first place. She'd return to being the boss in a few hours. Powering on her Bluetooth speaker and finding a smooth jazz station on her phone's music app, Lisa adjusted the volume low enough to where they could hear the music and still have a conversation.

Aunt Wanda squealed again and waved a copy of a book in the air. "A new romance I can't wait to read."

"And you know what that means?"

They said in unison, "Book club."

Book club for Lisa started when she attended college. It was one of the ways she and her mom used to stay connected. They'd choose a book for the month and discuss it. When Aunt Wanda found out, there was no way she would not be part of their monthly discussions. Then, Lisa invited Ginger, and ever since then, it had been the four of them.

"Mind if I help?"

"Now you know I don't."

Lisa almost forgot that Aunt Wanda was as much of a chatterbox as she was and would use the opportunity to snoop. "So, you say you saw Jayden this morning, huh? He stopped by?"

Lisa shrugged, and in the most nonchalant voice she could muster, said, "Yes, ma'am. He did. Just to wish me well since it's my first day running the bookstore."

"*Ummm-hmmm.* My son has always been thoughtful, especially when it comes to you."

Lisa knelt and rummaged through the display supply box. "Probably second nature since we've known each other forever."

"That's how you see it?"

"And so does he. We're just friends, Auntie Wanda."

Aunt Wanda waved toward heaven and then jammed her fists into her hips. "Y'all are forty years old and still telling yourselves that lie. Why do you reckon the two of you haven't gotten married to other people?"

Lisa frowned. "Because we haven't met the right people yet."

Aunt Wanda twisted her lips, followed by a slow headshake as if to say, *Y'all don't have the sense the Good Lord gave you.* And Lisa knew that's what she meant because she'd seen that look and heard her say it one thousand and one times. One thousand and two counting today.

"Have a little faith, auntie. Jayden will get you those grandbabies you've been praying for."

Aunt Wanda mumbled something that sounded a lot like, "Yeah, as soon as y'all get your acts together," but Lisa didn't address it, only chuckled. She was used to Aunt Wanda's behavior by now. It seemed about every six months, she would try her hand at pairing Lisa and Jayden together. They both found it entertaining but hadn't considered dating each other. Well, that wasn't entirely true. Lisa had considered it a time or two but had never mentioned it to him. Something about it felt awkward. Besides, they were comfortable with each other. No need to complicate their relationship. She loved him, and he loved her.

As friends.

"I'm glad you and Jayden find it funny to toy with an old lady's heart."

"You can't take it personal. He and I are just friends, and we always will be. I don't think I can imagine my life without him in it. He's always been there. I'm not sure if there's more I can ask for."

Aunt Wanda threw both palms in the air, flipped them back and forth, then broke out into the hook of Beyoncé's song, "Single Ladies (Put a Ring on It)." She swayed her hips and moved her shoulders to the rhythm.

Lisa doubled over in laughter. Tears sprang to her eyes. Aside from the fact that Aunt Wanda was moving just as well as the entertainer herself, the dance caught her off guard. Why did she leave her phone on the counter? This would have been the perfect moment to record her shenanigans.

Lisa regained her composure and played along. "You don't think it's weird for me to ask my best friend to put a ring on it?"

"Honey, I am sixty-five years old, which means that I've seen a lot in my day, including how you two act around each other and how you look at each other. I know love when I see it." She shoved a hand into her hip as if to solidify her point.

Still kneeling next to the box, Lisa looked up at her. "Of course I love him. He's my best friend, aside from Ginger."

"Don't go bringing Ginger into this. She's come to her senses."

"Maybe you should have this conversation with Jayden and see what he thinks about you trying to hook us up."

"How do you know I haven't? Maybe he's waiting for you to be sure of him."

Lisa's breath caught, and her gaze stilled on her.

Is that true?

"You've just proven my point. The color nearly drained from your face. And if I put my hand over your chest right now, I'd bet your heart is beating two hundred times a minute."

Lisa subconsciously grabbed her chest. Yep. She was right.

"Auntie, I think we need to ban you from reading romance novels for a while. They're messing with your head."

Aunt Wanda shrugged and gave a knowing smile as if to say she'd proven her point. She hummed along with the jazz music and moved book stands and posters in place to start her display.

Doggone it. She got Lisa again. Fell into her trap.

But what Aunt Wanda desired for her and Jayden appeared way off base. And now she'd planted the seed in Lisa's head. Not that Aunt Wanda hadn't done it before, but this time, the ground was more fertile because of the strange emotions she'd experienced when he'd come to visit earlier. Could her best friend be the love she'd been waiting for?

Nah. That would be too weird.

∞

Jayden stood and smoothed his hand along his red power tie. He sucked in enough air to make his chest rise, then released it in a slow, methodical manner. Even though he had been invited to a meeting he suspected was about his partnership, he still grabbed his electronic tablet to take notes. Jayden never attended any meetings without it. Taking notes was one of the things that made him good at his job. Deadlines, meetings, questions, follow-up tasks, and everything else were all kept on his handy little personal tablet.

He strolled out of his office to the designated conference room where only the partners had their meetings. According to his conversation with Joe earlier, his title would soon change from senior manager to partner. Two years ago, he likely would have shut the door to his office and punched the air in excitement upon hearing the news, but not today. Maybe it was time for a new challenge. He couldn't be certain.

Jayden was known for showing up early to meetings. Usually the first person. But today, he was last. When he crossed the threshold into the conference room, he was surprised the flooring transitioned from carpet to wood. Whereas other conference rooms were much like a fishbowl with floor-to- ceiling glass, this one had more privacy because of frosted glass.

All six partners were seated around the oversized mahogany table, outfitted with chocolate leather chairs. Each one greeted him when he walked in, wide congratulatory smiles on their faces—at least he took them to be congratulatory.

Mitch Bordeaux, one of the senior partners, pulled the leather seat out to his right. He'd been around the longest. Nearly forty years. The lines under his eyes and deep wrinkles in his forehead were evidence of his weariness, yet his smile communicated that he enjoyed the work. "Come on in, close the door behind you, and have a seat."

Jayden accepted the leather chair—the chair he'd prepared for his entire career. He'd dreamed of sitting at this table for the past seventeen years.

Worked hard for it.

Put in late hours for it.

Sweated for it.

The partners' table—an elite place for those who survived, strived, and desired to be there above all else. And now that he was finally here, it didn't have the same grandeur or bring about the fulfillment he thought he'd experience. A silver platter with several shot glasses and a bottle of whiskey sat in the middle of the table. Nothing he'd drink though. He'd never been one to consume strong alcohol.

Mitch opened the meeting. "We've invited you to this meeting to discuss your potential partnership with Dallas & Smith. I know this has been an ongoing discussion between you and your mentor, Joe. However, this is not a decision we take lightly, and neither should you. As you know, becoming a partner means you become part owner, and with that comes great responsibility."

Jayden nodded his understanding. These were all things he knew and considered, but he found himself wondering why hadn't he ever thought about starting his own firm. And even more importantly, why was he having these types of thoughts now? He'd made it, hadn't he?

Mitch gestured to the partners on the opposite side of the table. "We're confident in your ability to lead and help grow the firm, Jayden. You're technically competent, take ownership of your projects, treat our clients well, ensure they're satisfied with the outcome of your contractual obligations, and mentor our new associates. Moreso, you've recently proven yourself even more when you brought in a new client account, Limestone."

The other partners erupted in applause.

"That's exactly the kind of person we need to join us in taking the firm to greater heights." Mitch pushed a stack of official documents in front of him. The top sheet read, *Welcome to the Dallas & Smith, LLP Partnership.*

Jayden skimmed the first page. The partnership buy-in of three hundred thousand dollars didn't bother him. He'd known about it for years. The firm offered several options to cover the buy-in: write a check, take out a loan, or finance through the firm's real estate holdings. But his knowledge didn't negate the unsettling in the pit of his stomach.

"Thanks, Mitch, and thanks to all of you for your confidence in my abilities to represent the partnership well."

Sitting across from him, Joe piped in, wearing the smile of a proud father. As his mentor, Jayden didn't expect anything less. "We've had our eyes on you for a while. Our clients love you, and your work speaks for itself."

"Thanks, Joe."

Nods and mutters of concurrence rang out from the other five partners.

Joe tapped the table. "Just to hit a few highlights in the partnership agreement, you'll continue to be a part of the federal tax practice area, advise our clients, develop and manage client relationships, and identify new business opportunities, contributing to the growth and development of the firm."

Mitch added, "This also includes making sure financial targets are met and that you ensure you have the right team in place to take care of your clients' needs."

Jayden nodded and commented here and there, but there wasn't much for him to add, and all he could think about was sharing the news with Lisa, especially after their brief talk this morning about how the partners had been taking their time giving him the opportunity.

Mitch removed the glasses from the silver platter and poured roughly two fingers of whiskey in each one, handing a glass to each partner. "Shall we toast?"

They each accepted a glass with a level of eagerness that Jayden didn't understand, especially an hour and a half before noon. He accepted his glass with hesitation because after all this time, he couldn't be sure if this partnership was the right path for him. And he couldn't pinpoint why he felt that way. Could it be that it felt so final, like he was pigeonholing himself?

He had sixty days to accept the offer, and that was sixty days to figure out what was going on with him.

For now, he shook off the uncertainty and raised his glass.

"May you work hard and enjoy the fruits of your labor," Mitch said.

"And once you see the size of your check, the long hours won't matter anymore," another partner added, and everyone chuckled, though Jayden knew there could be times when his checks were smaller, based on profits and performance.

"We toast to a lifelong partnership filled with an open road of opportunity for you, young man," his mentor Joe added.

Jayden lifted his glass. "Cheers." That instance became his first exception to his no-drinking-hard-liquor rule. When the burning sensation went down his throat, chasing itself to his chest, he remembered why he had the rule in the first place. The stuff was gross.

A few minutes of small talk followed. Afterward, each partner filed out of the conference room, with Jayden and Joe being the last two exiting.

Joe patted him on the back. "Well done, Jayden. Well done. How about you come over for dinner Friday night? I'll need to confirm with the wife first, but I'm sure it'll be fine. You can bring a guest if you'd like. We'll be celebrating in your honor."

"Thanks. I appreciate that. We'll be there."

And by *we,* he meant Lisa. She'd always been his plus one. Firm Christmas parties. Family events. Whatever the occasion, if employees were allowed to bring guests, she was the one. It was now lunchtime, so as promised, he left to pick up lunch and to go share the news with her. Maybe she could help him make sense of what was going on in his heart.

Chapter Three

Lisa and Aunt Wanda wrapped up two displays—one for Rhonda Mcknight's new release and the other for Michelle Stimpson. Between setting up books and posters, chatting about everything, including Lisa's relationship status, and swaying to jazz and R-and-B music here and there, Lisa was unsure of how much time passed. Not even once did her mind wander back to the property tax problem that weighed on her like an anchor. Judging from the rumble in her stomach, she'd guess it was near lunchtime. And speaking of lunch, she and Jayden had plans—plans that now made her a little leery because of Aunt Wanda's earlier assessment. They must have eaten lunch together over a thousand times during their lifetime, so today shouldn't be any different. Except Aunt Wanda now had her second-guessing herself with what-ifs shuffling through her mind like a dealer mixing a deck of cards.

What if Jayden did have feelings for her and she had somehow missed all the signs?

What if she had deeper feelings for him that she hadn't recognized?

What if he was actually the man of her dreams, as they'd put it in the romance novels she often read?

Don't be silly.

She and Jayden laughed at the idea of the two of them being a couple whenever his or her mom brought it up.

Lisa shrugged off uncertainty and slid her cell phone from her back pocket. He was number three in her favorites, right after her mom and dad. She called, and he answered on the first ring. Aunt Wanda was out of earshot in the mystery and suspense section, ensuring the books were shelved correctly. Good. She could talk to Jayden without Aunt Wanda ear hustling to prove her invalid point.

"Hey. Are we still having lunch today? If you're tied up, I can go grab something now because I'm starving," she rambled without giving him a moment to greet her or respond to her question.

Jayden released a light chuckle. And for some odd reason, her heart performed a flip.

A tiny flip.

Hearts shouldn't flip for friends.

It'd never done that before. *Okay. No more allowing Aunt Wanda to fill my head with her agenda.* "Well, hey to you and your stomach. I'm pulling into the parking lot right now."

"Oh, good. I hope you brought enough because your mom is here with me."

"Really? I didn't think she'd be coming out until tomorrow. I can give her my food and just grab something on the way back to the office. I'll be inside shortly."

"Okay. Bye for now."

Lisa slid the phone into her back pocket.

A few short minutes later, Jayden entered the store, the door chime announced his presence, which also summoned Aunt Wanda back to the front where she'd left Lisa.

His smile looked different than it did that morning—even brighter. However, his eyes didn't match. The chestnut orbs honed in on her, and she could see the hesitancy. Something was bothering him. Though she'd pinned that this morning, she didn't know what it could be. He held up the Treebeards bag as he walked to her. "What'd I say this morning about my degree? I'm right on time, too."

She chuckled and relieved him of the bags. "Whatever."

He hugged and kissed his mom. "I didn't know you'd be here. I would have brought you something, too, but you can have mine. I'll eat on my way back to the office."

Aunt Wanda looked between the two of them and fanned her hand. "Don't worry about me. I'm meeting Barbara Ann for lunch. Besides, I wouldn't dare impose on what you two have going on here." She winked at Lisa.

Jayden hiked an eyebrow and looked from Lisa to his mom, obviously wondering what he'd missed. Lisa shot him a glance and shook her head. That shake meant, *Leave it alone.*

Lisa strolled over to the table where her laptop sat idle. She closed the lid and slid it to the side, placed the bag on the table, and removed the Styrofoam containers. "I didn't know Mom was getting out today. Where're y'all goin'?"

Jayden and his mom followed her, with him taking the seat across from her. Aunt Wanda stood, acted as if she was peering at the food, but whispered in Lisa's ear, "Watch his face."

Aunt Wanda stood tall again, and Lisa's eyes trailed her movement. She nodded in Jayden's direction, a sly smirk etched at the corners of her lips.

Oh, boy.

"We haven't decided yet. Somewhere quiet where we can talk. You know how we do. We're narrowing down a list of eligible bachelors from the church on your behalf. She wants grandchildren, too."

And that's when Lisa saw it. The crinkling of his forehead, the twitch of his eyes, and the flare of his nostrils—all subtle and quick. She would have missed it if Aunt Wanda hadn't told her to watch his facial expression. And she almost wished she hadn't seen it because now she didn't know what to do with herself.

Lisa pretended she didn't notice Jayden's discomfort with what his mom was proposing. And Lisa knew her mom would not actively interfere in her love life. Now, Aunt Wanda would, like she was doing right now, but not her own mother.

"My mom knows she'll get her grandkids in due time. You will, too, Aunt Wanda. You can't rush the process. Jayden is on a mission with his career. He'll settle down soon, marry, and get you those grandbabies. I'm sure of it. He's cream of the crop. It won't take him much time when he's ready." She winked at Jayden. "I've got your back, dude."

"Thank you for understanding, Lisa," he said, but stared at his mother.

They exchanged knowing looks, silently sharing a conversation about his relationship status, which they'd had on many occasions, both verbally and nonverbally.

"Yeah. Lisa's been understanding for almost forty years," she said, tapping Lisa's shoulder. Aunt Wanda's comment hung in the air, thick as the gravy on the mashed potatoes Jayden brought her. She sashayed to the storage closet to grab her purse. On the way back through the store, she waved and winked on her way out the door.

Aunt Wanda's words shouldn't bother her, but they did. She'd done this sort of thing on hundreds of occasions, but today was different. Normally when she got the urge to play matchmaker, she'd say her piece and move on, but she hammered the idea so much today that Lisa almost believed it—almost believed that she and Jayden were meant to be together, or at least should try.

Mortified.

Embarrassed.

Shocked.

All feelings coursing through her right now. With the air trapped in her lungs, she wondered why she couldn't let Aunt Wanda's words go. They weren't true. She hadn't been waiting around for Jayden to fulfill his career goals and definitely hadn't been smitten with him all her life and waiting for him to ask her out.

"Has she been like this all morning?" Jayden asked, snapping her out of her self-centered thoughts. His eyes were unreadable, and he seemed unbothered with what she'd just said, so they were good.

Lisa stirred her mashed potatoes and chopped her Salisbury steak into tiny pieces. "In rare form. Your mom is on a mission to get what she wants."

"I don't know if there's a time when she isn't." He reached across the table, palms up. "Let's bless the food."

Lisa slid her hands into his and bowed her head. Before this second, she hadn't noticed how—dare she say it, perfect—their hands fit together. On contact, he offered a gentle squeeze and opened the prayer, but she couldn't focus on what he said. No, her thoughts traveled to what she may have already eaten that had her experiencing these strange feelings. Was it the coffee he brought her that morning? Did Ginger put something in her scone? Both silly notions. This was Aunt Wanda's doing—her sideways plan to make Lisa consider Jayden as something more. She wouldn't fall for it.

Jayden finished the prayer. "Amen."

Forgive me, Lord, and please bless my food. "Amen."

Lisa lifted her head and met Jayden's curious gaze. Seconds ticked by before she realized her hands were still securely tucked in his. They'd sat like this before, too, but this time was different, and she didn't know why. She'd be lying if she said it didn't scare her—

not the hands, but the look in his eyes and how the corner of his lip lifted. Had what his mom said gotten to him too?

Inch by inch, she pulled away, picked up her fork, and poked around at the cut-up pieces of meat in front of her. "Things must be slow around the office this morning. I didn't think you'd make it back for lunch. I'm glad you did, though." She scooped a helping of mashed potatoes, gravy, and Salisbury steak onto her fork and took her first bite.

Jayden hadn't touched his food. In fact, his fingers were linked in front of him. "Actually, I couldn't wait to get back to you."

With her fork raised halfway to her mouth, she paused, waiting for the rest of the sentence. Her heart pattered like the sound of someone flipping pages in a book. He had to be messing with her because of everything his mom just said, right? Or maybe he wasn't, and she was interpreting it all wrong. They were friends. Nothing wrong with friends being excited about seeing each other.

Lisa put her fork down. "Is that so?"

∞

He hadn't intended to cliff his sentence, but it was true. Even though he'd only admit it to himself, he missed her. Stopping by to see her before going into the office that morning had been the best part of his day. And that said plenty considering he'd been offered partnership in the firm. But he couldn't cross that line with Lisa and make things awkward. They were friends and had been that way forever. Changing the dynamics of their relationship didn't make sense.

But it was her rich hazel eyes that caught him off guard just now. She'd looked at him with expectancy, warmth, compassion, and a hint of something else he couldn't name, and he lost his words. He could gaze into them forever. And as friends, he could guarantee that forever. Anything more would complicate their relationship and put them at risk of losing each other if things didn't work out.

Jayden cleared his throat. "Yeah, today's your day, remember?"

"Oh."

He detected disappointment in her voice, like she was waiting for him to say something more. "And I also have a bit of news myself. You're the first person I wanted to share it with."

Lisa's eyes illuminated. Her face was animated. "They're making you partner?"

He took his phone out of the inside pocket of his suit jacket and tapped across the screen until he pulled up page one of the offer document, an image he'd snapped so he could show her. Jayden handed her his phone.

She skimmed it and squealed. "I'm so happy for you." Out of her seat in seconds with her arms wrapped around his neck, Lisa squeezed him and kissed his cheek. "I'm so proud of you, Jayden. We've gotta celebrate. Whatever you want to do, name it, and I'm down for it."

He hiked a brow. "Whatever?"

Lisa released him and reclaimed her seat. "Yeah. You have a one-time pass, so use it wisely. I'll even go with you to the golf range, and you know I don't like that."

"Give me some time to think about it. You remember my mentor Joe and his wife, right? They're having a celebratory dinner for me at their place Friday evening. Mind joining me?"

"Are you kidding me? I want parts of every celebration happening for you, so of course I'll be there."

"But this doesn't count as the 'whatever I want to do' deal, does it?"

Lisa laughed. "No, silly. This dinner is hosted by Joe and his wife. I," she said, pressing a finger into her chest, "want to do my own celebration for you."

Jayden picked up his spoon to taste his chicken and sausage gumbo. "Just checking."

"Why do I get the feeling I'm more excited about this than you are?"

"What do you mean?" He knew what she meant. She sensed his uncertainty, probably recognized it in his face.

"I just thought you'd be happier. And the fact that you have to think about how you want to celebrate concerns me. As far as I know, getting to the partnership level has been what you've wanted since you started at the firm right out of grad school, so the Jayden I know would've prepared for this moment, right down to how you'd want to celebrate the occasion."

"I'm happy. Maybe still in shock a little." He shrugged and thought for several seconds. "I half expected them to move the goal post and require me to fulfill some other requirement before they made the offer."

Lisa closed the container of her half-eaten Salisbury steak and potatoes and pushed it aside. She steepled her hands under her chin and contorted her lips, the look she wore when she was about to dig deep for some unspoken truth. With a major in English and a minor in psychology, she'd appointed herself as his counselor and safe space over the years.

Here it comes.

She gave a slow nod, measuring her thoughts and words. "Okay, that's fair, and I understand your concerns, but it's me you're talking to. What else is bothering you?"

Jayden closed his own Styrofoam container and pushed it aside. "That's the problem. I don't know, and I wish I could pinpoint it, but I can't."

"You need an outlet—a little time to do something different to clear your head. Ginger and Brock's wedding will be here soon. Maybe the trip to Jamaica is exactly what you need."

Something different? Maybe focusing on his writing for a while could be helpful. He'd never been more at peace than when he spent those hours hovering over the keyboard crafting that story. Yet, that was the one secret he'd kept from Lisa.

"You might be on to something. I'll think about it."

She crooked her head and studied him. "Is there any part of you that wants to walk away from this opportunity?"

He pinched his thumb and forefinger together. "A part so small that it isn't worth mentioning. And the fact that it even crosses my mind is insane because I've officially been on the partnership track for the last five years. I guess I feel trapped in a sense," he said, moreso thinking out loud than responding to Lisa.

"Trapped?" she echoed, scrunching her eyebrows. "How so?"

Lisa was the only person he could be vulnerable with—share his truest thoughts and feelings—but right now, he felt too naked. Too raw. And he wasn't sure he wanted to share his truth with her today because it brought about too many emotions—and emotions weren't what he was good at. Lisa being Lisa, got up, held out her hand, and he accepted. She led him to the reading sofa and sat facing him with one foot curled under her.

She cupped one of his hands in both of hers. Her voice was gentle and nonjudgmental. "Why do you feel trapped all of a sudden?"

Jayden released a heavy sigh. At the risk of sounding like he was going through an early midlife crisis, he said, "It's just that when I look at the personal lives of the other six partners, I don't want my life to look like that. Part of me believes that if I go down this road, I'm headed for the same fate. You'd think I'd have thought about all of this before now. Crazy, right?"

She smiled and shook her head. "No, it's not. You know what you want, and recognizing the problem before it even becomes a problem is a good thing. I believe you'll do whatever it takes to keep your future marriage and family together."

Jayden pulled her into a one-armed embrace, buried his face into her fruit-scented hair, and kissed the top of her head. The softness of her. The way she fit into the crook of his arm. Familiar yet perfect. "That's why I love you, woman. What would I do without you?"

"Not sure, but you'd definitely be lost somewhere."

They shared a laugh, and he released her.

"You have no idea."

Funny but fact. Her support over the years is what sustained him. What he wanted, truly desired, was her. All of her.

But how could he tell her that and keep their friendship intact?

Chapter Four

Lisa needed the perfect outfit for her evening out with Jayden to celebrate his partnership promotion. She posed before her floor-length mirror holding a sleeveless black dress with a ruffled neckline against her curvy frame. It was her special black dress, one she wore to every event that required her to dress up. The hem hit right above her kneecaps. Not form fitting or even what she'd consider date material, not that she went on many of those, but it seemed to fit every semi-formal occasion. In the other hand, she held a sleeveless black belted jumpsuit with a V-neck. She was leaning more toward wearing the jumpsuit because it could be dressed up or down, depending on her shoes, jewelry, and hairstyle.

Her doorbell rang, and she glanced at the clock on her nightstand. Jayden shouldn't be here for another hour, and she wasn't expecting any visitors. Lisa tossed the clothes on the bed and strutted through her three-bedroom home to the living room where she peeked through the wooden two-inch blinds. Ginger, her best friend, stood on the porch. She hurried to the door, flung it open, and threw her arms around Ginger's neck.

"Hey, Gin."

Ginger returned the squeeze. "Hey."

Lisa released her hold on Ginger and stepped aside to allow her to come inside. "Not that it isn't always good to see you, but I wasn't expecting you today. Isn't Saturday one of the busiest days of the week for Ginger's Goodies?"

"Yes, but Jessie can handle it. Besides, your mom called and asked that I meet her here."

Lisa leaned back and frowned. "Really? Not sure why she'd say that because I'm getting ready to leave in about an hour. Book club is next week. Maybe she got the dates mixed up."

Ginger shrugged and folded her lips in such a way that Lisa could see she was holding back a smile. And not just any kind of smile. It was the kind that meant she was up to something she had no business meddling in, which meant Lisa's business.

Her doorbell rang again a few minutes later, with Mom and Aunt Wanda on the other side of the door. Ginger let them inside.

She loved all three women with everything in her—they were her favorite people on earth. However, they were interrupting her plans to be ready when Jayden came to pick her up.

"Did I miss the memo? Book club is next week. You all are welcome to water, soda, snacks, or whatever you can find in the kitchen, but I have to get ready."

Like sardines in a can, the three of them sat together on her sofa. Mom curled her lips into a mischievous smile and spoke up. "Oh, we know you do."

Aunt Wanda flicked her finger toward Lisa and continued where Mom left off. "We just came to make sure you look good. None of that hair scarf business—that boho chic thing you have going on. It's cute and all, but it won't work for tonight."

Do they seriously not have anything else to do?

Lisa tightened her bathrobe and folded her arms across her chest. "Y'all can't be serious. I know how to dress. Plus, it's only dinner at one of the partner's house. It's Joe whose house I've been to many times before tonight."

She looked to Ginger for a little help, but instead, Ginger's words came out more like singing, and not in her favor. "Well, tonight is sort of different. Aunt Wanda seems to think that since Jayden has reached partner status, he's more inclined to act on his feelings for you. And I am here for it, honey. All of it," Ginger finished with a chuckle.

"We are friends," Lisa said, emphasizing her declaration with pointed looks at the three of them after each syllable.

"Well," Ginger started again, "maybe a little more than friends. You two are literally in a relationship and don't even know it."

Lisa shot Ginger an I'm-going-to-deal-with-you-later look.

"Think about it: When is the last time you or he dated anyone else? Would you have been upset if he asked someone else to go with him tonight instead of you? Honey, he told you about his promotion before he shared the news with his own momma. If that ain't a relationship, I don't know what is."

Ginger was such a traitor right now.

"It's called being a true friend, which someone seems to have forgotten how to do," Lisa said and picked up a pink throw pillow to toss at Ginger. She caught it mid-air and grinned.

"That's not answering the questions," Aunt Wanda interjected with one eyebrow raised. This woman was relentless. She'd bet all the books inside of their store that this was her idea.

Lisa sat on the arm of her recliner and touched her forefinger to her chin, pretending to think. "*Hmmm.* It's been a while since I've dated anyone at all. Hello. Remember the pandemic? I think that's true for most people who went into it single."

Ginger mumbled, "That was ages ago. She's just going to hold on to the pandemic as her excuse for another forty years."

Mom and Aunt Wanda laughed.

Lisa ignored them and picked up where she left off. "I don't know who Jayden is or isn't dating—he doesn't tell me everything—and I wouldn't be upset one bit if he'd chosen to take someone else tonight instead of me. It's his right. His promotion. He can celebrate however he chooses." She shrugged, nonchalance in her demeanor. And that was hard. She probably would have avoided his phone calls for the next week or two if he'd taken someone other than her. She was his best friend, and that meant important moments were reserved for her. That had always been their unspoken rule.

"I'm just honored he asked me. This is a big deal for him, so if y'all will excuse me, I need to get ready."

She could hear them murmuring behind her back, but she ignored them. If they thought they'd see her sweat or she'd give them the satisfaction of showing that there *might* be something there when it came to Jayden, well, they'd better work harder than that. It was cute that they banded together, though.

Lisa showered and dressed in the black jumpsuit. She may have chosen another outfit, but the trio of women in her living room stole her time with their shenanigans. A dab of the perfume she'd worn for years and Jayden's favorite. A coat of her favorite shade of red lipstick. A pair of pearl earrings. And a moisturized twist out with curls for days. At Aunt Wanda's advice, she decided against a matching headband and allowed her curls to flow freely.

With both hands on her hips, she strutted into the living room, runway style, pivoting to the left, right, and back to show off her outfit.

"That's what I'm talking about. Make him pick his heart up off the floor," Aunt Wanda said, high-fiving Ginger and Mom, who both erupted into laughter.

Lisa smiled and shook her head. While it was kind of fun, it was also insane. Why she entertained them, she did not know.

Ginger wiggled her eyebrows up and down and gave her a thumbs-up.

"Thanks, but we are not going to treat this like a date. It is not a date. A friend is supporting a friend. That's it," Lisa said to convince herself as she walked out of the room. Fooling around with them, she'd almost lost her head.

This was not a real date.

∞

Jayden slowed his truck to a stop near the curb in front of Lisa's red brick, one story home. Thanks to his yard man who also took care of Lisa's lawn, her landscaping looked great. He couldn't even park in Lisa's driveway because his mom's car and what looked like Lisa's friend, Ginger's car crowded the double space. Had Lisa forgotten his plans to pick her up this evening? What felt like a hundred tiny needles pricked his heart, and his chest constricted at the thought of Lisa forgetting about him. He didn't mind going to Joe's alone, but he'd been looking forward to this night all week—time with her celebrating his accomplishments and hers as well. There was no one else he'd want to share this moment with other than Lisa. She'd been by his side for years—in the words of his mother, almost forty years.

He shifted his truck into park, cut the engine, and grabbed the bouquet of white roses from the passenger seat. True, it wasn't a real date, but white roses were her favorite and safer than red roses, in his opinion.

Before he could make it up the concrete path to the front door, Ginger flung it open.

"Hey, Gin."

She turned around to announce, "He's got flowers," then faced him and returned his greeting. "Good to see you, Jayden. You're looking mighty dapper in your blazer and khakis."

"Appreciate it."

Ginger stepped back and opened the door wider for him to enter.

His mother and Lisa's mother, Aunt Barbara, sat on the couch next to each other, whispering. When his mom locked eyes with him, she all but shouted, "Hey now. My son is on his A-game. Lisa, come in here and get your flowers."

Like an angel, she appeared in the entrance to the living room dressed in all black, wearing the brightest smile. "Hey, Jay. You're right on time."

Her voice seemed lighter and sweeter, not that it wasn't usually that way, but it sounded different to his ears somehow. Or was he imagining it? Shiny, big curls framed her face, and her eyes were as bright as headlights on high beam. And for the first time ever, he was tempted to smear her crimson lipstick with his own lips. He swallowed, hoping that would clear his mind. Where did that thought come from?

"You are so beautiful. Thanks for agreeing to be my date tonight."

Date?

Her eyes widened even more, and a flicker of horror, fear, or something passed through her features. She parted her lips, probably to correct him, but didn't say anything. She flashed a smile, and a wave of relief washed over him. He didn't mean *date* date. They'd been friends long enough, so she knew what he meant by it.

"Anytime. I'm ya girl."

He handed her the flowers he'd been squeezing. "Oh, here you go."

"Oh, Jay, you didn't have to do this. It's your night."

"Well, I want to celebrate you, too. You own a bookstore now."

She blushed and nodded. "It's true. Kinda surreal, but I'm happy about these new adventures we're both starting. Give me a minute."

Lisa waltzed into the kitchen to grab a vase and fill it with water. She positioned the flowers in direct view of her kitchen window. When she finished, he hooked his arm, and she linked hers through it. He'd forgotten they weren't alone until he turned to see three pairs of nosey eyes and goofy smiles.

"Alright, ladies. Lisa is mine for the next few hours. I'll have her back before the clock strikes twelve," Jayden announced, mostly to get a rise out of them. His mom would eat up that kind of talk.

Ginger stood and walked over to hug Lisa, then gave him a side hug. "Take your time. Like you said, she's yours." She winked and strutted out the door.

"We're leaving, too," Aunt Barbara said and stood to her full height of five feet five inches. She had the same honey skin and wide eyes as Lisa. She glided toward him, while his mom gave her attention to Lisa. "You two have fun, and be safe. Congratulations, Jayden. I'm so proud of you." She enveloped him in a tight embrace.

"Thank you. You think I could get one of your homemade apple pies as my reward?"

Aunt Barbara made the best apple pie he's ever tasted. Growing up, she baked him one upon request when he scored all A's on his report cards. That pie had always been his special treat, and he could taste it now with a scoop of ice cream and a drizzle of caramel syrup.

"You ain't said nothing but a word. I've got you."

She glided toward the door, her orange kente-print skirt nearly dragging the floor.

His mom had her arms wrapped around Lisa's shoulders, whispering something in her ear. Jayden wasn't sure why she'd gone through the motions of doing so because he could clearly hear her, and they all knew that she was working her plan to pair him and Lisa together.

Being the gracious woman she was, Lisa smiled when his mom pulled away. "I'm glad y'all were able to stop by."

Jayden hugged his mom. "You two can stop treating us like we're going to prom now." If he remembered correctly, senior prom night played out in similar fashion with both of their parents huddled on the sofa, taking pictures and barking out curfews. Even then, his mom hinted at the idea of him and Lisa becoming a couple. He'd think she would have let it go by now.

Aunt Barbara and his mom left the house; he and Lisa stood in the middle of her living room floor where the space was now quiet but stuffed with sentiments unspoken.

Lisa released a heavy sigh. "They are a lot."

Jayden chuckled. "Tell me something I don't know. Ready?"

She gave the kind of smile that said she'd go anywhere with him, and he'd known that to be true. "Let's go, partner."

Jayden took her by the hand and led her outside. She used her free hand to press the lock button on her electronic keypad. He'd linked their hands because it was natural for him, but what wasn't natural or normal was the electricity from her touch. Something stirred within him, and if he were honest with himself, he liked it. Only he didn't know what it was or how to respond. This thing wasn't the numbers he dealt with daily. One of the things he loved about math was that it was absolute.

Facts.

And that was easy to understand.

There were solutions—to him often easy.

But whatever this was—was the opposite.

He opened the door for Lisa and waited for her to climb inside and secure her seatbelt. Before he closed the door, their eyes met in mutual understanding of what was happening between them—something foreign to them as friends. However, starting tonight, Jayden vowed to explore the unfamiliar territory.

Chapter Five

The very thing Jayden spent his entire adult life seeking did not bring him the satisfaction he'd hoped it would. And the point sunk further into his mind at every congratulatory wish he received at the dinner party hosted by Joe and his wife, Pam, earlier that evening. Two other partners and their wives were there, too, which surprised him. He'd expected dinner with just the four of them, but Joe had invited the other partners. The two who didn't have plans, Cameron Burroughs and Matthew Smith, attended.

A catered dinner from Perry's Steakhouse and Grille had steaks, chops, and vegetables on the menu. No one had a single complaint about the food. Neither did he. The conversation was light with a great deal of it focused on him and his path forward. He didn't care too much for the spotlight, especially when he wasn't sure if he'd accept the opportunity, a crazy thought considering how much he'd worked for it. Two years ago, Jayden wouldn't have given it a second thought and would have returned the signed partnership agreement the following day. But present-day Jayden continued to have thoughts of how he truly wanted the rest of his life to look, and working long hours each week seemed less appealing as the days passed.

The best part of the evening was Lisa. She had this spark about her that enhanced every room she went into. The partners' wives liked her and often sent her small token gifts around Christmastime. And he loved that his colleagues and their families welcomed his dearest friend into their circle as much as they'd welcomed him. But there was this small part of him that sporadically reared its head and whispered, *You don't belong here.* And although he'd forged his own path, he'd bought into that thought over time, even more so now that he'd reached this should-I-stay-or-should-I-do-something-else juncture.

Back home that evening, Jayden changed into a t-shirt and a pair of comfortable sweats and parked himself in his home office. He didn't have plans to do any work, but that plush leather chair behind his executive-style desk had become his home inside his home. He clicked on the TV to watch game highlights while also powering up his laptop. Creature of habit.

Smiling back at him was a five-by-seven selfie photo of him and Lisa taken when they had lunch at Memorial Hermann Park for her birthday a few years ago. She'd given it to him saying that he needed some life in his office. The gold and chocolate tones needed a pop of color. When he refused the potted plant, she'd given him the photo of them instead.

With the Houston Rockets game playing in the background, Jayden clicked around his screen until he landed on the Amazon publishing platform. Honestly, he only wanted to write and not have to do all the extra stuff, but he could do it if he had to—and he'd done so. With all these random feelings he had about the partnership situation, it was nice to have something else to lean into while he thought through his next steps. Should the book not do well, no one would know because he'd used his pen name, Justin Love.

Three consecutive buzzes interrupted him. Lisa's photo and number illuminated his phone's screen. Guilt settled in his belly. He hadn't shared with Lisa that he'd finished and published the book.

Jayden turned his attention away from the laptop and held his breath for a moment. Lisa didn't normally call late at night. "Hey. What's up? Is everything okay?"

"Yeah. Just checking on you. You didn't seem like yourself much of the evening. On the surface you were fine, but I can sense when something is bothering you."

He released a breath and rested his weight against the back of his seat, his eyes locked on the ceiling. "You're always looking out for me. I love that about you." But what he didn't like was her need for him to talk about his feelings.

"Well, that's what you get when you've been knowing someone forever. Is it the promotion?"

"Something like that. Maybe. I don't know."

"I wish I knew what to say to make you feel better or at ease, but we can work through it together so that you can freely celebrate your accomplishments with zero guilt." She paused for a moment. "Do you feel guilty? Well, maybe guilt is the wrong word. Are you feeling like you're missing out on something else, or is there something else you haven't accomplished that you need to do before you can move forward? Know what I'm trying to say—coulda-shoulda-woulda type thoughts?"

"You seriously want to have a counseling session with me at..." He peered at the time at the bottom of his laptop screen, "at eleven thirty?"

"Sounds like you're fully awake, so why not? Plus, you being unsettled is bothering me. We need to figure this thing out."

Jayden chuckled. "I hope you have some caffeine because it's gonna be a long night if you think this can be worked out quickly when I can't even pinpoint the problem."

"Can I be real with you, Jay?"

"Always."

"I feel like you're holding something back from me. You know you can tell me anything, right? No judgment."

Lisa knew about his plans to write a book. He'd always talked about it, yet he hadn't told her that he'd written his first manuscript, had it edited, shopped it around to several agents and editors, and self-published it with an Amazon publishing account. If no one else would celebrate him, Lisa would, especially when it came to that. But at this point, she might kill him for holding out on her. Perhaps he had his own issues with a writing career that he needed to deal with. After all, he had a master's in accounting, a Certified Public Accounting license, and he was a signature away from becoming partner in one of the largest accounting firms in

Houston. How could a writing career compare? He'd tell her when he perceived the timing was right.

"Don't do that to me, Lisa. This just may be something I need to work through on my own. Can you give me time to do that?"

Even though his tone was as gentle as he could make it, Lisa was offended, and he knew it because the line went silent for roughly thirty seconds, but it felt more like a minute. History had shown that when she got quiet on the phone, she was upset about something, but it would be a few days before they hashed it out.

"Well, you just let me know if you need to talk. I'm going to bed. Have a good night, Jay."

"Night."

He'd planned to take some time to research Amazon ads, but was no longer in the head space to do so after his conversation with Lisa. Once he worked through his career issues, he'd tell Lisa everything…eventually.

∞

The next morning, Lisa was still trippin' and taken aback by the way Jayden had pulled away from her. He hadn't done that in the past, not that she could remember. However, Jayden was not her significant other, which meant that he didn't have to share everything with her. And she was fine with that idea as long as she didn't know he was holding back. She could see it in his eyes. He'd pushed his guard up. But, he must have forgotten she'd known him since they were both in diapers, which meant that she knew him well. His tell was his avoidance of the issue. Jayden was tactical, practical, and faced issues directly, not passively in any way. If she had to guess, he knew exactly what was bothering him, but had his reasons for not wanting to share them with her. That, she was okay with, if he'd just say so, but what she wasn't cool with was the fact that he felt like he couldn't say that after almost forty years. Maybe they weren't as close as she thought.

Or perhaps she could be overreacting and projecting her uncertainties on him. Taking a break from her laptop screen, she pushed away from her kitchen table and strolled over to the single-serve coffee maker to brew her second cup of coffee. It sat on the right side of the sink below the kitchen window. The vase filled with a dozen white long-stemmed roses was positioned to the left. She smiled at Jayden's thoughtfulness, which contradicted his behavior on the phone last night.

What was or wasn't on Jayden's mind was the least of Lisa's worries. For the entire week, she'd avoided her pending property tax issue. She'd combed through their bank statements and Melvin's spreadsheets. There was no record of any payment to the Fort Bend County Tax Assessor's office. None. But what she did notice was the payments to Melvin. A lot more than what he should have earned based on their agreement, which should have been zero considering he'd been helping her mom free of charge.

After the last drip, Lisa removed her mug and doctored up her coffee with French vanilla cream and sugar. She inhaled the fresh aroma of ground Jamaican coffee beans before she took her first sip. It was time to call her mom.

Lisa scooped her phone off the table near her laptop and unlocked the screen. A text from Jayden came through before she could make her call.

J: Sorry if I came off rude last night. Not my intent. I promise to talk to you when I get it figured out.

L: No need to apologize. I'm here whenever you're ready to talk.

J: Thanks. I'll catch up with you later.

Lisa nodded, but didn't respond. She placed that call to her mom.

"Good morning, Mom. How are you?" She took another sip of coffee and braced her weight against the granite countertop.

"I'm okay. My back is bothering me a little bit, but that's nothing new. What's going on? Are you calling me because you want to take me out for breakfast?"

Lisa chuckled. "I wasn't, but that sounds like a good idea, and I can take a hint. Where do you want to go?"

"I could go for one of those hashbrown scrambles at Snooze."

Lisa peered at the microwave clock. "Can you be ready in the next hour? I'll shower and change then come pick you up."

"Honey, I'm already dressed. I'll wait for you."

An image of her mom outfitted in one of her many African-print maxi dresses came to mind. She had her way of dressing them up or down, which pretty much made her ready for all occasions. "Okay. See you in a bit."

Lisa must have adapted her boho chic style, as Aunt Wanda put it, from her mother. She fished out her favorite comfort style, a white top and one of her own African-print maxi skirts with a matching headband from her closet. She cleaned up and dressed in thirty minutes.

Twenty-five minutes later, Lisa navigated her car through the quiet neighborhood she'd grown up in. Old Katy. Her parents moved into the neighborhood when she was five years old. At that time, it was a new development, so most of her neighbors were families with children around her age. Now, everyone had grown up, and only a few younger families were in the subdivision. It didn't seem as lively as it once did. She parked in the driveway of her childhood home, a three-bedroom traditional structure with a white porch swing that had seen better days. She didn't get a chance to cut the engine because her mom was already outside locking the door dressed as Lisa suspected.

She waltzed to the car, climbed in, and secured her seatbelt.

"Let's get this show on the road. I'm starving."

Lisa turned to her. "Since you're up bright and early, I'd think you would have made breakfast for you and Dad by now."

Her mom flicked her hand. "Oh, I already made him breakfast and lunch."

Lisa cocked an eyebrow. "And you didn't eat?"

"Kinda had the feeling you'd be calling today. You had about fifteen more minutes before I called you."

Lisa shifted her car in reverse and checked her rearview mirror for clearance. "And why's that?"

Her mom's lips twitched into a smile. And not just any type of smile. The kind she often shared with Aunt Wanda when they were conspiring against her. "Because I want to hear about your date. I don't want to wait until book club to get the details with everyone else."

Lisa laughed. "So you've climbed aboard Aunt Wanda's ship, I see. You, of all people, know that wasn't a real date."

"How about you define real date so we can decide if that's what you and Jayden had."

"Well, *ummm,* a real date is when two people agree to go out with intentions of getting to know each other better or exploring their relationship or just hanging out together because they enjoy each other's company. When people go on a date, it's because they like each other in a romantic sort of way."

If she didn't feel and sound like a tenth grader trying to explain that to her mom.

And that was only because she'd had to choose her words carefully. She couldn't say anything that would prove her mom's point.

Mom gave a slow nod. She often did that when it was something she wanted Lisa to think about, not because she was trying to understand what was said or done.

"So how was the non-date with Jayden?"

"It was nice. Things were as they always are with us: easy. I don't have to try to make a good impression, and neither does he. We can be ourselves. The other partners and their wives were good company, but I knew that before going because I've met them all. The food was catered from Perry's Steakhouse, so you can imagine how delicious the steaks were."

Mom twirled a finger. "Hold on. Rewind. I thought it was just one partner and his wife. You're telling me that the other guests were there with their wives, too? Don't you find it strange that you two were the only two not married—that you were his plus one to what seemed like a couples' dinner?"

Lisa shook her head. "No, because it wasn't like that. And Jayden and I are only friends, so you and Aunt Wanda have to chill, Mom. You all are kinda making things weird for us—well, me. I can't speak for Jayden."

Her mom, and especially Aunt Wanda, were part of the problem. What Lisa didn't mention was the fact that he'd held her hand on the way to the car, both going and leaving the dinner party. Or the electric sensation that washed over her when their hands met. And she didn't know when anything had changed between them or if anything had changed at all, and her mind had conjured up these feelings because of the seeds Aunt Wanda had planted.

Palms up, her mom said, "Okay. I won't interfere. It's just that Wanda has painted this beautiful picture of you two in my mind, and I'm loving it. You two will figure things out in your own time."

Under her breath, her mom mumbled, "I just hope it doesn't take forty more years."

Lisa chuckled. "I heard that."

Feigning innocence, she said, "Heard what? I said I'm leaving things alone. I can't control Wanda, though. The only way to make her back off is for one of you to date someone else."

Lisa shrugged and smiled. "It could happen."

Mom didn't seem convinced, and thankfully they ended the conversation. Lisa turned into Snooze's parking lot.

After they were seated and had placed their orders, Lisa began the hard conversation.

"I've got something to tell you about the bookstore."

Her mom held her latte mug mid-sip and returned it to the table. "What's wrong?"

"I received a letter from the county tax office. Our property taxes are three years delinquent. If we don't settle the account in less than sixty days, they're going to foreclose on the property."

Her mom shook her head, her wide eyes filled with flickers of anger and disbelief. "That can't be right. Melvin paid them. He assured me. And with your father getting sick during the pandemic, I wasn't in my right mind to double check. Did you look through our records?"

Lisa nodded. "Twice. The spreadsheet you've kept says that they've been paid, but the bank statements show otherwise."

Her mom clasped her hands together and rested her forehead on her fists. "I didn't know I was handing over a mess to you. We can get this fixed."

"I don't want you to worry. I just wanted you to be aware and to make sure you didn't know anything about it. Confirmation that I wasn't missing anything. I'll handle it. I promise."

A promise she couldn't be sure she could keep.

But Lisa couldn't allow anything to stand in the way of her living her dream. She finally owned her own bookstore, and Melvin nor the tax assessor would take it away from her.

Chapter Six

Between the Lines didn't open for another three hours, but Lisa arrived early to meet Jayden and go through the documentation he needed to prepare the bookstore's income tax return. Hopefully similar issues wouldn't pop up like the one she had with property taxes—owing the government money. There wasn't enough money to go around.

Lisa downloaded the prior years' returns online, according to Jayden's instructions, and gathered worksheets from Melvin her mom kept. She cleared the same table they'd used for lunch last week and placed her return printouts, bank statements, and receipts in a neat pile next to her laptop. Jayden preferred to have the documents in electronic form, but she needed to touch them. With everything she was dealing with surrounding the property tax issue, physical documents gave her a sense of security.

Lisa sat facing the door, waiting for Jayden. She sipped her coffee and skimmed news articles and the social media accounts of some of her favorite authors. Unsure of how long she'd been caught up in the lives of others, the door chime signaled his entrance, pulling her out of her haze.

"Good morning. Ready to work?"

"Morning." Jayden's lips spread into a smile, and his eyes darted to the six-inch tall stack of papers on the table. "Tell me you did not kill trees when you could have just attached everything in an email or even shared the documents in the cloud."

"I did what was necessary."

He walked over to where she sat and wrapped an arm around her shoulder, squeezed, and placed a kiss on top of her hair. "Just remember that next time, everything in electronic format is fine."

With her foot, Lisa pushed the seat out from the table. "I'll try to remember that."

Jayden put his portfolio bag in the chair across from Lisa, took the seat she'd pushed away, placed his hands on the hefty stack, and blew a stream of air.

"Three years of bank statements," Lisa said, "just like you asked." She slid the second stack to him. "Receipts." And a third stack. "Melvin's workpapers."

"While I understand you printed these more for your sake than mine, can you e-mail me Melvin's spreadsheets?"

"Sure." Lisa clicked around on her laptop to send him what he'd requested. "Missed you at church yesterday."

Jayden removed his laptop from his bag. "Yeah. I watched online. Had a bit of work to catch up on. We're in the thick of busy season, with everyone required to work at least fifty-five hours a week. I hadn't quite met my quota this past week with all the excitement of the promotion."

Lisa despised busy season because they didn't spend as much time together. And when she did see him, it was usually because she stopped by his house to check in, taking him food to ensure he was caring for himself. Though an avid exerciser, he even skipped his fitness routine during those months. She sent everything to Jayden in electronic format, closed her laptop, and shifted to face him.

"Speaking of promotion, have you made a decision to go all in?"

He looked up from his screen, and their eyes met. There it was again. He was holding back from her. She didn't have proof—it was just the feeling she got.

Jayden shook his head. "Nah, not yet and I'm not sure what it's gonna take either."

"Have you prayed about it?"

"I have, but I'm still not sure where God is leading me. I need more time to decide, that's for sure."

He didn't offer anything more, but Lisa wanted to ask more questions. However, she recalled him saying he would tell her when the time was right, so she wouldn't press the issue. Instead, she brought the conversation back to the issue at hand.

"So now that you have the records, what are the next steps?"

Jayden took both of her hands in his. "Okay. What did I do to upset you?"

"What are you talking about?"

"That look on your face says you're upset with me. You're not acting like yourself."

I could say the same thing about you.

"Jay, you're here to work, and I don't want to waste your time, that's it."

He smoothed his thumbs in circles over the backs of her hands. "Treating me like I'm your friend instead of a stranger you hired is not wasting my time. C'mon. I don't like it when things aren't cool between us."

Perhaps she was being funky about his need to work out whatever his issue was. Jayden's chestnut eyes were filled with warmth and compassion. Goodness, she hated when he looked at her like that—like he would do anything for her. Like he cared for her more than as a friend. It wasn't until now that she realized she'd been under the Jayden spell for a long time. Her heart received the memo, too, because it drummed faster than Allyson Felix's feet on a race track.

Lisa swallowed her anxiety, her voice firm and steady. "Jay, we're good. Promise."

Jayden held her hands for a moment longer, his eyes studying hers. He squinted as if deciding whether to believe her. She added a smile for good measure.

He released her hands, and she missed his touch already. Jayden straightened in his seat and returned his attention to his screen. "There are a few things that need to happen here. Before I prepare the return, I need to get comfortable with what Melvin did in the prior years. After that, I'll reconcile your bank statements to the spreadsheet you've given me, and prepare the return."

"And how long will that take?"

"Give me a few days. Is that good enough for you, or would you like me to work overtime and get it back to you tonight?"

Lisa chuckled. "Melvin filed an extension so I wouldn't put that kind of pressure on you, but the sooner you let me know if we can expect a refund or not, the better." Her stomach dipped at the thought of owing the IRS, too. It must have shown on her face because his expression turned serious.

"What's the matter?"

Lisa shrugged. "Nothing twenty thousand dollars can't fix."

Jayden's head swung in her direction. He bugged his eyes. Probably the same expression she had when she first read the letter.

"Twenty thousand dollars? Come again."

"You heard right." Lisa took a deep breath and rehashed the story to him, as she knew it. "Last week, I received a letter from the county tax office.. Between the Lines has three years of unpaid taxes. The balance includes penalties and interest."

Jayden scrunched his eyebrows. Deep lines appeared on his forehead, skin normally smooth and wrinkle free.

"And they're just now contacting you? That alone seems strange. What did Melvin have to say about it?"

"I haven't been able to get in touch with him—MIA. Plus, he moved to San Antonio, last I heard."

Jayden shook his head, obviously just as disturbed by the news as Lisa. "I don't understand how he could overlook something like that."

"My thought is that he took advantage of my mom while she was caring for my dad when he got sick. He knew she wouldn't look too closely with her mind preoccupied with my dad's health."

Lisa buried her head in her hands. "I feel like this is my fault. I should have stepped up more. My only concern was making sure we kept a steady flow of sales, and I let my mom and Melvin continue doing what they needed to do. Yes, I made sure the monthly utility bills were paid and monitored the bank account, but that's about it."

"I'm sorry you're going through this, but you are not to blame here. When I go through Melvin's work for the prior years, I'll look for any discrepancies to see where something may have gone wrong, so you'll be getting a bit of an audit and tax prep."

She'd gone through the bank statements and spreadsheets twice already, but it wouldn't hurt to have a second pair of eyes— trained eyes.

He reached out and covered one of her hands with his. "Hey, try not to worry. I'll see to it that everything works out in your favor. Owning this bookstore has been your dream, and we're not going to let something like this stop you from having it. You know I've got you, right?"

Lisa nodded, relief pouring over her. Though she wasn't quite sure how this would work out, and Jayden probably wasn't certain either, knowing he was with her until the end comforted her soul. He had her back. Always had.

"I know. Thanks for saying that."

"Those aren't just words. I mean it. Even if I've got to loan you the money, we'll get the situation resolved."

"Jayden, you don't—"

He shook his head to stop her. "No buts. What kind of friend would I be if I knew I could help you but didn't?"

Lisa silently prayed that Jayden would find something in those records she'd missed because she couldn't ask him for twenty thousand dollars, loan or not. That was too big of an ask. Even for him.

"You're right. I'd do the same for you."

And she would.

So why was it so hard for her to even consider allowing him to do something as grand for her?

∞

Twenty thousand dollars was a hefty amount of cash, but a small price tag when it meant helping Lisa. Jayden filled his lungs with air, taking in the smell of paperback books. A rush of nostalgia settled in. Between the Lines had become his second home growing up. Before he joined the basketball team in junior high, he and Lisa came to the bookstore every day after school. From time to time, he vacuumed the floors, dusted the bookshelves, shelved books, and helped create displays. His mom was there to help her best friend, and so was he. It's where he practiced multiplication and fractions and read every book he could get his hands on. Between the Lines was where he'd fallen in love with the written word and where he and Lisa had decided they'd be best friends forever. At the time, they were seven years old, yet here they were. He smiled at the memory. This place meant just as much to him as it did to her.

He could understand Lisa's hesitation to accept the money, no matter the terms. It wasn't twenty dollars or even two thousand dollars, which she likely wouldn't ask of him either. As his closest friend, what kind of friend would he be if he could help and did nothing? There was a Bible verse to back him up on that. Something to the effect of helping your neighbor when they asked and not when it's most convenient. He'd do anything for Lisa. At this point in their lives, he'd think she knew that.

Jayden studied her. "Would you accept the loan from me if it meant saving the bookstore?"

"If it meant keeping Between the Lines open, yes, but I'd do everything in my power to pay you back, and most likely before the end of the loan term."

He laughed. "No pressure. We could call it an investment instead of a loan. I could be a silent partner or something like that and accept a percentage of profits."

Lisa threaded her arms across her chest. "You're serious, aren't you?"

"Did you think I wasn't? You know I'm not gonna let you go down without a fight. I care about you and this bookstore way too much. It's just as much a part of me as it is a part of you."

"I know." She scrunched her face. "It just seems like a lot. A loan from you would be a last resort. If I have to go find Melvin myself, I will. But for now, I think I've got a plan that would help a little."

Jayden pushed the laptop away and gave Lisa his full attention. "Really? Let's hear it."

"I'd already had my mind set on this huge grand re-opening celebration. Now I'm thinking I can plan it in a way that will help raise money to pay off the debt, in case we can't recover the money. Before you say anything, I know we won't make twenty thousand dollars, but I think we can earn enough to pay the tax assessor a portion in good faith. I just can't believe this happened."

In truth, Jayden wanted to write a check right now to make it all go away, but this wasn't his battle to fight. He couldn't overstep. Not only was she independent, she'd always known this opportunity would come. In a sense, he'd be taking it away from her by attempting to solve the problem on her behalf. He reminded himself to be sensitive to her plight.

"I'm sorry this is happening, but I'm willing to help with the grand re-opening in any way I can. What do you need me to do?" The thought crossed his mind again—to tell Lisa about the book. Maybe he could sign and sell copies of his books? Donate all the proceeds to the store? That she'd probably accept.

But he decided against the idea. Now wasn't quite time to tell her about the book, not when he had other things to figure out.

Lisa's eyes lit up, and she did that thing where she talked with her hands flailing all over the place. "I'm going to reach out to some local authors to gauge interest. I'm also thinking of bringing in other vendors—food trucks, jewelry, homemade candles and soaps. This is gonna be one huge market event. Do you have any other ideas about vendors we can invite? We need something unconventional."

"What about Ginger setting up a table to sell cookies? I'm sure she'd love to help. Or someone who isn't selling anything, but maybe advertising. Like a tax professional, gym rep, or real estate agent. It also couldn't hurt to have something to give to people for showing up."

"Like a bribe?"

Jayden chuckled. "Something like that. Folks like free and are more likely to show up. And music. You need music. If you can get a few popular local artists or musicians to come play, that'll be great, too. That's more traffic with them sharing with their networks where they'll be performing."

Lisa pushed his knee. "You're so good at this. How did I not know?"

"I have the ideas, and you're more likely to get it done. That's why we're the perfect team."

Lisa lifted her laptop lid and awakened the screen. "You've got a point. I should be writing this down. If you think of anything else throughout the day, shoot me a text."

"Will do."

She pecked away at her keyboard, jotting down the ideas they'd just discussed. "I'm going to start reaching out to vendors today. I'll have your mom help when she comes in later."

"She's definitely gonna love helping set this up."

"Don't I know it? It'll give her something else to focus on besides me—at least for a little while anyway."

Jayden returned his attention to his own laptop to refocus on why he'd stopped by in the first place—to gather the records from Lisa so he could prepare the bookstore's income tax return. It was safer not to comment on his mom's matchmaking because in truth, something was happening between him and Lisa. They just hadn't discussed it yet.

He took a cursory glance at the bank statements, previous accountant's workpapers, and the monthly expenses spreadsheet Lisa had sent over. Satisfied that he had what he needed to get started, he closed his e-mail. There was no way he would get anything done this morning with his thoughts all over the place. Jayden pulled out his phone to schedule the task for tomorrow night.

His book had been posted to Amazon's self-publishing platform for two months, and now, of all times, he got the urge to peek at his progress—his sales and estimated royalties. And that thought alone was weird considering he hadn't shared with Lisa that he'd uploaded the book. His eyes bugged, and his heart slammed against his ribcage with the same impact as an eighteen wheeler crashing into another one. The thud was so loud that he could hear it in his ears. And so loud he thought Lisa might be able to hear it, too. He shifted his eyes in her direction to double-check, but her gaze was focused on her screen as her fingers danced across the keypad.

Not much surprised him these days, but he racked his brain attempting to analyze how his book was ranked number one in its category with the estimated royalties to match. Not to mention that he had over five thousand reviews, most of which were positive because his star rating was four and a half. He wanted to jump out of his seat and shout—scream that he knew he could do it. Snatch Lisa out of her seat and spin her around. And kiss her senseless because he was so happy.

But instead, he sat there. Still. Dumbfounded. Wondering if it was sheer luck and how long it would last. And what if sales remained steady? Did that mean he should pursue his writing more seriously? Was it time for him to shift away from his accounting career? Was this the change he needed? Jayden was a calculated man, and making a decision that would impact his life off something that could change in any moment didn't make sense. Being a full-time writer wasn't sustainable, was it? And did he even want to be a full-time writer? Perhaps a part-time writer and part-time accountant?

This was the precise time he should have opened up to Lisa and shared the great news, even if it was possibly temporary, but he couldn't. Jayden wanted to see where this would go. He shouldn't be taking this journey alone, but that was this sliver of fear that he'd disappoint her or himself. At least that was the excuse he'd convinced himself was true. The truth was that for the first time in his life, he considered doing something that didn't quite make sense, wasn't safe, and didn't provide a steady paycheck. And he needed to rationalize and be comfortable within himself, sure that he was doing the right thing before he brought Lisa in on it. She wouldn't sway him one way or the other, but for his own sake, Jayden needed to be certain of the route he'd take.

Chapter Seven

As Ginger's maid of honor, Lisa should have been more attentive to the bride-to-be during the wedding gown search. They were now at the second bridal shop, and instead of giving Ginger her full attention, Lisa's thoughts huddled around Jayden. What was his deal? And why couldn't she get past his choice to leave her out of the loop in whatever he had going on?

At the last bridal shop, Ginger tried on at least five dresses. Honestly and shamefully, Lisa couldn't be sure. It may have been three or even seven gowns. Lisa focused more on Ginger's eyes. They weren't lighting up, and Lisa couldn't sense her excitement. As much as Ginger and Brock had been through, Lisa knew and understood the assignment. Ginger wanted this day to be special and to send Brock's heart galloping across the sand since they'd planned a beach wedding. None of the dresses she'd tried thus far had done the trick.

Lisa and Ginger walked into Belle Ame bridal shop located in the heart of Houston's Galleria area five minutes before Ginger's scheduled appointment slot. Ginger chose this shop because it was owned by three sisters, and much like herself, she took pride in supporting women-owned small businesses. When she walked in, Lisa felt as if she'd entered the venue for an actual ceremony. To her left was a floral arch framed over the dressing room entrance area. To her right was the sitting area with two blue sitting chairs, and photos of beautiful brides clad in their magazine-worthy wedding gowns hung on the wall behind them. A vase with the same flowers as the arrangement of the over-the-door arch sat on a small table between the two chairs. A love song, probably one that could be a bride's processional, played through the speakers, and the shop smelled of lavender.

One of the sisters was there to meet them when they walked through the door. The short, slender woman was dressed in a black laced shirt and white capri pants. She looked as if she was ready to attend a wedding event herself. Her jet-black silky hair was pulled back into a ponytail, accentuating her perfect makeup, and she had the most welcoming smile. The atmosphere already felt different from the last shop.

"Good afternoon. I'm Judy. Which one of you is Ginger?" Her smile was bright and wide. She clasped her hands, clearly ready to transform Ginger into the bride she'd always dreamed she would be.

Ginger cheesed and raised her right hand. "That would be me."

"Just the maid of honor and cheer squad," Lisa said and wriggled her fingers in the air.

"Alright. Let's get to work." She motioned for them to follow her to the back of the store. "Now, you mentioned that you liked sweetheart necklines, lace, and gowns from Marchesa Bridal." She sized Ginger up, her eyes roaming from Ginger's head down to her feet. "I have picked what I believe to be the perfect gowns that fit your wish list, and we can start with those unless you already have one you'd like to try on first."

"No, please bring them all," Ginger said, glancing at Lisa for approval.

Lisa simply nodded. She knew nothing about wedding dresses or designers. In her mind, she figured she'd always wear something simple—sleeveless and fitted down to her waist. The rest of the dress would be free flowing. She hadn't thought of anything past that point and hadn't had any reason to. She was as far from wearing a wedding dress as the earth is from the moon.

Judy stopped at a clothing rack near the dressing room where five dresses hung with a sign labeled *Ginger*. "Based on your size and likes, I've selected these for you. Of course, if there are others you'd like to try on, I can grab those for you as well."

Lisa fished through the rack. "These are gorgeous, Gin. Which one are you trying first?"

"It's hard to choose. You pick."

Lisa grabbed the first gown and handed it to Ginger. "Let's see you in this."

Judy winked and smiled. "Great choice."

Ginger sauntered into the changing room, and Lisa took a seat on a plush tufted blue chair.

Judy clasped her hands. "Would you like something to drink? Champagne? Water?"

"I'll take a glass of champagne."

"And you, Miss Ginger. Would you like something to drink?"

"Water, please," Ginger said over the shuffling of fabric behind the changing room door.

Lisa called to her. "Need any help?"

"Not yet. So far, so good."

Lisa settled into the seat and relaxed. Another love song streamed through the boutique's speakers. The faint smell of lavender wafting through the air calmed her senses, drew her more into the moment. At the first bridal shop, she couldn't bring herself to focus on her friend or to get into the groove of the occasion, but here, everything fell into place. And Ginger possibly felt it, too.

Judy returned with a bottle of water for Ginger and the glass of champagne for Lisa. She accepted them both and put Ginger's water bottle on the table next to her. Ten minutes later, Ginger emerged from the changing room, taking Lisa's breath away.

"You look amazing, Gin. I think I'm in love with you."

They shared a laugh; Judy laughed as well. Ginger smoothed her hands down the dress and stood on the pedestal in the center of the floor. Mirrors on every side, she turned to size up her reflection. "This is so beautiful."

"Brock might not make it through the ceremony if he sees you in this."

Ginger chuckled. "Yeah, that's the effect I'm going for anyway."

Judy walked up beside her and flared the train. "We have a seamstress we recommend for alterations so that you aren't tripping down the aisle. And the length is the only thing I'd change. I'd say this dress was made for you. You're a beautiful bride." She took a step back and looked Ginger in the eyes. "I always like to look at the bride's face to gauge how much she likes a dress, and looking at you, I can tell you love it, but I sense some hesitation. What is it?"

Ginger looked over her shoulder, her eyes focused on her backside. "You all don't think it's too sexy?"

Lisa sipped her champagne and flicked her hand like there was a fly she had to get rid of. "Girl, bye. It's just the right amount of sexy. You look amazing, but you don't have to commit if you're not ready. Try on the next one."

Ginger stepped off the pedestal and skirted back into the changing room.

Judy leaned over and whispered, "How much do you want to bet that she'll pick that one?"

"Oh, absolutely. I can tell she really likes it. She's just worried about showing too much, which she really isn't. As far as I'm concerned, we can stop right now. That was the one."

Judy fist bumped her. "I agree. Every bride goes through this though. She needs to be sure there's nothing better. And while there might be a more beautiful dress, that first one was made for those curves."

Lisa nodded. "Yep. That man is gonna eat her alive when he sees her in it."

"Y'all do know I can hear everything, right?"

Lisa snickered. "Okay, good. I was a little worried I wasn't talking loud enough."

Ginger poked her head out the door and laughed. "You think you're so funny. I'm gonna talk mess about you when you're looking for the perfect dress to meet Jayden at the altar in."

Judy's eyes lit up. "*Ooh.* Do I need to book an appointment for you after Miss Ginger is done?"

Lisa fanned her hand. "Oh, no. Don't listen to her. She's delusional. Jayden and I aren't dating. We're just friends, and it's been that way our entire lives."

Judy pressed, trying to make sense of Ginger's statement. "But you're secretly in love with him or something?"

"No."

"Yes." Ginger poked her head back out of the door answering simultaneously. "And he is, too. They're just slow in seeing what's right in front of them. Very slow." Ginger disappeared again.

Lisa shook her head. Disbelief filled her. Aunt Wanda's scheming seemed to have sunk into Ginger's mind, too. "Like I said, delusional. Who marries their best friend?"

Judy posed in front of her. "Literally seventy-five percent of brides who come in here say they're marrying their best friend."

"But Jayden and I are different."

Why was she defending herself to someone she didn't even know?

Ginger stepped out of the changing room in a lace bodice mermaid dress and exchanged looks with Judy. Her lips were twisted, and she raised one eyebrow as if to say Lisa had proven her point.

"You look gorgeous, Gin. What do you think of this one?"

Ginger shrugged and smiled, but not the same one she had when wearing the first gown. "It's beautiful."

"But you like the first one better," Lisa added.

Ginger twisted, turned, and modeled in the mirror. "I do. This is so nice, but it isn't me, and I'm not sure I'd want to wear this in the sand."

After trying on dresses three and four, Ginger declined to try on the last one. She couldn't get the first one out of her mind and was convinced that was the perfect gown. Ginger changed back into her jeans and V-neck fitted tee and met Lisa and Judy at the cash register.

"Here is a list of seamstresses that we recommend. They all do fabulous work. One of them should be able to take a few inches off the dress to fit your height in your short time frame."

Ginger accepted the list and handed Judy her credit card. "Oh, good. They're all in the area."

After ringing Ginger up, Judy propped her elbow on the counter with her chin on her fist. "Miss Lisa, I'm curious about this best friend of yours. I guess I'm just a sucker for love stories, so tell me why he isn't the one for you. Religious differences? Is he not handsome? Doesn't treat his family well? What gives?"

"No, none of that. Jayden loves his mom, and he's one of the most handsome guys I know. We've attended the same church together all our lives. Our moms are best friends, so we've become best friends by default. Our relationship has just never gone in a romantic direction, that's all."

Ginger thrust her phone in Judy's line of view to show a picture of Lisa and Jayden.

"Wow. He's hot. Can I have his number since you don't want him?"

Lisa fumbled over her words. "I didn't say…I don't know if he's…"

Judy rose to her full height and removed a business card from beneath the counter. "Oh, I see. Well, take my card for whenever you're ready."

Ginger plucked the card from Judy's hand and dropped it into Lisa's purse. "You were saying? You've known Judy less than a couple of hours, and she's figured it out. I don't understand how you're so blind to it."

Lisa turned to Judy on her way out of the store. "It was nice to meet you, Judy. Thanks for your help."

Judy waved. "Nice to meet you, too. I'll be waiting for your call. See you, soon."

∞

The sixty-hour work weeks were taking their toll on Jayden. Five years ago, he took long hours as a badge of honor—they made him feel productive and successful. But the idea of working on a Saturday these days brought on a feeling of claustrophobia. When would it end? Though it was firm policy to work a minimum of fifty-five hours during the busy season, which normally ran late February through April and late August through October, the truth was that he was always busy. He'd set himself up early in his career to take on extra projects, pick up other colleagues' slack, and to be the one to call on whenever anyone needed help. The result? No personal life.

This morning, he put off work for his Saturday basketball games at the YMCA. Working out had been his primary stress reliever over the years.

Jayden strolled into the locker room, changed, and headed straight onto the basketball court. Dribbling basketballs and gym shoe screeches reached his ears. Sounds he missed.

Brock Pearson, Ginger's fiancé, called out to him. "Well, look who decided to show up and catch this L today."

Jayden chuckled. They greeted each other with a fist bump.

"Haven't seen you in a while. The boss let you out to play this morning?" Brock said, dribbling the ball at his side.

They stood shoulder to shoulder, Brock dressed similarly in a muscle tank and basketball shorts. He'd met Brock through Lisa's best friend, Ginger. They often went out as a group of four. From outside looking in, it appeared they were double dating, but things weren't like that between him and Lisa. Yet.

Jayden rolled his shoulders, then his neck from one side to the other, completing his stretch. "It's been rough, man. I had to get away this morning. What have I missed in the last month?"

"Nothing but my team dominating yours."

Jayden threw his head back and laughed. "It's a good thing I'm back. Time for me to make things right."

"I know you've been out of the game for a while, but don't expect me to take it easy on you."

Their teammates joined them, mostly men from college and their professional circles. Only two of them they'd met while playing at the Y.

"Good to have you back, Jay," called one of them.

Jayden dabbed each of them up, greeting them in return. "What's up, bro?"

Brock shifted his head toward the opposite end of the court. "We gotta play half court today. They just got started, so no telling how long they'll be."

Jayden alternated pulling each foot behind him to stretch. "It's all good. We don't need full court to put y'all back in place."

Brock tossed a coin in the air. "We'll see about that. Heads or tails."

Jayden called, "Heads."

The coin landed on tails. "Game time, my man. Let's see how long it'll take you to knock that dust off."

Brock headed to the side court and passed the ball to his teammate. Playing four on four, each of Jayden's teammates guarded the offensive team. For the next hour, Jayden dismissed his concerns about his future, regarding the partnership, writing, and where things were possibly headed with Lisa. The game was the only thing that mattered. He missed the freedom that came with focusing on dribbling and shooting a basketball, the camaraderie with other players, and spending time enjoying the moment. When was the last time he'd enjoyed the present moment? *In the car with Lisa to and from the dinner party hosted by Joe and his wife.*

Jayden hadn't set foot inside a gym in over a month. The sweat dripping down the sides of his face and the endorphins kicking in from the physical activity was like manna from heaven. At the end of the game, each of them chugged water or Gatorade and wicked sweat from their skin with towels.

Brock fist bumped him. "Good game, man."

"Appreciate that. We let y'all win this time, though."

Brock laughed. "Man, stop. You were pressing hard trying to score the last two points y'all needed."

Jayden couldn't admit that because that would be admitting defeat, although his team did lose. Brock was on top of his game this morning.

"You've just been practicing while I was out grinding. I figured you needed the time since baseball is more your thing."

"What are excuses?"

Jayden laughed, thinking about a line they had to repeat when they pledged their fraternity. They didn't join at the same time. Brock pledged the year before Jayden and at a different school. Jayden, Lisa, and Ginger attended University of Houston, while Brock left the city to attend University of Texas at Austin on a baseball scholarship.

"Hey, we don't have to go there today."

Brock tipped his water bottle in Jayden's direction before finishing it off. "That's what I thought."

Back inside the locker room after showering, Jayden and Brock dressed and left the building. Outside in the parking lot, Jayden turned to Brock. "What do you and Ginger have planned this weekend?"

"Nothing much. She and Lisa are out picking out her gown for the wedding. You?"

Jayden slipped on his sunglasses to shield his eyes from the late August Texas sun. "I'm headed home to work."

"You sure they're gonna let you leave town for the wedding in Jamaica?"

"No way I'll miss seeing you and Ginger tie the knot. Ginger might understand if something comes up with work, but Lisa would probably kill me."

Brock tossed his gym bag in the trunk and pressed the button on the liftgate to close it. He leaned against his Beamer and folded his arms across his chest. "And why is that? Something goin' on between you two? If you ask me, it's about time."

Jayden shook his head and rolled his eyes. "So you, too, huh?"

"Simple question. Simple answer."

Jayden tossed his own gym bag in the back seat of his truck. "What's the question?"

"When are you going to ask Lisa to marry you?"

Jayden threw his head back and laughed. "Man, stop trippin'. You know we aren't even dating, right?"

Brock cocked his head to the side and lifted an eyebrow. "You didn't answer the question."

"Haven't gotten that far yet. Since you're the one about to get married, I'll get my advice from you when I'm ready."

"Do you want to live without her?"

"Man, what kind of question is that?"

"The one you need to answer. That's the start of my free advice. Think on that on your way back to work. Later."

Brock climbed into his car and started the engine. Jayden waved goodbye, rounded the tailgate, and climbed behind the wheel of his truck. Weird how their families and friends had a sudden interest in hooking them up. So what, he didn't want to live without Lisa. There was never a time when she wasn't part of his life. That didn't mean he had to marry his best friend.

Chapter Eight

After successfully securing the Limestone account for Dallas & Smith, LLP, Jayden was tasked with schmoozing another potential client. The partners in his firm had their sights set on doing business with Ceasar, a local oil and gas company. And now that they were in the market for a new accounting firm, Jayden was all over it.

Jayden valet parked his vehicle and handed his keys to the concierge outside of McCormick & Schmick's, which was typically their restaurant of choice when entertaining potential clients. He buttoned his suit jacket and smoothed his hands along the front, strolling into the restaurant like a man on a mission—and he was, on a mission to secure another account for his firm. A firm he still couldn't quite commit to. If he could go through the motions bringing in money for Dallas & Smith, why was he hesitating to sign on the dotted line?

"Jay, good to see you, man."

Jayden stood at the hostess booth, about to give his name for the reservation when he heard a familiar voice.

"Marlon? What's up, man?"

They shook hands and embraced each other in a one-armed hug. Marlon stood about three inches shorter than Jayden. A few streaks of gray were already noticeable in his otherwise dark head of hair and his beard. Jayden and Marlon attended the same small church in Katy.

"I think I'm the man you're supposed to meet with today. Stepping in for Tyler Washington. He had something come up."

Jayden's smile spread wider. He'd known Marlon for ages. Convincing him to hire Dallas & Smith should be an easy task. "It's all good. Nice to see you."

A blond hostess dressed in a black dress interrupted their small talk. "Gentleman, will any other guests be joining you?"

"It's just the two of us. Reservation for Jayden Reynolds."

She scanned the electronic tablet on the stand. "Okay. If you'll follow me." She led them through the dimly lit restaurant, where several patrons dressed in suits were already seated. They stopped at a booth for two at the back of the restaurant. Not that it was loud, but Jayden preferred the level of privacy it offered. Once they were seated, she handed them two menus. "Your server will be right with you."

"Thanks," Jayden said.

Scanning the menu, Marlon said, "You know, Jay, I admire you—putting in the work and climbing to the top. I take it that since you're here, you've finally made it to partner."

Jayden unbuttoned his jacket and released a long stream of air. "Thanks, man. It isn't quite final yet. I have to sign the agreement and buy into the partnership, and it's a done deal."

"Man, that's awesome! Congratulations. Your mom is always bragging on you down at the church, you know. You work all the time, but we keep up with you through her."

Jayden laughed and knew that to be true. His mom was his cheerleader and personal news anchor, sharing all his accomplishments at every opportunity to anyone who would listen.

"I appreciate it. Thanks, man. And you're doing well yourself. You're VP of tax at Caesar, right?"

"For the last four years. Our company has grown so much over the past few years that we've decided to outsource the preparation of our returns, which is where you guys come in. To be completely honest, we've met with the Tryon group, and we like what we've heard so far. Their numbers are in alignment with our budget, so what makes Dallas & Smith the right fit?"

Right down to business. Jayden could appreciate that.

Their waitress, a young black woman with curls pinned on top of her head in a high bun, stopped by with two glasses of water and an order of bread. She smiled and offered to answer any questions about the menu. After they declined, she promised to return after they had a few more minutes to decide on their orders.

"For starters, we're large enough to provide a team of employees to work on site, full-time and year round. You'll have our team at your disposal. As soon as you guys have the workpapers ready, our employees can start the returns. Not only that, but they'll also be available to answer questions about any uncertain tax positions and working to help reduce audit exposure."

Marlon rubbed his beard. "Okay, okay. I like that. Let's talk workspace and fee structure."

Their waitress returned to take their orders. Both men ordered steak, potatoes, and a side walnut salad. When she left, Jayden explained Dallas & Smith's fee structure. Satisfied with what he heard, Marlon requested Jayden send over the engagement letter so he could talk it over with his team.

"Thank you for your time, Marlon. I appreciate the opportunity for Dallas & Smith to provide tax services to Caesar."

"You're quite convincing. I'm surprised you aren't doing this for yourself."

Jayden sipped his water. "What do you mean?"

"You know, start your own firm. You're putting in quite the work for these guys. You ever thought about working for yourself?"

"Trying to get rid of me already? We haven't even signed the contract yet."

Marlon laughed. "No, nothing like that, but I am curious. Has it ever crossed your mind?"

A few times. And lately, now that there was the possibility of him not accepting the offer of partnership, he'd considered it a lot more. But did he want to put himself out there like that? More so now than ever, Jayden wanted to focus on his purpose and passion. Yes, he loved helping people work out their financial situation, but did he want to help the big guy or the little guy? And even more importantly, did he want to start over at this point in his life? The fleeting thought of his lack of love life crossed his mind. If he ever wanted one, he may not have a choice in the matter—he'd need a different career to have enough time to cultivate a relationship.

Or perhaps time to grow his relationship with Lisa.

"I don't know what the future entails," Jayden finally answered. "We'll have to see where God leads."

In a professional meeting with anyone else, Jayden wouldn't have mentioned anything about his faith, but he knew Marlon on a different level, so he felt comfortable with his statement.

"Well," Marlon said, jabbing a finger toward heaven, "He won't steer you wrong. You just need to be sensitive to His voice. God speaks in many ways, but sometimes we've already made our minds up about how he will answer and that thinking will cause us to miss what He's saying to us."

Jayden took another sip of his water. "You're preachin' right now, brother."

Marlon released a soft half chuckle. "Nah, none of that. Just speaking from experience."

Curious, Jayden asked, "And what experience is that, if you don't mind sharing?"

"I never mind sharing because my story can help someone else. Before I took this position, I was tax director at LNG downtown—crazy hours, working weekends, very little downtime for myself, let alone Natalie and the kids. It was destroying my marriage. Sure, the money was great, but based on the number of hours I worked, I wasn't coming out ahead financially or with my family. I prayed for something different for a while, but didn't really act on it, meaning I wasn't actively looking for another position. But after praying about it for a while, I started to notice little things. My employer didn't value me or my time. All they wanted was the job done."

Marlon pressed his finger into the table to emphasize his point. "Do you know I've had to cancel family vacations or work while on vacation? I quit after being asked to cut my last vacation short to come back into the office. That wasn't the kind of life I wanted to have. Granted, I don't encourage anyone leaving their job without another position already lined up, but that was the right move for me. You know Natalie. Man, she was hot when they called me while we were away in Disney World. First, she was upset that I brought my work phone on vacation to begin with, but she threatened to leave me and take the kids if I went back to work when that was supposed to be our family time."

"Wow."

Marlon's story sounded a lot like his, except he didn't have a family. But would his firm really call him on vacation? There were a few people who came to mind who probably would do such a thing. Not to mention they probably wouldn't think it to be an issue because Jayden often made himself available.

"Wow is right. It was a crazy time, but God provided. Now, I only work forty hours a week with great pay. I took a pay cut coming to Caesar, but I don't regret it. My marriage is solid, and my family is good. I even have the time to coach my son's soccer team."

"I'm happy it worked out for you."

Marlon winked like he knew something Jayden didn't. "And it'll work out for you, too."

"Coaching a little league soccer team? How is that experience?"

Marlon chuckled. "Not really something I ever saw myself doing, but I like that I get the chance to be there for him and watch him grow in sportsmanship."

"That's good for you. I'm sure Chase is happy to have you around at every practice and game."

"I hope it's a memory that he'll cherish when he gets older, but it probably doesn't mean as much to him now."

"And your little girl? I'm sorry I can never remember her name. How is she? And Natalie?"

At this point, Marlon pulled out his cell phone to show Jayden pictures of his little girl, Alaina, at her latest ballet recital. Then photos of his son Chase after his team won their little league soccer championship. And last, photos of their family during the last vacation. The smiles illuminating from the screen filled Jayden's heart with warmth and want.

Jayden wanted that—the family, the children, and the career that would allow him to manage it all. Sitting across from Marlon made the realization clearer by the second.

The waitress returned with their entrées. And although they didn't speak more about Jayden's future career path, the idea sped through his thoughts like a car on a racetrack with no brakes. Could this conversation have been God speaking to him, shining a light on what his future might look like if he continued on this path? At some point, he wanted to settle down and become a family man, but could he be different than the other partners in his future marriage if he accepted the partnership? Since he'd worked so hard for this opportunity, was it God honoring his request or a chance for him to choose something better?

Lord, if You want me to take a different path, then I need You to make it clear. I want to walk in Your purpose, but you have to show me what that is.

Their lunch meeting concluded with promises from Jayden to have the engagement letter sent over to Marlon's office by close of business that day. And although out of the way, Jayden drove to Between the Lines to see Lisa. She knew more than anyone how much he wanted this partnership. What would she think about him taking a different path?

∞

Lisa had already gotten seven authors to commit to the grand re-opening celebration event. Poised behind the checkout counter, she sent follow-up e-mails to the authors who had tentatively accepted. Ginger agreed to be on site selling Gingers' Goodies, and after hearing about the book store's delinquent tax issue, promised to donate all her proceeds back to Between the Lines. Lisa fought her on the issue but lost, thankful to have a friend like Ginger. Lisa booked Anthony Rejiv, a highly sought after local saxophonist, to provide entertainment. Three local food vendors would also be on site—barbecue, Louisiana-style Cajun, Tex-Mex. Things were coming together, but she hated the fact that this had become more about saving the bookstore than providing a nice event for the community. Under different circumstances, she wouldn't have charged the vendors fees, but in this case, it was necessary—whatever would help get her closer to raising a small percentage of the tax bill.

"Hey, hey. How's my favorite person in the whole world?" Jayden's voice rang through the building, drawing out a smile on her face. The overhead wind chimes signaled his entrance where he stood in the doorway holding up a bag from McCormick & Schmick's.

"The kind of food in that bag will be the true test of if I'm your favorite person or not."

Jayden chuckled and placed the bag on the counter. Lisa rounded the counter and wrapped her arms around his waist. He squeezed, and the wave of comfort that washed over her made her heart flutter. How could she be comforted and excited at the same time?

He kissed the top of her hair and sniffed. "*Ummm,* you smell good. New shampoo?"

Lisa pulled out of his embrace and cocked her head. "Actually, yes." It was just shampoo, so was that even something you thanked a person for noticing?

"Well, I like it. Works well with your perfume." He slid the bag over to her. "I brought you the same thing I had—steak, potatoes, and walnut salad."

She peeked inside the bag. "*Ooh. Yum.* I believe you when you say I'm your favorite person now."

Jayden brushed her curls over her shoulder, his fingertips lightly touching her collarbone. That little touch caused a shiver to course through her body. She fought hard to keep her shoulders from trembling in response. Lately, every time he touched her, she felt *something*. "Did you really have any doubt? Tell me now because if you did, I need to step up my game."

She leaned against the counter and held his gaze. "Well, I do like the sound of you stepping up your game, so I'm gonna go with yes. Plenty of doubt."

He laughed, and even that sound may as well have been lyrics from one of her favorite love songs.

Jayden licked his lips, and his eyes held this mix of playfulness and seriousness that she hadn't seen or at least noticed from him before. "Consider it done."

The electricity charging through the area could have powered the entire building. Uncertain about where this was headed, Lisa had to break their connection.

"So, I take it the food was good since you brought me some." She went back to her space behind the counter. A safe space. "Not that you need a reason, but did you only come by to bring me food?"

"Yes and no."

Alarms sounded in Lisa's head. Something was wrong. She locked eyes with him and waited for him to explain.

"I have something I want to run by you—get your opinion."

She gestured toward the center of the store and smiled. "Okay. Do we need to sit on my therapy couch?"

That playfulness slash seriousness returned to his eyes, which she wasn't sure how to read. "I think so."

Lisa vacated her safe space and rounded the counter. Jayden caught her hand, and she led him to the sofa in the middle of the area. She squeezed, but only to stave off the jitters. He held on until they sat, but had no problem staying in her personal bubble with their knees touching. And she didn't mind. Whatever this something different was slowly happening between them, she liked it.

"Talk to me."

"I've been praying about the next steps I should take in my career now that I've finally been offered the partner promotion, which in a sense is probably a terrible time to be thinking about this. But what if this is not what God has for me?"

He hesitated, and she had to refrain from interjecting with her opinion. She took his hands back in hers to encourage him to continue. Vulnerability had never really been Jayden's strongest area.

"And I met with Marlon today."

"Marlon from church?"

"Yeah. And he said some things that confirmed what I've been thinking."

Lisa nodded. "Okay, I'm listening."

"I'm not sure why now, but I've been thinking a lot about my purpose and being in the place God wants me to be."

"I take it you don't think where you are is it?"

Jayden's chest rose and fell. This career issue was obviously weighing on him. Is that why he'd been that way with her after his celebratory dinner at Joe's house?

"With me second-guessing my decision about signing on the dotted line, I don't think joining the partnership is the right choice. I have no peace about it, and honestly, it's hard for me to accept because I've been working so hard for this. This moment is years in the making."

Lisa nodded and squeezed his hand for reassurance, but all it did for her was cause these strange stirrings in her heart. Her emotions ran wild. "So, let's talk this out. If you didn't accept their offer for partnership, would you stay in your current position?"

"No. I'll start my own practice."

Her hands flew to her mouth before she thrust her arms around his neck. "Oh, Jayden, I'm so proud of you."

"I haven't made a decision yet, but based on your reaction, I take it that means you think it's a good idea."

"Are you kidding me? That's an excellent idea. You work harder than anyone I know, so why not do it for yourself?"

Jayden nodded and stroked his bare chin. "You sound like Marlon."

"Yes, about that…I jumped in and interrupted you. What was that conversation about?" She pinched her thumb and forefinger together and moved them in a zip-your-lips motion. She'd try not to interrupt again.

Jayden slouched back on the couch, his fingers linked in his lap, and eyed her skeptically, like he wasn't sure he should share the conversation with her, of all people—the person who knew almost everything about him.

"Marlon said some things about work interfering in his marriage. Listening to him and knowing what I know about the relationships of the partners in my firm, I don't want that to be my life. At some point, I want to get married and have a family. Work can no longer stand in the way of that."

Jayden grabbed her hand as he finished his last statement, and Lisa nearly had a heart attack. Granted, it could have been because of all the ideas Aunt Wanda had put in her head, but right now, her head and heart could only connect Jayden's words with his touch. And knowing him, he didn't mean anything by it—it was just his way of connecting.

"I know you'll make the right decision. I'll be praying for you, too."

He slid to the edge of the sofa. "Thanks, favorite person."

Lisa rubbed his shoulder. "You're welcome. Jayden, you know I support you no matter what you choose to do, and ultimately, I believe God will show you the way. Just be open."

He stood and extended his hand to help her up. "Being open seems like it may be the new phrase for my life." He pulled her close. "I'm gonna get back to the office. Thanks for lending your couch."

"Anytime. And only for you, no charge."

"Clearly I paid in advance with the food."

"If I were charging you, that wouldn't be enough."

Jayden chuckled and strolled toward the door. "I may need to join the partnership just so that I can afford you."

Lisa walked him to the exit. "Don't do it on my behalf. Still couldn't afford me."

He walked outside, descended one step, and turned so they were eye level. She hadn't expected him to turn around. The intensity in his eyes caused her heart to speed up. She had to get it together. Her emotions, her heart, her mind, her pulse, none of it should be reacting to anyone in this way, especially not to her best friend. "And why's that?"

"Because I'm priceless."

He lowered his eyes to her lips and leaned in close enough for her to feel his breath on her face. And before she swore her heart stopped, the blood pulsed through her veins like frozen fruit in a blender. "That, you are."

Lisa couldn't even find the words to respond before he did an about-face and left her standing in the doorway. She was a little unsure if he was flirting with her earlier, but now there wasn't any room left for doubt. What was even crazier was that she wanted him to kiss her. Even braced herself for his lips. And dare she think it? Disappointed that he didn't do so? What did this mean? And how was she supposed to act around him now?

Chapter Nine

Five days. Five phone calls. Four voicemails. Zero returned calls.

All Lisa needed from Melvin, Between the Lines' previous tax preparer, was the truth—one conversation to set her mind at ease. Though unlikely she would recover the money she knew he'd taken, she couldn't help but hold out hope. Her business, her store, her dream was on the line.

Aunt Wanda sashayed over to the counter. "Aren't you driving to San Antonio tomorrow for the booklovers convention? Why don't you just drop by Melvin's house?"

The reader convention had been the farthest thing from her mind since she'd learned about the property tax issue. In truth, she probably would have skipped it since she had more pressing things to worry about now, like keeping the Fort Bend County Tax Assessor's office from foreclosure proceedings. For now, she thanked God they hadn't done so, because three years was a long time to allow the taxes to go unpaid. If she didn't have this tax situation, she would have been in San Antonio a day early for the booklovers conference with either her mom, Ginger, or Aunt Wanda, but she just wasn't in the right spirit for it at this time.

"Mom isn't up to going, and you're staying behind to manage the store. Ginger has to run her own shop, so I don't know if I'll go this year." And that sucked because this would be the first live conference in three years.

Aunt Wanda's eyebrows danced. "I think you're forgetting someone whose always available whenever you call him."

"It's the middle of busy season for Jayden. He doesn't have time for last-minute trips."

Aunt Wanda shrugged and sang, "That doesn't apply to you."

Lisa laughed. "I'll ask, but I know what he's going to say." She dialed Jayden and pressed the speaker button. "Speakerphone is for your benefit."

"Good morning." The instant she heard his voice, the emotions she'd experienced when they stood at eye level outside of her bookstore yesterday resurfaced. She swallowed and forced herself to keep a straight, unbothered expression because Aunt Wanda watched her like prey. Lisa could swear that woman could smell if anything was different with her and Jayden.

"Good morning to you. How's your morning so far?"

"I can't complain. It's a little better now that I hear your voice. What's up?"

Lisa glanced over at Aunt Wanda, who quirked an eyebrow. *He's just being Jayden.* Although, a little flirtatious lately, Lisa knew he didn't mean anything by it.

"I have a favor to ask, and it's okay if you can't do it because I know you're busy with work," she said in one breath. "I'm driving to San Antonio to attend the booklovers conference, and since Melvin lives there and is avoiding my calls, I'm going to make a surprise visit. My plan was to make it a day trip. Can you come?"

"When do we leave?"

Lisa stumbled, "I, *ummm,* I thought you were busy with work."

"I am, but I can't have you walking into a situation with Melvin unannounced. What if something happened to you? I can't have that, so when do we leave?"

Lisa cut her eyes at Aunt Wanda, who now stood close with her arms folded across her chest. Her presence known. She had that I-told-you-so look on her face, a sentiment she likely wouldn't let Lisa live down. Ever.

"Tomorrow morning."

"And what time tomorrow morning do I need to pick you up?"

Lisa pursed her lips and thought for a second. She hadn't quite gotten that far because she hadn't committed to the trip until now. "*Ummm,* seven?"

"I'll be there."

"Thanks, Jayden. I appreciate it."

"No, problem. I meant what I said." Jayden's voice dropped an octave, sending shivers down her spine and back up to her neck. The tiny hairs at the base of her neck stood at attention.

If Aunt Wanda weren't there working to piece together things she didn't already know, Lisa would have asked him to repeat what he said about stepping up his game. She liked this flirtatious side of him. If nothing else, it was fun. However, they had at least six hours in the car together tomorrow, driving to and from San Antonio. Hopefully this little flirting they'd been doing wouldn't make it weird.

"Yeah, and I'm holding you to it. Get some work done, and I'll talk to you later."

"You can count on it. Later."

Lisa ended the call, rounded the counter, and walked to the children's book section. She organized books on the shelf as if Aunt Wanda hadn't followed her waiting for her to admit she was wrong.

"You can't ignore the fact that I was right. Now, I birthed that man. You can't tell me that I don't know him."

Without turning to look at her, Lisa responded with a steady voice. She couldn't let on how much Jayden had started to affect her. His touch. His voice. Everything about him. That feeling made her nervous, and *nervous* had never been a word anyone would use to describe her. "You were right, Aunt Wanda. You're always right about Jayden."

"Don't I know it? You're the only woman I know that he's always wanted to please."

Lisa turned to her and frowned. "Jayden has dated plenty of other women. Let's not forget Chelsey." She was jealous, but would never admit it to Jayden because he had the right to date whoever he wanted. They weren't an item, never were. But Lisa couldn't stand the way the woman hung all over him, always touching him. Chelsea wasn't good enough for him anyway, but Lisa didn't say so—at least not to him. She never interfered in his love life or gave her opinion unless he asked for it.

Aunt Wanda fanned her hands. "I ain't thinking about that woman. She cared about him more than he cared about her. And if you ask me, he was just trying to make you take notice of him. Besides, that's not the point. I didn't say he never dated anyone else, I said he always wanted to please you." She wagged her finger in Lisa's direction to emphasize her point.

Lisa turned and rested her weight on the bookshelf. She'd likely regret asking because Aunt Wanda's memory was like an elephant's—never forgetting a thing, especially if it served her agenda. "How did you come to that conclusion? Name one time, other than today, that he wanted to please me?"

"How much time do we have? Because I've got a whole book of examples."

The door chimed, and two women walked inside, cutting their personal chat short.

"Welcome to Between the Lines, ladies. Are you looking for any book in particular?"

The short brown-skinned woman with straight hair smiled and nodded. "Point me to the romance section."

"My kind of woman," Lisa responded. "C'mon. Follow me. And what about you?" she said to the taller friend. Short haircut, leggings, and an oversized sweater for the iffy weather—yesterday, it was hot—she looked like she was minutes away from making herself comfortable on the bookstore's sofa with a good book.

"Any chance you have that new romance novel from Justin Love?"

Lisa's brows crinkled, and she stopped walking. "No. I haven't heard of him."

"You've gotta read his book, *At Last*. I think it's only been out a couple of months, and it's number one on Amazon. How have you not heard about it? Everyone is talking about it. I have a copy on my Kindle, but I want the paperback. Hopefully I can get it signed one day since he's local. It has like over five thousand reviews, and they aren't lying when they say how good it is." She palmed her chest and sighed. "Trust me. Do yourself a favor and read it."

Aunt Wanda sauntered over. "We're usually on top of all the new romance novels. How is he local, and we haven't heard of him? If it's as good as it sounds, we need to get it."

Lisa nodded. "Right. I can order it for you and have it ready for pickup by next week. How does that sound?"

"Please do. Thank you." Lisa appreciated local readers who supported her store. The young woman could have easily ordered the book online and had it on her doorstep in two days.

"Please take a moment to look around to see if we've got anything in the store that catches your eye. Who are some of your favorite authors?"

"Rhonda McKnight, Michelle Stimpson, and Toni Shiloh," the shorter friend said.

"We've got similar tastes," her friend added.

"Say no more. I have books by them and similar authors we recommend." Lisa led them to the romance section and left them to browse. "I'll get Justin Love's book ordered for you right now."

Lisa navigated to the book's Amazon page. She nearly choked when she read the book's tagline.

When falling in love with your best friend wasn't the plan...

She noted the reviews, but chose not to read them because she didn't want anyone else's views to influence her own. His author bio was short, but did mention that he lived in the Houston metro area. She left that page and put together an order from Ingram. Lisa purchased copies for her store and one for herself. Just how did falling in love with your best friend work out for the characters in that book? Because she couldn't see that making sense in her own life.

Aunt Wanda rounded the counter and peered over her shoulder. "I already looked it up on Amazon, read the reviews, and started the sample chapter. I'm hooked. Let's make it our book club's next read."

Lisa turned her attention away from the screen. "Well, it is your turn to choose the book, so that's fine with me. I'll add copies for all of us."

The two women finished their shopping and came to the checkout counter with eight books between them. Lisa asked, "Did you find everything okay? Is there something else I can order for you that we didn't have in stock?"

"I think we're good for now," the taller friend answered.

Lisa accepted their payment and completed their transactions.

"I'm also adding a flyer into your bags about our upcoming grand re-opening event. Plenty of local authors, food, and music. Come by, and tell your friends and family."

They read over the postcard-sized flyers. "I love book signings and food, so I'll be here," the shorter friend said.

"If you could get that Justin Love to come, I bet that will draw a crowd. I think I might be in love with him," the taller friend said and chuckled. She fanned herself. "*Whew.* The way that man wrote that story, he has to know a thing or two about love and how to treat a woman."

"Right," her friend agreed.

When they left the store, Aunt Wanda said, "Can you put a rush order on those books? I want to read it now."

Lisa chuckled. "I know, right? They're talking this book up like they're on his marketing team. Now I can't wait to read it either."

With the order complete, she navigated back to his Amazon page, which mentioned his website to get in touch. The man was secretive or in need of a designer. His website was one page, which she assumed was a work in progress. The same short bio that she read on Amazon along with information about his book was the gist of the webpage. She took the advice of the readers who left her store and hit the contact button. In her message, she extended an invitation to attend the bookstore's grand re-opening.

If this book was as good as they said, maybe Justin Love was just what she and the bookstore needed.

∞

Five thousand amazon reviews. The high he felt from the response he'd received from his newly published book overcame the low he experienced from working thirteen hours yesterday. But he'd done so because he would be out of the office today with Lisa on the trip to San Antonio. Now was probably a good time to tell Lisa how great his book was doing and that he'd finally published it, especially since she'd invited him—well, Justin Love—to attend Between the Lines' grand re-opening. He hadn't made any plans to do author appearances, but he wouldn't turn her down. He'd go to the ends of the earth for her. So, without hesitation, he accepted.

Now, he needed to find the right time to tell her about Justin Love. But that had to be after he figured out everything—his career and the moves he'd make.

Jayden climbed out of his truck and jogged up the cement path to Lisa's front door. Her smile was as wide as the opening. "Hey, hey. Good morning."

She was dressed in leggings and a track jacket with her curly hair pulled into a ponytail on top of her head. Even dressed down, Lisa looked amazing to him. She wrapped her arms around his waist, and he pulled her close. Lately, every time they hugged, Lisa felt more and more like home—like that was how things should be. Her in his arms every day. But that thought alone was a lot to think about, to take in, and even as the person who wrote a seventy-thousand-word novel, he couldn't seem to find the words to say. Could it be that he was afraid she wouldn't feel the same? Or afraid that confessing what he felt would push her away from him? Losing her wasn't a risk he wanted to take.

Instead, he'd hold on to hope that showing her how he felt was better than telling her.

"Good morning to you, too. You ready for me?"

His choice of words weren't lost on Lisa because she bugged her eyes, and her mouth dropped open. She recovered quickly and exchanged her bewilderment with a smile. "Been ready. Just let me grab my purse."

For once, Jayden didn't follow her inside. He paced the cement porch, the rising sun piercing through the clouds, and it seemed to be shining its light directly on him, following him across his short path. It was almost like a nudge from God to talk to Lisa about everything, or maybe that was his own guilt getting to him.

Lisa stepped outside and turned to lock the door. "Let's get this show on the road."

Taking her hand became more automatic lately, but Lisa didn't object, so this morning wasn't any different, even though his truck was about twenty feet from the door. That new electric feeling didn't seem to be wearing off any time soon either. Part of him needed to test it a few more times just to be sure it was truly happening.

Once Lisa was safely inside and Jayden joined her, he started the engine and turned to face her. "Are you hungry? We can stop to get something to eat if you'd like."

"We can grab something quick if you don't mind. I'd rather keep this show moving. How about we stop by Ginger's bakery on the way?"

"I'll never object to that."

Fifteen minutes later, Jayden parked in Ginger's Goodies' parking lot. The old house that she'd transformed into what locals referred to as the pink bakery couldn't be missed. Pink lights shone around the business sign to alert customers that she was open. Jayden hopped out of his truck, rounded the bumper, and opened the door for Lisa. This time, he held his palm up, and she accepted it. They strolled inside like they were more than just friends, and to anyone looking at them, they'd likely believe that to be the truth.

At seven o'clock in the morning, the bakery already had a healthy load of customers sitting at the round counter-height tables, sipping coffee, and feasting on Ginger's keto and gluten-free baked goods. The intimacy of the atmosphere was what her customers enjoyed, and Jayden couldn't blame them. Smooth R-and-B music came through the speakers, and the aroma from her kitchen was comforting and brought about this sense of peace. He only ate the treats when he was with Lisa, but even he felt the need to sit and enjoy this time with her, talking about everything and nothing. But today wasn't the day to relax at Ginger's bakery, they were on a mission.

"Look at what we have here." Ginger beamed and darted her eyes from Jayden to Lisa then down to their intertwined fingers.

"Morning, Ginger," Jayden said.

"Hey, Gin. How's it goin? Whatcha got for me?"

"The better question is how are things going with you two?" She wagged her finger back and forth.

Lisa looked at Jayden, then frowned at Ginger. "Nothing much. We're hitting the road to San Antonio. Just stopping by for treats and to support our favorite baker on the way out."

Ginger squinted at Jayden for several seconds. Whatever she wanted to say, she didn't, but he could just about guess. He'd known her for at least half of his life. She pushed her lips out, hiked her eyebrows, and shrugged. "Oh, okay then. So we're acting like nothing is happening. Okay. Cool."

Ginger turned away and walked to the baker's glass case. Jayden and Lisa followed on the customer side. "I have blueberry scones ready. Butter croissants. Chocolate croissants. An assortment of muffins. What would you two like?"

Lisa peered through the glass case. "Everything is good, but I don't want to stuff myself and eat mindlessly on the road. What do you want, Jay?"

"I know you want the scones. I'll get one of those, too, and try the chocolate croissants."

Lisa held up two fingers. "Two scones and that chocolate croissant. A medium cup of coffee, too, please."

"Is that all?"

Jayden added, "A coffee for me, too. Cream and sugar."

"I've got you. Coming right up."

While Ginger bagged their orders and poured their coffees, Jayden turned to Lisa. "Anything else you want to do while we're in San Antonio after we leave the book convention and pay a visit to Melvin?"

"How about The Riverwalk? It's been ages since I've been out there. Maybe if we have time, we could even do the boat ride."

"What about lunch on The Riverwalk? Plenty of choices. Of course Mexican, but also seafood, Italian, barbecue, and American." Jayden almost forgot that could be considered romantic, especially depending on the restaurant. But gauging by Lisa's reaction, she wasn't thinking of it that way. Her smile touched her eyes before her lips.

"That sounds like fun. I would even suggest a movie, but that might be squeezing in too much, and we both need to get back for work tomorrow."

"Cool with me. I'm at your service."

"Not just today, but every day," Ginger added, though more of a statement under her breath.

Lisa rubbed his back, looked up at him with the most beautiful eyes he'd seen on any woman. Her lips parted, showing off the top row of her even pearly whites. "Yeah, Jayden always seems to come through."

Ginger had that same grin she had on her face the day he picked Lisa up to attend his promotion dinner hosted by his mentor, Joe. She smirked like she knew something neither of them knew. "He does, doesn't he?"

"Well, I promised Lisa I'd step my game up, so that's what I'm doing."

Ginger looked toward the door, seemingly checking for customers, then braced her elbows on the countertop with her chin resting on her fists. "Step your game up? Oh, please tell me more. I feel like I've missed something since I saw Lisa when we went gown shopping."

Jayden and Lisa laughed. Without responding to Ginger, Jayden paid for their orders, they said their good-byes and left. They both knew what Ginger was insinuating—that the two of them had decided to take their relationship to the next level—but their growing attraction was a topic they were good at avoiding. And he knew his why, but what was hers? Part of him also liked the fact they were allowing things to develop naturally without putting a label on what was happening, but the danger with that thinking was his feelings could be one-sided.

Jayden opened the door for Lisa before taking his seat behind the steering wheel.

She held up her palm. "Let's say a quick prayer for God's protection on the road."

He took her free hand in his. "Lord God, thank You for this opportunity. We ask that You keep us safe on the road traveling to and from our destination. Be our eyes when we can't see. Give us clarity. Give us peace in our interaction with Melvin, no matter the outcome. Let Your will be done, in Jesus' name. Amen."

Lisa squeezed his hand before letting go and rummaging through the pink Ginger's Goodies' bag. "Amen."

He shifted the truck into gear and navigated out of the parking lot onto the main road. In his peripheral vision, Lisa looked comfortable, like this trip was the most natural thing in the world for them. Perhaps a year ago, it probably would have been.

But today was different.

They were different.

Their relationship was different.

Today was the day he admitted to himself that Lisa was the one for him. His heart was completely wrapped up in her. Now he just had to figure out how, when, and if he could tell her.

Chapter Ten

Lisa and Jayden entered reader heaven when they stepped inside of San Antonio's Henry B. Gonzalez Convention Center. The romance booklover conference crawled with readers shuffling through the aisles. The scene before her made her heart smile. Tote bags filled with books hung on almost every shoulder. One reader wheeled around a suitcase. Long lines for autographed copies and others sitting in smaller groups discussing their favorite books.

Lisa tugged Jayden's arm. "Oh my goodness. Is that who I think it is?"

"Who?"

"Come on. Let's go see."

They maneuvered through the throng of readers, bumping shoulders with a few people along the way, murmuring "excuse me" and "sorry" more times than she could count until they arrived at Sebastian's table. Sebastian was her favorite male romance author, who simply went by his first name alone. He couldn't write anything wrong in her eyes. He wrote the kind of novels that made every woman swoon and fall in love with his characters, and dare she think it, possibly even him. How she spotted him one hundred feet away, she wasn't sure. The line was long, but so were most of the author lines for readers to get their books signed. She didn't mind the wait. Meeting authors, taking selfies with them, purchasing books, and getting them signed was why she was there.

While she waited, she peered around the authors at surrounding tables, wondering if by chance, this Justin Love would be in attendance. She hadn't read his book yet, but with all the great reviews and buzz surrounding it, Lisa couldn't help but wonder. But it was difficult to see through the crowd. She stood at an average height of five feet, five inches. It seemed everyone else around her was blessed with several more inches because the only thing she could spot was other attendees' shoulders.

Jayden leaned over and spoke in her ear, close enough to where she could feel his breath, which caused a tingle to race down her spine. "What can I help you find? You look like you're about to strain your neck."

Lisa glanced up at him and half-chuckled. "Nothing. Just looking to see who else is in attendance that I might not have known about."

"Anyone in particular?"

She thought for a moment. "Justin Love."

Jayden's eyes widened. A flicker of emotion flashed in his eyes, though she couldn't pinpoint which one.

Lisa continued, "He's a new author. And now that I think about it, he wouldn't be here because they announced the author line-up months ago."

Jayden shrugged. "Okay. Who are we going to see next? It's a madhouse in here."

"I know. But it's been years since they've hosted the conference, so I'm not the least bit surprised."

"Yeah, that's true."

After waiting another thirty minutes, Lisa and Jayden were finally at the front of the line.

Lisa removed two of Sebastian's latest books from her bag. "You are one of my favorite authors. I can't tell you how excited I am to finally meet you."

A genuine smile framed his face while his almond-colored eyes focused on her, like she was the person who mattered in that moment. He had a head full of dreadlocks neatly hanging below his shoulders. Sebastian had released four books each year for the last five years, but he looked like he spent more time in the gym's weight room than behind his keyboard. "I'd be lying if I said I didn't love to hear that. What's your favorite book?"

She pushed his second-to-last book in front of him. "*All I've Ever Wanted,* but really I've enjoyed everything you've ever written."

"Sounds like I'm talking to my biggest fan. Who should I sign this to?"

"I'm Lisa—Lisa Atkinson."

While he autographed the books, she played with the thought of inviting him to her bookstore's grand re-opening. Well, he could only say yes or no, right?

"Can I have a photo with you?"

He pushed away from the table, stood, and spread an arm for her to come close. "Absolutely."

She turned to Jayden and thrust her phone into his hand. "Do you mind?"

Sebastian posed next to her like they'd been friends forever and even handed his own phone to Jayden to snap a photo.

"You've been awesome. I won't take up too much more of your time. You have a long line of fans to get to." She hesitated before leaving his table. "I own Between the Lines bookstore in Katy. I would love to host a signing for you sometime. In fact, we're having a grand re-opening soon."

"Will you e-mail me the details? If I can attend, I'd certainly come out to support my biggest fan."

She could have melted where she stood. Everything in her fluttered at the possibility of Sebastian agreeing to attend her event. "I'll shoot you an e-mail later this evening." She had everything in her inbox and phone now, but didn't want to appear desperate so she'd hold off until later.

"It was nice to meet you, Lisa. Me or my publicist will be in touch after I receive the event details."

Lisa stopped by as many author tables of both well-known and new-to-her authors as she could make time for. Two were

Houston-area authors whom she discussed her grand re-opening event with and who were interested in attending. After about three hours, Lisa checked the time. "It's almost two o'clock, and as much as I'd like to stick around until they kick us out, we still need to see Melvin and spend a little while on The Riverwalk before heading back home."

"Sounds good to me. But you know this is only a yearly event. Are you sure you've seen everyone you want to see?"

They strolled down the cluttered aisles, and Lisa looked from one side of the aisle to the other. If she had it her way, she'd stop and talk to every author in the building. If her book club were there, they could divide and conquer, giving them the opportunity to discover more authors and new books. But despite all the fun she was having, the tax situation was much more pressing.

"Yeah. I'm sure." She had to deal with Melvin sooner rather than later, especially while she still had the guts to confront him.

Lisa led Jayden toward the exit. He stopped before opening the door. "You sure you don't want to go say goodbye to your favorite male romance author back there?"

"No. He's already signed my books, and I have pics." Lisa glanced up at Jayden. "Wait a minute. Are you jealous?"

"Why would I be jealous of him being so close to you during the photo opp? He was just a little too familiar, is all I'm saying."

Lisa laughed and shook her head. "I can't believe you're jealous. And here I was thinking that you were being a good sport by carrying my bag of books and snapping pictures. *Tsk. Tsk.*"

Jayden pushed the door open. "I am not jealous. I'm just saying. I didn't know you liked him that much."

"My whole book club likes him. I'm sure you've heard us talking about him from time to time, right?"

"Nope. Honestly, I tune you out."

Lisa doubled over in laughter. "Wow. Jealousy does not look good on you."

When she recovered, they strolled through the parking lot to his vehicle. The afternoon sun beamed in full force. Lisa had to use her hand to shield her eyes from the sun's rays.

When they made it to his truck, Lisa jammed a fist into her hip and turned to face him. "Jayden Reynolds, I can't believe you. You don't have to be jealous of Sebastian or anyone else. I don't plan to replace you as my best friend any time soon. Besides, I don't even know him."

Jayden opened the door for her and continued the teasing. "So if you knew him, then my best friend status could be in jeopardy?"

"I don't think anyone would want to put in the time you put in."

Jayden closed the door. "You've got that right."

∞

Jayden couldn't resist teasing Lisa, but the truth was that his jealousy had reared itself. Though she may have been joking, he didn't like the way this Sebastian fellow was hugged up on her. Author or not, fan or not, he was way too close for Jayden's liking when they posed for the picture. But he had to shake off his issues because he didn't have any claim to Lisa. They weren't dating, only friends, so he had no right to be jealous, nor should her interaction with any other man concern him. But it did.

The other issue that bothered him was that he should have been inside that convention center behind one of those tables signing books and meeting readers. With Lisa taking pictures with him and gushing over how much she liked his—not Sebastian's—work. The longing in him to pursue his writing career grew stronger these days, but he still couldn't be sure if it was time for him to do anything about it.

He rubbed a palm over his face as if that would wipe away the dissatisfaction he felt and climbed in the driver's seat and started the engine. "Okay. What is Melvin's address?"

Lisa called it out to him as he punched the address into his vehicle's GPS.

Jayden buckled his seatbelt and navigated out of the convention center's parking lot. "Let's talk about what you plan to say to Melvin when we get to his place."

Lisa dug through her purse and removed the notice from the tax office. "Simple. I'm going to show him this letter and ask him about the property tax payments."

He nodded. "I understand that, but what's your backup plan? Have you thought about this from every possible angle?"

"Of course I have, but the answer should be simple. Either he paid them or he didn't. And obviously we know he didn't pay the property taxes because we wouldn't be in this situation. I want to know what happened to the money."

"Are you expecting him to write you a check or hand over cash to you today?"

"I'm sure that's wishful thinking. And while I'd also like to wrap my fingers around his neck and shake the money out of him, I want him to look me in my eyes and tell me why he did this to my mother. She trusted him. And at a time when she was taking care of my dad and believing that the monthly bills, which I handled, and the property taxes would be one less thing for her to be concerned about because Melvin supposedly took care of them. It's low down and dirty of him to take advantage of her—of me—like that."

Jayden took his eyes off the road and glanced at her when they arrived at a red traffic light. "Have you thought about my offer?"

Lisa's chest inflated. She blew a slow stream of air before responding. "I have, and I appreciate it, but I stand by what I said. I want to do this on my own first. Will you promise me that you'll let me come to you before swooping in to save the day?"

The traffic light signaled it was time to resume driving. "Only if you'll promise me that you will come to me."

Lisa chuckled. "You know I will."

"Nah, I don't know that. That's why I'm making you promise me. You're stubborn, Lisa, and in this situation, you don't have to be. This is simply me offering you the opportunity not to worry so soon, not when you've just started running this business.

Your efforts can be better focused on doing all the things you love like buying books, hosting signings for authors, connecting authors and readers."

Was he selfish in a sense? True, he understood her need to work the situation out on her own, but why put herself through this extra stress when she didn't have to? His motives were pure. He didn't expect anything from Lisa in return. That whole making him a silent partner idea was to make her feel better about it.

"That sounds like a dream."

"It is. It's your dream, remember? Growing up, all you'd talk about is what you would do when you owned Between the Lines."

"And have you forgotten about your dream?"

Jayden knew precisely what Lisa meant, but he hoped it wouldn't come up. Not when he'd taken the step to do something about his dream and hadn't told her about it. He didn't want to have to lie to her because he planned to tell her when the time was right— when he figured out what he'd do about accepting this partnership. When he figured out what he should be doing at this time in his life. At least it seemed Lisa was clear on her purpose and her place in this world. He needed to find his.

"What dream are you talking about? Becoming partner?"

Lisa smiled wide as if revealing it to him would change his entire world. "Nope. Not that one."

Jayden hiked an eyebrow. "Becoming a writer?"

"Bingo. While I dreamed about owning the bookstore, you said you'd write enough books to have your own section in my store.

Now that I have the store, it seems only right that it's about time for you to start churning out books. I'll save a special space for you in the store when you're ready."

A slow smile spread across his mouth. Thoughts of the many conversations they'd shared about what their future would look like once they were adults filled his mind. On many occasions, after school at Between the Lines, while doing homework, Jayden talked about the books he would write. He'd once said that he'd write at least one book in every genre, but he was just a kid, not really knowing or understanding the craft or what it would take to do such a thing. But still, he had hope—until he saw his parents stressing over bills at the kitchen table one night when he was eleven years old. He was supposed to be in bed, but he'd gone to the kitchen for a glass of water, well actually soda, but it had to be water once he saw his parents in the kitchen. He hadn't thought much about money before that time, but the image of the two of them with the calculator, checkbook, and stack of bills never left his mind. He swore to himself then that he'd do whatever it took to make money to ensure his parents had a better life. And he made good on that promise, though his dad never lived to see it. Five years ago, he'd purchased a home for his mother. The smile on her face had been worth every long hour he'd worked leading up to that point.

"I can't believe you still remember that."

"Not sure why you're so surprised. We talked about it nearly every day. You even started writing a book. Remember that? You gave it to me for safekeeping."

Jayden tossed his head back and laughed. "I do remember that. I'm glad that's nowhere to be found."

Lisa shifted her eyebrows rhythmically. "Oh, but it is. I have it at home."

"Stop playing."

She spread her hands in the air as if she were painting a picture. "It's going in the Jayden Reynolds collection. Maybe I'll frame it and put it on the Jayden Reynolds' shelf whenever you decide to make your dreams a reality."

"I'll take that. It's nice you've kept it all this time, although I don't know if I'll believe it until I see it."

"I'll dig it up for you. Maybe that'll motivate you or spark a fire in you to do what you've always wanted to do."

The words were on the tip of his tongue to tell her that he'd done it, and so far, it was going well, although it had only been a short time. But instead, he slowed his truck to a stop in front of a white, one-story house with cement steps leading toward the entrance and said, "We're here."

Chapter Eleven

Lisa practiced calming breaths while Jayden rounded the truck to open the passenger-side door for her. She'd allowed Aunt Wanda to boost her up for this moment—to believe that when Melvin saw her face, this tax situation would get resolved. Now that the moment was here, her nerves were frayed like the pieces of a shaken pom-pom. She'd rehearsed her speech at least twenty times last night in her bathroom mirror. First, she would listen to his side of the story, though nothing would appease the fact that he'd stolen from her family. Second, she'd try to level with him using familiarity and emotion. Third…well, she hoped that it wouldn't get to that point because Jayden might have to drag her out of there.

Between the Lines was her dream, and Melvin wasn't about to mess it up for her.

Jayden stood there with his palm up like a king waiting for his queen. Although unnecessary, she would never tire of the way her friend tended to her every need. Perhaps that was why she'd never been in a rush to get into a relationship with another man. Had Jayden practically met all her needs for as many years as she could count, except for her desire for romance? But even as a self-proclaimed romantic, she wasn't in a hurry for love either.

Unsure of where those thoughts came from, Lisa squeezed her eyes shut for a moment to push them away. The issue at hand was Melvin and Between the Lines' property taxes. She took hold of Jayden's hand and held on tight as she stepped down out of his truck. The grass was freshly manicured, with no plants or flowers in sight. Tranquility swept over her. Hopefully that was a sign for what would happen next.

"You ready for this?"

Lisa nodded and released a heavy breath. "Yep. As ready as I'll ever be."

Jayden rubbed circles on the back of her hand. He meant it to calm her, but his touch had the opposite effect, much like it had a lot lately. Her heart pounded even more.

Get it together. Be strong. Show Melvin you're serious.

"I've got your back, no matter what happens."

With Lisa's hand still tucked securely into Jayden's, together, they trudged up the red-brick path leading up to the three cemented steps to Melvin's wooden oval-glass-panel door. Jayden rang the doorbell. Lisa held her breath and waited.

Nothing.

After about thirty seconds, Jayden pushed the doorbell again and tilted his head left and right to peer into the glass for motion. "I hear footsteps."

After what seemed like an eternity, but in actuality was another thirty seconds or so, Lisa heard the locks disengage. The door creaked open, and a whiff of Old Spice cologne and wrinkled caramel skin greeted her.

Melvin Mason smiled wide, showing the gap between his two front teeth, though she could have sworn there was first a look of panic, but that could have been in her head. His beard and mustache were filled with many more streaks of white than the last time she'd seen him, which was about six months ago.

"Lisa. What a surprise." He peered around her as if looking for someone else. Melvin thrust his hand toward Jayden for him to shake. "And Mr. Jayden Reynolds. Come on in."

Melvin stepped aside to allow them entry and clasped his hands together. "To what do I owe this pleasure?"

As if he doesn't know.

Lisa rummaged through her purse for the tax letter that had given her grief over the past couple of weeks. "Mom transferred ownership of the bookstore to me, and there's something I need to talk to you about."

Melvin's eyelids drooped, and he turned toward the doorway that led to the kitchen. He called over his shoulder. "Oh. Can I get you two something to drink?"

Jayden looked at her, cocked an eyebrow, and nodded in Melvin's direction. He mouthed, "He's stalling."

Lisa was well aware of that, but didn't want to be pushy. She was determined to handle this situation in a civil, professional manner. She answered for them both. "No, thank you."

About a minute later, Melvin hobbled in the room carrying a wooden tray with three glasses of iced water. He set them on the table and gestured toward Lisa and Jayden to take a seat on the chocolate sofa. Melvin sat across from them in a recliner.

"Congratulations on becoming the owner of the bookstore. Your mother always talked about you taking over one day. She'd said that everything she did was for you."

"Thank you, Melvin." Lisa placed the letter on the table and pushed it toward him. "What do you know about this?"

He picked up the letter and read through it. It took him longer than Lisa thought he needed. It was short and clear. Between the Lines owed property taxes for the last three years plus interest and penalties.

Jayden sat on the edge of the sofa with his hands clasped and elbows resting on his knees, ready to pounce at any moment. And judging by his facial expression, all he needed was for her to give him the green light to jump in. But thankfully, he remained quiet and deferred to her.

The thickness of silence in the house didn't help the situation either—no humming of the refrigerator, radio, ceiling fan, or air conditioning unit.

If she had to guess, the flat-screen television on the wall was about sixty inches. The sofa she sat on was as comfortable as one newly added to a furniture store's showroom floor. The wooden coffee table and end tables were freshly polished. Even the pictures on the walls looked new. Had he used some of their money to spruce up his home? Not that she'd ever been in his home, but she couldn't help but wonder.

The watch cuffed around his wrist wasn't cheap either, not that she was a watch connoisseur, but she knew an expensive one when she saw it. The Rolex was probably funded by her bookstore, too.

"Melvin, Between the Lines owes property taxes to the Fort Bend County Tax Assessor—taxes that you were supposed to pay. What happened? Where's the money?" Lisa's voice came across with much more authority than she'd planned. Maybe even a little harsh. And the only reason she became aware of her tone was because Jayden leaned away and hiked an eyebrow, then smirked and nodded his approval.

At first, Melvin didn't respond. He placed the letter back on the table and slid it to her. He shrugged so nonchalantly that her blood bubbled and sizzled. "The money is gone."

"Where is it? What did you do with it?"

"I took what was rightfully mine."

"You mean you stole the money from us. My mom trusted you. How could you do this to her?"

Melvin slid to the edge of the recliner, jamming his finger in the table to emphasize his point. "Your mother owed me for all the years I put in helping her. Keeping her books. Preparing her federal income tax returns. Making sure she paid her property taxes. I did all of it."

"So what changed? Seems you had no problem being benevolent before. Why didn't you just ask her to pay you? You know she would have done so if you asked. Instead, you were the one who chose to do it out of the kindness of your heart—or at least that was the lie you told her. What changed?" Lisa asked again, this time through gritted teeth.

"Why don't you ask her?"

Lisa thought for a moment. He could not be insinuating that her mother led him on in a romantic way. Or that her mother had an affair with him. That she would not accept and would not believe under any circumstances.

She leaped out of her seat and closed the space between them, her chest heaving and pressure elevated. She was doing exactly what she said she wouldn't do—lose control. "No. I'm here because I want you to tell me to my face why you stole from us. How can you justify your actions?"

The air in her lungs struggled to get out as she tried to regulate her breathing. She didn't want a shouting match with Melvin. She wanted the truth. And to be honest, a check.

Melvin stood. His demeanor was still all too calm for her taste. "I think it's time for you to leave, young lady."

"I'm not going anywhere until I get the truth and my money back." Even as she screamed and carried on, she knew Melvin would not be writing her a check that day, or any day for that matter. And the reality of her keeping the bookstore faded like a colored garment doused with bleach. She couldn't let that happen. Lisa geared up to give him a piece of her mind, and this time, she wouldn't be nice and civilized about the situation. But before the words reached her lips, she felt Jayden's warm touch on both of her arms.

∞

Jayden had to stop Lisa before she ripped the man to pieces physically and verbally. He never should have allowed the situation to escalate between them—well moreso, Lisa. Melvin was unbothered. Before walking into this situation, Jayden knew—and he believed a part of Lisa knew as well—that she would not walk away with any money or satisfactory answers from Melvin. But he understood Lisa's plight. She had to try. And as he told her, he could not let her do this alone. He advanced behind her and stilled her with his hands on her arms.

He leaned and whispered in her ear. "He's not worth it."

Lisa looked over her shoulder at him with wet eyes.

Melvin brushed passed the two of them and opened the front door. "Listen to your boyfriend. I have nothing for you, so you need to leave. Before I call the cops."

They'd have to find another way to deal with him, because nothing would be accomplished standing in Melvin's living room.

She nodded and traced Melvin's steps toward the front door with Jayden next to her. He enclosed her hand in his to keep her calm. When they made it to where Melvin stood, Lisa stopped and faced him. "Nothing good will come from what you've done. And one way or another, you will pay for this."

After she said her peace, she tugged on Jayden's hand. Her shoulders were now more relaxed, and so was her grip. While she still held steady, there was no longer any force to her hold.

Back inside of his truck, Lisa covered his hand with hers when he moved to shift the gear. If she only knew what her touch did to him.

Lisa released a huffed. "Thank you, Jay. Part of me figured this might be a waste of time, but I had to try even though deep down, I knew he wouldn't just write me a check. If he was that sensible, he wouldn't have stolen the money in the first place."

"Just tell me how you want to handle this, and I'm with you. We can talk with Brock, you know, and get his help or recommendations for a lawyer."

"I know. I know. But that can take time. And time is what I don't have much of." She blew a long stream of air and lifted prayer hands to her chin. "It'll work out somehow. I just have to have faith—and a little money."

Jayden thought to bring up his proposal again, but he'd wait until Lisa wasn't as emotional and could think rationally about the situation.

"Everything will work out, and I'm not just saying that just to be saying it. I mean it. Plus, you've got me, and we're going to come up with a solution together. You know I won't sit down and allow you to lose the one thing you've wanted all your life."

Lisa's eyes softened, and a smile tugged at the corners of her lips. "Of course you won't. I appreciate that about you, too." She held his gaze for several seconds before breaking the connection, both with her eyes and hand. Shoot, she'd snatched her hand away like he'd scorched her. Jayden was close to being crazy enough to pay to find out what was going through her mind. The unspoken thoughts. Thoughts that he didn't usually have to wonder about, but lately, things had been different.

"How about I take you to The Riverwalk? We can go for a boat ride—temporary distraction that may help you relax."

Lisa smiled with her bottom lip folded between her teeth. "I'd like that. But you know it doesn't matter what we do, right? You always seem to have this magic to help me calm down, regardless of the situation."

Though Lisa spoke out loud, Jayden couldn't help but think that was something she'd come to realize in that moment. Her brows and forehead were wrinkled before she relaxed her face. Understanding settled in her eyes.

"Comes with having my degree in Lisa Atkinson."

She erupted in laughter.

"I won't argue that point today because you might be on to something. You've slipped across the graduation stage without me even knowing it."

Jayden shifted his truck into gear. "I've got you, woman. That's one fact that's never up for debate."

And she had him, too.

All of him.

He couldn't dare give his heart to another woman when Lisa carried it around with her every day. The only problem he had now was if he'd ever do anything about it. Given the predicament she was in and what he knew he had to do to help her, this was yet another situation where the timing wouldn't be right. He didn't want her reciprocating his feelings out of obligation. But this was Lisa. She already loved him. Jayden only needed to know how much.

Chapter Twelve

Jayden and Lisa strolled along The San Antonio Riverwalk. They must have picked a near-perfect time to visit the city's landmark because the crowd wasn't as large as they expected, but there were enough visitors for them to bump shoulders with folks from time to time. The Texas heat showed mercy that afternoon as the sun peeked in and out of clouds coupled with a cool breeze drifting in the air every so often. The only thing that would make this moment more perfect would be kissing her.

Where did that thought come from?

Walking alongside her with his hands stuffed in his pockets, Jayden nudged Lisa with his shoulder. "Want to grab something to eat? Fish?" He nodded in the direction of a restaurant up ahead.

Lisa shook her head. "No," she said, sighing. "I don't really have an appetite right now."

Jayden's heart shattered for her. The most insane part of this situation was that she didn't have to go through this if she just allowed him to write her a check—or maybe he could go down to the tax office and pay the past-due property taxes on her behalf.

He took her hand in his, an action he'd taken a thousand times, but lately the connection he felt with her grew stronger every time they touched.

Lately, holding her hand felt more right than it ever had.

Lately, Jayden felt more and more like he was meant to spend his life with her.

Lately, kissing her had become more than a fleeting thought—that was all he wanted to do to test their connection.

Focus on Lisa.

"I'm sorry. What can I do to help you feel better?"

"You can start by dropkicking Melvin."

Jayden did his best back hand fist strike. "Like this?"

Lisa burst into laughter. "You did not just break out one of your mixed martial arts moves."

"Made you feel a little better, didn't it?"

"It did. Thank you."

"You're welcome. Don't think for a second I won't put this black belt to use. Technically, I'd be defending you, so I won't be breaking any black belt code."

"I appreciate you for acting like you're willing, though you and I both know you wouldn't hurt the old man, and I wouldn't really ask you to do anything like that."

"For you? I'd do anything."

Lisa looked up at him and held his gaze for several seconds, as if searching to confirm that truth. "Yeah, I believe you. We've been friends forever."

That isn't the only reason.

"Which is why I don't want to see you like this, Lis. I hate it when you're all sad and long faced."

She bubbled in laughter. "I am not long faced."

Jayden raised an eyebrow.

"Okay, maybe I am. I'm just trying to wrap my mind around things, you know?"

"Yeah, I understand, but don't forget you have me to help you."

She leaned in and gave him a quick peck on the cheek. "Never."

She appeared about ten percent better, if he had to put a number on it. He took hold of her hand again as they continued their stroll. They passed shops and restaurants until they found themselves on the far end of The Riverwalk where they were met with mostly trees and the beautiful stone path ahead. The farther they walked, the fewer people were on the path.

Jayden ventured off the trail and rested his frame against one of the oak trees lining the route. He pulled Lisa in close. "Let me do this for you—pay the tax bill, and move on. You shouldn't have this weight on your shoulders when this is a time when you could be celebrating owning the store. It's what you've wanted for a very long time."

Lisa wrapped her arms around his waist. She rested her head on his chest while she squeezed. "I appreciate you wanting to save the day, and I may just have to take you up on your offer, but not yet."

He held her close, massaged her untamed curls, and kissed the top of her head. "I understand—sort of. You have this need to figure out the situation yourself because the bookstore is now yours, and I get that, but I hate to see you hurting and not being allowed to fix this for you."

She squeezed him tighter. "You really are the best, aren't you?"

Maybe the best when it came to her. This wasn't an offer he'd make to anyone else other than his mother. "Just know that I've got you."

Lisa released him. "Okay. Enough mushy stuff." She laughed. "Let's find a booth to get tickets for the boat ride."

He allowed her to tug him back along the path they'd walked. His palm grew warm at their attachment. Lisa must have felt the same because her gaze locked on their hands before she raised her eyes to meet his. She gave the kind of smile that told him they shared the same thoughts, but he needed to hear the words.

"Am I crazy, or is something different between us?"

Lisa bit down on her bottom lip and shrugged one shoulder. "So you sense it, too?"

"Yeah. I can't quite pinpoint the moment it happened, but—"

"There's been a shift," Lisa finished. "I figured maybe it's because your mom has been not-so-subtly pushing her agenda."

They slowed their pace. Silence passed between them while Jayden settled into his thoughts. He'd loved Lisa for a long time, but he didn't want to lose the friendship they had nor did he know how she'd receive or even if she'd reciprocate his feelings.

He tested the waters. "Or maybe she's just trying to get us to see what's been there all along."

Lisa blushed, and his heart hammered like his fingers across a calculator. "I can say for sure that I have feelings for you, which feels great and wrong at the same time. Honestly, I don't know how to feel or what to do with these emotions."

He didn't either. And at the risk of her thinking that he'd further lost his mind, in one fluid motion, he acted on impulse. Jayden pulled her close and synced her lips with his own. Searching. Caressing. Connecting.

A moment he'd dreamed about that kept him awake for hours on end for the past few nights.

A moment he'd wanted to be more private than standing in the middle of The San Antonio Riverwalk for the city to witness—but right now, he didn't care.

A moment in time that would remain drilled into his mind and heart because when Lisa reciprocated, he forgot about where they were. Nothing else mattered.

Any uncertainty he had about his feelings for her and her place in his life were snatched away the second their lips touched. As far as he was concerned, her heart belonged to him. Always had.

∞

Lisa broke the kiss.

If her thoughts were swimming in her head before, they were drowning now. Her best friend had just kissed her, and she'd kissed him back.

Friends didn't kiss, especially not like that.

And when did Jayden learn to kiss like that?

How did he turn her into some silly swooning teenager in a matter of seconds? Or was it minutes? She grabbed her chest and stared up into his intense gaze. Not apologetic but one of adoration.

Oh. My. Goodness. I think I'm in love with my best friend.

She had to be cool. They could figure this out together.

Lisa used her thumb to wipe her lipstick away from his lips. "There. All good." Those were the only words she could muster. Because what did one say after kissing one's best friend like they were the love of your life?

The one moment when she wished she could say good night and ease inside her house to think through things or even call Ginger, she could do neither. She had to face the situation—meaning Jayden—right now.

Jayden took a deep breath. Surely, he had to recalibrate his thoughts, too. "Still want to go on that boat ride?" His voice sounded deeper than before. Or, in the words of her mom, was she hearing what she wanted to hear?

His question should have prompted a yes-or-no answer. However, she needed to weigh her options. If she said yes, they'd take the ride and would listen to the tour guide. She wouldn't have to talk, and that would give her time to assess her feelings. It was only about thirty minutes, but something was better than nothing. If she said no, they'd go home, and she'd likely have to address the kiss sooner rather than later. And with a three-hour car ride ahead, there would be no avoiding the situation.

"Sure. Why not?" Her own voice had adopted another pitch or two—or three.

This is crazy.

They walked in comfortable silence to the ticket booth where Jayden purchased their tickets and led her to the pickup area. There was a line of about eight passengers ahead of them. When their turn came to climb into the boat, Jayden stepped inside first. He turned around to reach for her and guided her inside the floating vessel. The water gently moved the boat from side to side. The two of them grabbed seats at the rear. When they sat, Jayden pulled her close and wrapped an arm around her shoulder. How was she supposed to focus and sort her feelings in the next half hour with him being so close?

For lack of not knowing what else to do with herself, Lisa stared at her feet. She'd give anything for a pair of magic shoes to click her heels three times and disappear back inside her house. Her phone buzzed. She shifted her crossbody purse into her lap and searched the contents until she fished it out. Ginger's photo and name flashed on the screen. With all that had transpired that day with the booklovers convention, Melvin, and now Jayden, she'd forgotten that she'd promised to call Ginger to tell her how things went.

She tucked her Bluetooth earbud into her ear.

"Hey. What's up?" She did her best to maintain an even tone as not to put Ginger or Jayden on alert.

"Calling to check in on you. I expected to hear from you a while ago. Is everything okay? Are you still with Jayden?"

"*Ummm-hmmm.* Everything is fine. We're about to take the boat ride along The Riverwalk. Can I call you later?"

Even she would be suspicious of her. Lisa held her breath, hoping Ginger didn't push.

"Alrighty then," Ginger half-sang. Lisa heard the hesitation in her friend's voice. "Are you sure you're okay? Where exactly is Jayden?"

She looked up at him and framed her mouth with a smile. "He's sitting right next to me." To Jayden she said, "It's Gin."

He leaned in close enough to where she could feel his breath on her ear. There went those tingles along her neck. "Hi, Gin. Don't worry. I'm taking care of her."

"See? We're good. I'll call you first thing tomorrow."

"*Ummm-hmmm,*" Ginger half sang again. "Something is definitely off, but I'll check in on you tomorrow. You all be safe. And don't try to spark any love connections while you're out of town. We all want to watch this love story unfold." Ginger burst into laughter before the line went dead.

Lisa shook her head, stuffed her phone into her purse, and settled into the crook of Jayden's arm. She might as well relax.

He squeezed her shoulder, prompting her to look him in the eyes. He held her gaze for several seconds, no doubt trying to assess her. "Are we okay?"

The boat pushed away from the loading point. The tour guide, a middle-aged Caucasian woman wearing a blue short-sleeved shirt, stood front and center and announced the housekeeping rules. No smoking. Stay inside the boat. Have fun. Her blond bob danced in the wind.

Lisa turned her attention back to Jayden. "Yes. Why wouldn't we be?"

"We are coming up on the Artisan River Theater, which opened in 1941 with an eight-hundred-person capacity. It's my favorite," the tour guide started.

However, Jayden kept his attention on Lisa. "Because we just shared our first kiss, and that wasn't our usual peck on the cheek or a kiss shared between friends. This was different. Where do we go from here, Lis?"

Dang it. This was supposed to be the ride-home conversation.

There she sat, afraid of saying the wrong thing. Afraid that whatever she said could be perceived the wrong way. But when had she ever had a problem communicating with him? This conversation should be easy.

She inhaled and released a slow and steady breath. So slow that he wouldn't be able to see the rise and fall of her chest.

"I don't know," she finally said.

"Can we at least not pretend like the kiss didn't happen, or that it doesn't change things for us?"

She shifted out of the comfort of his arms and turned to face him. This was a delicate situation, so she couldn't say the first thing that came to mind. "I'd never want to block out any shared moments between us, you know that. But why does anything have to change? Can't we just go with the flow?"

"I think you and I both know we've been going with the flow for far too long. It's time for us to be intentional."

How could she say that she was scared without saying she was scared?

"Do you two lovebirds in the back need your own boat?" The tour guide's comments caused the rest of the passengers to whip their heads around and stare at the two of them before erupting into laughter.

"I'll gladly buy her a boat if she wanted one," Jayden said.

*Oooh*s and smiles came from the group.

The tour guide fanned her hand. "Oh, I'm just kidding ya. Carry on. This isn't the first time I've been offended by riders not paying attention to my fun facts."

The group laughed even more. When the tour guide returned everyone's attention to the landmarks ahead, Jayden cupped her chin and guided it toward him so that their eyes met again.

Okay. Where were we? Oh, yes. Figuring out a way to not show or admit I'm scared but needing Jayden to know that truth without pushing him away.

"Lisa, I love you. I can't think of a time in my life when I didn't love you, but I don't want you to feel pressured into being with me because of one kiss. I need you to want me because you share my feelings."

Dang it. He'd picked up on her hesitation and took it the wrong way, hadn't he? Taking her hesitation as a possible no.

She held his gaze. "Jay, I love you, too. You know that, right?"

"I do. But I am not certain of the context of your love. If you say you love me like a brother, I—"

Lisa giggled. "Well, for starters, I wouldn't kiss a brother."

He half-chuckled. "I suppose that makes me feel better."

She planted a soft kiss on his lips. "Good. I love you, Jay, I really do. I have for a long time. Because we've been friends forever, I don't even know how to make the transition to being more than friends."

Jayden tilted her cheek with his fingertip. "The question is are you willing to try."

The way his eyes bore into hers made her want to say yes to whatever he asked. Part of her felt ashamed for the way her brain and heart had been responding to him lately.

"I am." So much weight lifted from her chest with those two words, like rising from the deep end of the pool to come up for air.

He closed the gap between them until his lips found hers again. Her heart chugged with the waves of the water beneath the boat. She'd never known kisses to be so good.

Good enough for her to look forward to them.

Good enough for her to want Jayden to kiss her every day if his lips would make her heart sing.

When he broke the kiss, she needed several seconds to process her thoughts.

"That's all I needed to hear," Jayden said, near breathless.

"But what if we mess this up and lose our friendship?"

"One thing is certain, we'll always be friends."

Although neither of them knew what the future held, Lisa experienced this sense of calmness and peace that assured her that all would be well with the two of them. She looked up to see the boat slowing and arriving at their pick-up location. She and Jayden waited until the other passengers exited the boat before they stood. Jayden led her to the front and allowed her to use his arm as an anchor to climb out first.

"You two are a beautiful couple. I was just having a little fun with you all back there," the tour guide said while Jayden waited until Lisa found secure footing.

"Thank you," Lisa and Jayden said in unison.

The smile spread across his lips was quite different than he'd had before. When he climbed out of the boat, he tipped the tour guide.

Back on The Riverwalk path, Lisa said, "She called us a couple. Is that what we are now?"

"Yeah. It's about time we put a name on what we've been doing."

She threw her head back and chuckled. "I like the sound of that."

Chapter Thirteen

Jayden had never felt so disoriented in his entire life. He'd semi gotten his love life in order—he and Lisa were finally together—but his career had come to a halt and a catapult at once. As far as his accounting career went, he'd planned to become partner since he stepped foot in the firm seventeen years ago. So how could he be so uncertain about this path now that the opportunity presented itself? While his writing was doing far better than he'd expected as a first-time indie author, there was no way to know if sales would stay up. In fact, he was almost certain that this path wouldn't remain lucrative—at least not enough for him to maintain his lifestyle. And especially not lucrative enough for him to care for Lisa and start a family.

Whoa. I love her, but where did thoughts of marriage come from? Is that where we're really headed?

Jayden maintained an open-door policy in the office. Literally. He seldom closed his office door because he wanted to be approachable and available to his peers and the new associates. However, today, he holed himself inside the space—a space that had always been roomy, but today felt like the air was slowly seeping out of the room. He prayed he wouldn't get a visitor who would ask him about signing the partnership agreement.

Three soft taps against the glass panel signaled a prayer that went unanswered. His mentor, Joe, was the only person who knocked on the window instead of the door. Jayden tore his eyes from the blur of the computer screen and nodded to him.

"How's it going?" Joe asked before he'd fully entered Jayden's office.

"Buried in workpaper review so that we can finalize these returns. Brimstone refused to sign the extensions, so we're up against the filing deadline."

Joe shook his head. "Always one problem child. The director seems to favor you over there. Surprised they didn't budge."

Jayden shrugged. "Can't always get my way, I guess. Thankfully, I have two of the best on this project, so we're making good headway. What's up?" He knew the answer to his question before he asked. No doubt Joe had come to his office on a mission. To get into his head. To find out what the holdup could be with him signing his life away.

Joe pushed the door closed and sat without invitation. He blew a heavy breath and seemingly assessed Jayden. "I was hoping you could tell me. What's with the hesitation? I thought you wanted this partnership. Is it the money? Are you looking to renegotiate your contract?"

He shook his head. "You know I've wanted this promotion for a very long time. If I can be honest, I'm not sure what's preventing me from signing. I just need more time to think and talk through it with Lisa."

Joe rubbed the stubble under his chin. He frowned, but then his eyes lit up. "Don't tell me you're finally gonna ask her to marry you." Without giving Jayden a chance to respond, he clapped. "Pam called it."

Jayden pushed his palms up. "Hey. *Whoa.* Slow down. That is not what I said. Don't start rumors."

They shared a laugh.

"You also didn't say that you didn't want to marry her either. Can't wait to tell Pam. We've had a little bet going on for a while."

Jayden laughed some more. "I'm sure you have workpapers to review, too. Don't let the numbers jumble your brain."

"Nah. One of us is trying to figure out life, and it isn't me. But for what it's worth, you've made me proud—the best mentee I've had in my thirty-year career here."

"I appreciate that, Joe."

"You're welcome, but I mean it. Just know you've got time and favor around here. So if you need to request an extension to think about it more and talk it over with Lisa, then just ask. But something tells me she won't mind her husband coming home with the bank you'll be bringing in."

"See, there you go again starting rumors."

Joe shrugged and stood. "Again, notice how you didn't set me straight either."

He moved to the door and stopped short with his hand on the knob. With a more serious expression, he said, "God knows the plans He has for you, Jayden. You only need to trust Him and believe. If you're truly hesitant, you should seek Him to find out why. You'll get your answer."

Joe left him alone with his thoughts. One of the things Jayden admired about his mentor was that they shared the same faith. And while it was inappropriate to discuss their faith and religion in the office, according to company rules, he and Joe were always comfortable sharing scriptures and faith-based messages with each other. Joe had always pointed Jayden to Jesus when he had difficulties at work, and that he could appreciate.

Jayden opened an electronic copy of the partnership agreement that he'd left unread in his e-mail inbox. He had a paper copy that he'd thumbed through, but hadn't made it around to the electronic copy. Not that it should matter. The documents were identical.

Dear Jayden,

It is our pleasure to welcome you into the partnership…

His stomach rolled into knots. And not the kind one got from excitement. Dread fell over him again. Crazy. He palmed his face to rid himself of the ill feelings. The knots came undone, but his heart raced when he continued reading.

"Jayden, I have more files for you to review."

He turned to see one of his second-year associates standing in the doorway—a welcomed distraction. "Come on in, Ephraim."

Ephraim reminded Jayden of himself when he started at the firm over seventeen years ago. Driven. Focused. Smart. The kind of associate every manager wanted on their team. The one who would look for work when he finished his assignments. The one who lent a helping hand to other associates, sharing the burden of the long work hours. As quickly as his heart swelled in admiration for the young man, his heart deflated at what his future might look like if he continued on this path. Overworked. Minimal social life. And almost missing out on the woman of his dreams. Hopefully Ephraim would meet someone as patient as Lisa had been with him.

"I heard the good news, Jayden. Congratulations."

"Thanks." Jayden extended his hand for the files. "What do you have for me?"

Ephraim handed him two blue folders and remained standing. "Extensions for Langston Brands and The Four Kings. I e-mailed the tax calcs to you. You'll also see an e-mail about the research I did for Brimstone's uncertain tax position."

"Man, you're way ahead of the game. You may have my job if you keep it up."

"I'd love nothing more than to follow in your steps." Ephraim thumbed toward the door. "I'm gonna head out to lunch, then I'm working with Maria on some research credits for one of her clients when I return. Let me know if you need anything else."

"Will do. Thank you, Ephraim."

Jayden flipped open the folders and closed them. He couldn't concentrate right now, so he did the one thing that always helped—pulled out his phone to call Lisa.

She was saved as one of his favorites.

He plugged a bud into his right ear and tapped on her name.

"Hey. What kind of x-ray vision do you have?" she asked when the line opened.

"What do you mean?"

"Give me a sec." She ended the call.

Jayden looked at the screen, dumbfounded. He could count the number of times she'd hung up on him. And those were times when she was upset. She didn't sound upset. They were good, weren't they?

His thoughts reeled until Colleen, the federal tax group's administrative assistant, poked her head in his door. She knocked at the same time. "Hey. I have something special for you today." She stood to the side, and her face lit up. "Or rather someone special."

Behind her stood Lisa with a to-go bag from The Union Kitchen. That woman always had a way of knowing what he needed.

∞

Lisa waltzed into Jayden's office, on official girlfriend duty, and placed the bag of takeout on his desk. She hadn't been to his office since he'd gotten promoted to senior manager three years ago.

"I would apologize for popping in on you, but it wouldn't be sincere."

Jayden tossed his head back and chuckled. "Yeah, I know. I'm glad you're here."

"I figured you would be. Plus, this is busy season, and you're hardly ever able to tear yourself away from this desk, so I had to make sure you ate."

Jayden advanced toward the door in two long strides and pushed it shut. He pulled her into a long, tight squeeze. "You never have to apologize for coming to see me. You know that, right?"

Of course she knew that. However, everything between them had been so intense lately—from the way he held her to the way he looked at her. Just everything. Even now that he'd broken their embrace and made eye contact so intense. An intensity that hadn't been there before. Or had she just failed to notice? Dating her best friend was weird.

She released a heavy breath, backed away, and took the leather visitor's chair across from his desk. "Yes, I know."

Jayden didn't sit in his seat. Instead, he positioned himself between her and his desk, leaning against the heavy furniture. "Are you good?"

"Yeah, of course. You?"

He took a deep breath. She could see the concern on his face. Narrowed eyes. Furrowed brows. Certainly some thoughts that needed out. "Yeah. Just a little pressure around here to make a decision."

And by decision, she knew he meant the partnership offer he'd received. He'd been working toward this point his entire career, so while she supported him, she found the hesitation strange. There had to be something she was missing. Sure, he talked about his future regarding marriage and family and what this partnership would mean, plus the fact that he could be working for himself. However, she'd already made up in her mind that she wouldn't sway his decision one way or the other.

"Well, let's talk and eat."

Jayden rounded the desk and claimed his seat. He blessed the food before rummaging through the bag. "Woman, what are you trying to do to me? You know I love the blackened dynamite chicken."

"Exactly why I brought it to you. I know this situation has been heavy on your heart for a couple of weeks. Nothing like food to help take your mind off things."

He popped open her container. "What do you have? Ah, come on. The chipotle wrap?"

Lisa reached across the desk and pulled her food container to her chest. "Hey, you like what you like, and I like what I like. Plus, I can always just eat some of yours if I'm still hungry."

They both broke out in laughter because taking bites of his food was something she often did.

Jayden settled himself and stuffed a forkful of the chicken into his mouth, careful to include the papaya salsa. "*Ummm.* This is so good."

Lisa bit into her wrap, chewed, and swallowed. "Good enough to make you forget your worries?"

"I wish. But you being here does make things better."

Lisa's lips spread into a wide smile. And not just any regular smile, but one that penetrated from her heart, up through her chest to her face. That had always been their truth—the other's presence made one feel better—but had never been spoken out loud until now.

Jayden took several more bites, but didn't finish his food. "I know you came all this way to enjoy lunch, but I could really use some air. Mind taking a walk with me?"

"I don't, but I'm starving."

Lisa and Jayden agreed that she'd finish half her wrap while he cleared e-mails, although, he didn't seem to be doing much but reading the same message repeatedly. He'd scroll down the screen and up again with the wrinkled forehead and scrunch eyebrows deepening each time.

"Okay, I'm done. Let's get you out of here." She packed her container back inside the to-go bag and stood.

Jayden grabbed his suit jacket. He was already wearing a long-sleeved dress shirt.

"You don't need the jacket. It's ninety degrees outside. You'll burn up."

He hesitated before taking her advice. Rounding the desk in three long strides, he advanced toward the door and opened it before she could touch the handle.

He turned to her. "You do know that I'd expect you not to let me burn up, right?"

She glanced over at his jacket hanging on the back of his leather chair. "I think I just prevented that from happening."

He shook his head. "Nah. I mean you'd have to cool me down—toss some water on a brother or something."

Lisa chuckled. "Oh, I've got you. I honestly thought you would have preferred a kiss." She shrugged and threw up her palms. "My bad."

"Oh, that would always be my preference, but the idea is to cool me down. A kiss from you would have the opposite affect." Jayden winked.

She didn't have a comeback after that. It was best that she dropped this line of conversation. Flirting with Jayden was fun, but still surreal. Lisa grabbed her wallet-sized purse and slipped it over her shoulder. She had no plans of returning to his office.

With his palm at the small of her back, sending heat equivalent to the rays the sun would soon provide, he guided her through the office corridor to the elevator bank.

She waved good-bye to Colleen.

"I'll be back in about an hour. If anyone needs me before I return, they can reach me on my cell," he called through the reception area to Colleen.

She nodded and waved back at them.

"You work too much," Lisa said when they stepped on the elevator and the doors closed behind them. Although they were the only two in the cabin, they stood close enough for their arms to touch.

"Why do you say that?"

"It's hard for you to take a break. Look at you allowing people to call you on your cell while you're out of the office. A break should be just that—no calls, texts, or e-mails. See you when I get back."

"Tell me about it, but it's the nature of the business. Kind of an unspoken rule—always be available."

"And you don't sound too happy about that."

"I'm not quite sure how to feel about it, but it's the life I've grown accustomed to. All normal around here."

They rode the elevator down to the ground floor in silence while Lisa allowed his words to sink in. Nothing was normal about always being available to your job. The elevator dinged, and three male employees nearly bum-rushed inside before Lisa and Jayden could get off. They exchanged pleasantries while Jayden held the doors open for her to step out first.

Lisa and Jayden had walked out of the building and gotten into a comfortable pace on the sidewalk of downtown Houston before she spoke again.

"And do you plan to always make yourself available to your job like this? And what happens when you become partner? Do things get better or worse?" Those last two questions were more of her internal thoughts. She hadn't intended to ask them aloud. But now that the door was open, they may as well walk through it and address his work priorities now.

"What are you really asking?"

"Now that we've made our relationship official, I just need to know what's ahead."

Jayden stopped walking. "Wait. Don't do that. I've always prioritized you. That doesn't change." His phone sounded three short beeps, and he whipped it out of his pocket to check the message before returning it to its place.

While he'd made it a point to be there for her in the past, things were now different. Checking e-mails and taking phone calls from work while they were hanging out always bothered her, but she never made a fuss about it because she'd become accustomed to him being a workaholic. Besides, she was only his friend, not his significant other. She didn't have a right to complain before now.

"Are you also telling me that things will always be this way with you and work?" She wasn't certain why, but her mind jumped ten years ahead. Would they be sitting around the Christmas tree creating memories with their children, and Jayden would stop to answer the phone for a client who had no sense of boundaries? Or away on a family vacation, and he'd bring his laptop along?

Jayden blew a heavy breath and stuffed his hands in his pockets. He didn't answer her for a long while. Any length of time that exceeded a few seconds was eternity for her, especially when she needed answers. And why she seemed to need them today, she didn't know.

"You know what, Lis? I feel like this is leading into an argument that I don't want to have with you right now. I just want to enjoy this moment. Can we do that?"

"Sure."

And there it was again—the shutdown.

Him keeping her out.

Things were never this hard with them before. Conversations came easy. Life with him was easy. But things obviously changed the moment her heart had been cast out into the deep, and she'd allowed Jayden to reel it in. All she wanted was the assurance that he would keep it safe. And *safety* was not the word that came to mind right now. Uncertainty and queasiness intertwined in her belly, leaving her unsettled. If Jayden were any other man, she would have left him standing on the scorching sidewalks of downtown Houston alone.

But Jayden had always been different from any other man she'd known. Or had he? Did she have some fantasy-type ideal about him that made her think that he was different? She should cut her losses right this second and run.

Run back to the way things were between them.

Run back to her normal.

Run back to the place where she'd hidden for so long, where her heart would be safe from the one man who had the power to crush it.

Chapter Fourteen

As soon as Jayden and Lisa made things official, their relationship seemed to have gotten harder. Where was the ease that he'd always known with her? While she didn't come right out and say she didn't like his job or his work ethic, she implied it with her pouting and semi-distant behavior yesterday. He'd always approached work in the same manner, giving his career the best part of him. She'd always known that fact and had been with him every step of the way. Why his career mattered so much to her now was beyond him.

He couldn't change his work habits, nor did he think he'd need to. Shouldn't she appreciate the fact that she had a man who was more than willing to work hard to provide for their future? Or perhaps she didn't know that she was part of the reason he worked the way he did. Either way, instead of working tonight, he'd chosen to take Lisa out to a couple's pottery-making class she'd always wanted to try. Never mind that they'd just only recently become official. They'd done couple-type activities all the time.

They talked during the car ride to the venue, but there was still a level of tension between them. Was the tension caused by his secret? Although, secret sounded like something bad. Writing a successful book wasn't what he'd call a secret, just something about himself he wasn't ready to share yet. And he had that right. Or was the tension caused by their disagreement about his availability to his job?

Jayden parked his truck in a nearby garage and reached across the console to secure Lisa's hand in his. "Are we okay?"

Her smiled reached her eyes, which caused his erratic heartbeat to settle. "Yes, of course. Can't believe you finally agreed to do this with me."

"The list of things I won't do for you is shorter than you think."

Lisa chuckled, fisted the air, and tucked her hand in her back pocket.

"What was that about?"

"Holding on to your comment in case I have to use it against you later."

Jayden burst into laughter. "You know me well enough to know I've got you. Let's go."

He grabbed a bag from the backseat, rounded his truck, and opened the door for her. Hand in hand, they walked through the outdoor shopping area until they climbed the stairs and arrived at Smashed Studio. The cozy space smelled of clay. The creations of other patrons lined the shelves. While the establishment touted no experience necessary, some of the pottery appeared to be made by non-amateurs.

"Look at this." Lisa pointed to clay shaped like a flower vase, then to Christmas-themed clay shaped like trees, penguins, and snowmen.

"Nice. I don't know whether to be inspired or intimidated."

Lisa hooked her arm around his waist and squeezed. "Let's just have fun with it and see what we come up with."

"That's why we're here, huh?"

"Right."

They took seats at high-top stools next to the window while they waited for the remaining attendees to arrive and their group session to begin.

Fifteen minutes later, a short brunette with an electronic tablet cupped to her chest called to the couples in the building. She raised her hand. "Are all of you here for the seven o'clock throwing class?"

Yeses and nods came from the group of fourteen.

"Great. We're resetting the studio and will be ready shortly. In the meantime, I'm going to come by and verify each couple's reservation."

Within ten minutes, she'd checked each couple in and given them the choice of where they wanted to sit. Each area had two stools and a small table and what Jayden assumed to be the materials they needed for tonight's event. After he and Lisa chose their seats, they draped each other in aprons and secured them in ties behind their backs. They took their seats side by side, knees to knees, and waited for further instructions. The event was BYOB, so Jayden brought them a bottle of cabernet, a red wine Lisa enjoyed, but he could do without.

He opened the bag he brought. "I guess it's probably time to open this bottle of your favorite wine. I even have two glasses."

"Look at you. Total boyfriend material."

They shared a laugh.

He used the cork to open the bottle and poured a glass for each of them—less for himself. "Well, I feel like I need to make things up to you. We haven't even been official an entire month, and we've already had our first fight."

Lisa accepted the glass he handed her and sipped with scrunched brows. "Fight? When?"

"You're going to make me relive it all over again, huh?"

She hiked a brow.

"How you feel about my job—or at least my work ethic."

She folded her lips and squinted as if mulling over his statement. Finally, she released a heavy breath. "Well, now probably isn't the time to talk about that, but at least we know that's something we need to work through."

Jayden lifted his glass and clinked it against hers. "Deal." He sipped and frowned. For the life of him, he could not understand why she enjoyed the dry, bitter liquid.

A different brunette appeared in the center of the room. She introduced herself as Brittany. "Welcome to Smash Studio. We're going to have a lot of fun tonight. Has anyone ever done this or anything similar?"

No one raised their hands.

Brittany smiled. "Well, the good news is that you don't need any experience to have fun here and create something amazing. This evening is designed to be a low commitment way to try throwing pottery. I'll be here to guide you every step of the way."

Lisa leaned closer to him. He could smell the wine on her breath, mixed with the feminine, powdery scent of her perfume. "What do you want to make? I was thinking we could try a vase or maybe even a bookend. Seems simple enough."

Jayden shifted on his stool and leaned in so that his forehead touched hers. "We each have our own lump of clay, so let's try both."

"Cool. Let's do this."

He had zero intentions of keeping anything they made here tonight. This event was solely a tool to spend time with Lisa and to ensure she wasn't still upset about the conversation they'd had when she came to his office. He had enough stressors in his life; he didn't need his new relationship with her to be one of them.

"You each have a piece of clay on your wheel. Our first step is to center the clay on it and to force it into a symmetrical shape. Gently tap the lever with your foot to spin the wheel."

Murmurs from the class floated around them as each student played with the potter's wheel and lump of clay. The clay was not as soft as he thought it would be. The feel was more like firm mud if he had to describe it. And he'd never been a fan of playing in mud, yet there was something satisfying about shaping and molding the lump.

"Remember that the bowl of water can be used to wet the clay as much as needed as you shape your creation," Brittany announced.

"I'm getting a kick out of this," Lisa said.

"As crazy as it may sound, me too."

Ten minutes passed, and both he and Lisa had created cylinder-shaped pottery, although not symmetrical in the slightest.

Lisa assessed their molded clay. "Hey, now these could easily be used for vases in the future, but what about the bookend?"

"Are you gonna change yours? This may be all I have in me."

Lisa twisted her lips. "I doubt that. Let's work on it together."

Jayden watched as she finished her pottery, shaped like one of the vases on display when he'd walked in the building, complete with professional looking ridges and all. She smiled at her molded clay. Her chest puffed, clearly proud of what she'd accomplished.

She slid closer to him. There wasn't much space between them to begin with. If she moved any closer, she'd be sitting on his lap. "Now, allow the master to help you out."

Jayden chuckled. "Always coming to my rescue. You probably shouldn't start anything you don't plan to finish. Shouldn't you try to manage my expectations?"

Lisa smirked. A *tsk* escaped her lips. "I don't buy into that stuff. I should be free to choose what I want to do and when I want to do it. My goal has never been to spoil you in any shape or form, Jayden Reynolds."

"Please don't ever spoil me then. I couldn't handle falling in love with you more than I already am."

Lisa grinned and nudged his shoulder. "Stop trying to sweet talk me."

The smile on her face and the lightness in her voice spun his heart like the clay on the potter's wheel before them. He hadn't seen this side of Lisa before now. Gushing. Smitten. Because of him. Something stirred deep within his heart that made him want to give Lisa the world on a silver platter. The fact that she'd always been an exceptional woman to him and for him without any extra effort and no hidden agenda made his heart swell.

Jayden cleared his throat. "Okay. I'll focus. Just help me, please."

She told him when to press the pedal and add water while she took the reins of throwing his pottery, manipulating the shape. She managed to shape it into a bookend, which he thought looked more like a chair.

"I need your hands now, Jay."

"Tell me what you need me to do."

"I'm going to press the top, but I need you to press your hand firmly against the back. We have to make sure this keeps its shape."

Jayden did his part to assist Lisa. Once the group finished, they were directed to do something to identify their pottery so that they would be able to pick them up after the firing process or either glaze them, their choice. They used a pointed stick to carve their initials into each piece with a heart separating them. The heart was Lisa's idea.

They lingered in the area for an hour longer, walking along the sidewalks, hand in hand, talking about anything and everything except his job commitments and his writing—probably the two most important topics that needed to be addressed, but Jayden didn't want to spoil the moment. However, he sensed the shift in Lisa's mood when she announced she was ready to go home. While she assured him she was fine, had had a good time, and only needed to rest, he didn't buy it.

Thirty minutes later, they arrived at her house, where he opened the car door for her and walked her to her front door. Jayden pulled her into his arms and squeezed.

"Thank you for tonight," Lisa said. Her words were muffled by her face pressed into his chest, but he heard her clearly.

"You know I'll never miss an opportunity to spend time with you." He released her and lifted her chin so that their eyes met. "Are you sure we're good? Do I need to come in so that we can talk?"

She pressed her lips together as if considering his question, yet her eyes did not waver. She looked at him as though peering into his soul, making him almost regret asking.

"Nah. We're fine."

Fine. He despised that word, and she knew it. But instead of hanging on to what she didn't say, Jayden drew her closer and pressed his lips into hers. They felt just as good as the first time he'd kissed her. His heart warmed all the same. Their connection was still intact. No matter what concerns she may have about his commitment to his job, she could never question his commitment to her.

"Good night. I love you."

This time Lisa smiled. She stepped out of his arms and unlocked the door. Looking over her shoulder before stepping inside, she said, "I love you back."

∞

As much as Lisa loved Jayden, she couldn't allow herself to become overly consumed with what was bothering him and what he was and wasn't sharing with her. She had a bookstore to revive. Literally. Taxes to pay and to reintroduce Between the Lines to the Katy community. The grand re-opening was scheduled to happen in four weeks, with Ginger's destination wedding in three. But today, she'd stay in the moment and let tomorrow's worries take care of themselves.

The bookstore was quiet that late afternoon—just Lisa and her Bluetooth stereo streaming the smooth sounds of John Legend. She sat behind the counter with her laptop open and took the slow day as an opportunity to review the confirmations for the grand opening. She had twenty confirmed local authors and vendors who agreed to donate a percentage of their sales to the bookstore— money she'd use to cover a portion of the past due taxes.

But would that undetermined amount be enough?

Pain seized her chest at the thought of losing the store when she'd only been the official owner for less than a month. The thought of taking Jayden up on his offer crossed her mind, but she'd only do so as a last resort. She needed to work through this on her own—or at least try to prove to herself that she had some business sense. She'd much rather save her favors for another time. Lisa could do this. She knew she could.

She needed something big.

Right now, a distraction would be great. Though she spent a great deal of her time pushing Lisa's relationship with Jayden, Aunt Wanda's presence was missed. And speaking of Jayden's mom, she really had to stop referring to her as *Aunt Wanda* now that she and Jayden were officially dating.

The chimes saved her from her spiraling thoughts and the pressures of running the store. Lisa shut her laptop and grinned when Ginger walked through the door. She wore jeans and a cute pink polo shirt with her Ginger's Goodies logo on the upper left side. Her silky ponytail swung over her shoulder as she closed the door. The rock Brock had put on her finger sparkled in the distance.

"I came to save you."

Lisa laughed. "I don't know how you knew I needed saving today, but you're right on time." She rose from her stool and rounded the counter to embrace Ginger.

"Because running a business is not for the faint of heart, that's how I know."

Lisa groaned. "Tell me about it."

"Plus, we have book club this evening. I've been looking forward to chatting about Justin Love's book. I could use a mental break from wedding and marriage planning."

Ginger plopped down onto one of the reading sofas and patted the empty space next to her. "How is the planning going for the grand re-opening?"

Lisa claimed the seat next to her friend, releasing a whoosh of air as she sat. "It's going."

"Talk to me. How can I help?"

"We could get dressed in all black and pay Melvin a visit."

Ginger burst into laughter. "Like that time we went spying on Ava back in college when she went on that date with Creepy Colin."

Lisa joined her in laughter. "That is exactly what I had in mind. I can't believe we did that."

"It was hilarious. Who did we think we were? And what would we have even done if he tried anything crazy?"

"*Duh.* We were going to use the moves Billy Blanks taught us in Tae-Bo."

Ginger held her belly and laughed harder. "Oh my gosh. That would have been crazy."

Lisa snorted. "I know, right?"

When they finally calmed down, Lisa wiped tears from her eyes. "Thanks. I needed that laugh."

"Me, too." Ginger paused a beat. "Now, tell me what I can do to help make this event a success for you."

Lisa thought for a moment. "Share it with your customers and social media followers. That's a good start."

"Already doing that. If you could print a few flyers, that would help. We can give them out at the mall shop and at the store."

Lisa made a mental note. She should have given her flyers before now.

"Thanks. I'll get those to you tomorrow. Shouldn't be too hard to design them online and get them printed at the drugstore."

Ginger nudged her shoulder. "And why don't you get Jayden to reach out to those partners' wives who love you so much. Maybe they can help spread the word. You're practically one of them already."

Lisa eyed Ginger.

She shrugged. Wide eyes and a mischievous smile followed. "What? You know I'm telling the truth."

The door chimes jingled. Both Lisa and Ginger turned their attention to the customers entering the building. "This is not over," Lisa added before she left Ginger parked on the sofa while she went to greet her customers.

Two pretty African-American friends, possibly mid-to-late twenties, entered the store. They giggled and waltzed inside with their arms hooked. The image of the two reminded her of herself and Ginger. Lisa smiled. "Welcome to Between the Lines. Anything I can help you find today?"

The shorter friend with gorgeous shiny curls answered. "Please tell me you have copies of Justin Love's book."

"As a matter of fact, I do. Just got a new shipment in yesterday. This book has been flying off the shelf. How many copies would you like?"

"We'll take four. He's our book club's read this month."

"Mine as well. What is your book club's name?"

They shrugged and looked at each other with wrinkled brows. "Brown Skin Queens," the taller one with straight hair and hazel eyes answered.

Her friend laughed. "She literally just made that up."

They all chuckled.

"No, seriously. We're just four friends who like to read. No need for a formal name."

Lisa glanced across the room at Ginger. "Sounds like another fabulous group of women I know. I'll be right back."

She grabbed the books off the shelf and returned to the counter. "Sure there aren't any other titles you're interested in?"

"Nothing for me today, unless you have some coffee," said the taller friend.

"A coffee bar is something I'm considering, but as of now, we're only brewing fresh reads."

"Good. She doesn't need any more caffeine. Carissa, you've had about thirty-six ounces today. That's enough for both of us."

"I literally only had three cups. You're exaggerating."

"Carissa, you use the twelve-ounce setting on the coffeemaker."

Carissa looked toward the ceiling and seemingly had an epiphany. "Dang. You ain't lyin'."

They broke out in laughter. "Michelle is right. We'll stick with the books."

Lisa completed their order and waved good-bye to them as they walked out the door. She pointed at Ginger. "Now, back to you."

"Who do they remind you of?"

Lisa smirked. "Us—ten years ago."

"Or now." Ginger patted the sofa. "Let's finish our conversation. You were telling me about how much you love Jayden and how glad you are that you two have finally confessed your feelings to each other."

Lisa laughed. "You're not that funny or slick. Jayden is a topic for another day. You were helping me think through ideas for the grand re-opening."

"Yeah, and I was also telling you to get the partners' wives involved because you're practically one of them."

She stared at Ginger for a long while. That bit of anxiety she'd been feeling when it came to Jayden and his potential stake in this partnership stirred within her. And that's when the realization hit her.

Lisa didn't want that life.

Chapter Fifteen

Lisa busied herself by preparing mocktails and the charcuterie board for their book club meeting, where they'd discuss Justin Love's novel. She wasn't sure why, but something about the book reminded her of Jayden. Perhaps comments from Ginger and his mom had something to do with that. Or even her mom. Maybe seeing how well Justin's first book was doing was a reminder for her to give Jayden a little push to go ahead and write and publish the book he'd talked about writing for so long. Of all the things the man put his mind to and accomplished, she couldn't imagine why he wouldn't step out on faith and write the darn book.

Oh yeah, she remembered: He was married to his job.

She had to shift her thinking because she'd get disturbed all over again. The way he handled the situation—or lack thereof— when the issue came up between them bothered her, too. Plus the fact that he continued to skate around the subject like it was nothing. But maybe the way he worked was a nonfactor for him. As he said, that's who he is. She mimicked his voice as she sliced the artisan cheddar cheese.

Lisa arranged the squares of cheese, deli meats, and grapes on her charcuterie board, one Jayden bought for her. When he noticed that every time book club was hosted at her house, she made charcuterie boards, he invested in a personalized board for her. Her name was engraved on the bottom left while the right side had a built-in cheese slicer. On either side, were black iron handles for easy carrying, and the bottom held a storage drawer for knives.

The doorbell rang, followed by a knock and simultaneous twisting of the knob. Ginger let herself in as Lisa instructed her to do when she called half an hour ago. She lifted a pink square box with her Ginger's Goodies' logo on it. "I've got the treats."

Ginger sashayed through the living room into the open kitchen. She placed the box on the opposite end of the island from where Lisa worked then walked over to kiss her on the cheek. "Hey, honey. Need help with anything?"

"No, but thanks for asking. I'm putting the finishing touches on this board. I've already made our drink for this evening."

Ginger walked to the refrigerator and opened the door. "Yeah, your margarita mocktail. Always good. But you do know that Aunt Wanda is headed over here with a bottle of wine."

Lisa chuckled. "Of course she is."

Ginger closed the door and rounded the island so that she stood across from Lisa. She picked a piece of meat and cheese from the board, popped them into her mouth, and chewed. "And speaking of Aunt Wanda. Thought of what you're going to call her now? You must know it's weird for you to call her *Aunt* when you're all in love with her son. She can't be your *Aunt* anymore. Just call her Momma from now on. I don't know why you haven't been calling her Momma from the get-go." Ginger burst into laughter.

Lisa plucked a grape and tossed it in her direction. "I don't recall you ever being this messy. What has gotten into you? It's crazy how folks get engaged or married, and they have all kinds of stuff to say about the single people."

Ginger laughed harder. "That's funny because you're the most unsingle single person I know."

Lisa tossed another grape at Ginger, which she caught with her right hand. "Hey, don't waste the food. It's not so funny when you're on the receiving end, is it?"

Lisa pursed her lips and cocked her head to the side. "I never treated you this way when it came to Brock. I stepped out of the way like a good friend, zipped my lips, and allowed you to take your time and make your own decisions."

Ginger made a show of stretching her neck and twisting her head as if looking for something. "Clearly you're having a memory lapse or you don't know yourself, but it's cool. Now that you and Jayden have made things official, I'm gonna chill. Can't say the same for your unofficial mother-in-law though."

No lies detected. Jayden's mom wouldn't rest until Lisa and Jayden walked down the aisle and Lisa was propped up in The Woman's Hospital giving birth. Well, the woman probably still wouldn't rest. Lisa could be pushing out twins, and she'd be asking if she thought she could have one more child. She never gave up.

Perhaps Jayden needed a bit of that spirit in order to write his book—or at least tell his boss where to shove it and perhaps start his own business, especially if he planned to work like crazy all his life. Might as well do so for himself.

As usual, Aunt Wanda—well, Jayden's mom—waltzed through the threshold with a bottle of wine she liked to gift to the host and open during the book club meeting. Lisa's mom followed. Their entrance signaled the end of the conversation she and Ginger were having.

"Hey, my dear." Aunt Wanda extended her arms wide.

Lisa carried the charcuterie board into the living room, placed it on the center table, and stood to receive the squeeze she knew was coming. "Good to see you."

Their separation seemed to serve as an invitation for her to charge into the kitchen for wineglasses. Ginger followed.

"Mom, you look good." Lisa squeezed her mom and kissed her cheek.

Aunt Wanda returned and proceeded to hand glasses to each of them. Using Lisa's electric wine opener, she wasted no time opening the bottle. She poured for each of them and raised her glass. "Before we get started, it's only right that we open this evening's book club with a toast to celebrate Lisa and Jayden taking the first step, no matter how long it took. Barb and I agreed in the car that you can call me 'Momma Wanda.'"

Ginger lifted her glass. "I'll sip to that, Aunt Wanda."

Lisa couldn't argue with anything she'd said. Yes, she and Jayden had taken more than enough time to get their acts together, although she could argue they didn't quite have things figured out. And she'd been mulling over how to address his mother. She chuckled. "Thanks, Momma Wanda." Lisa sipped. "But wait… It's not like we're getting married or anything like that. We're just dating. If things don't work out and he marries someone else in three years, I don't think his wife would take too kindly to me calling you Momma."

Aunt Wanda gripped her chest and pretended to faint, though she didn't let her glass slip. Barbara quickly stepped behind her to keep her from falling. The movement was so smooth, Lisa wouldn't doubt if they'd rehearsed before coming over.

"It's okay, Wanda. Sip your wine," Barbara said to calm her.

Aunt Wanda took a large gulp. "Oh, my father in heaven, she's already sabotaging my future, setting me back a few more years. Barb, please help the child. O ye of little faith."

Ginger cackled. Tears welled in the corners of her eyes. "I swear I can't get this kind of entertainment anywhere else. I live for this."

Lisa couldn't help but join in. She crashed on the sofa next to Ginger; recovering a moment later. "Okay, okay. I get it. Stay in the moment."

Aunt Wanda's eyes bulged while she took another large gulp, finishing her first glass. "Don't play with my heart like that."

"Honey, Wanda has you and Jayden on her vision board for the year. Try to be sensitive," Mom said and winked.

Why any of them went along with this madness, she did not know.

"Okay," Lisa sang. "Well, help yourselves to the mocktails and the charcuterie board. Anyone want to open the discussion? If not, I wrote a few questions."

Ginger made herself more comfortable on the sofa, one leg tucked under her bottom and an elbow resting against the back of the couch. "I'll start. This is more of a general observation about the story and the writing as a whole. The words seemed to have come from a deep place, almost as if the writer was pouring his heart out on the page. I mean, it felt more like a love letter, if that makes sense."

Lisa nodded. "I know what you mean. We've had many requests for this book in the store over the past few weeks, and I can see why. I think the author wanted readers to see themselves as the object of affection, to look past the character and understand that we are all worthy of love. And that our special someone is out there. The biggest lesson I took from the book was to not give up hope."

Ginger added, "Yeah, but he's created a problem because women will be in search of a man to love on them like Malaki loved Jasmine in the book. To be honest, I side-eyed Brock a few times thinking, why can't you be like Malaki?" she added a laugh.

Mom, Lisa, and Aunt Wanda laughed, too.

"Honey, please, you're almost living a real-life fairytale with Brock," Lisa said.

She shrugged. "Yeah, I know." She giggled like a teenager gushing over her crush at a high school sleepover.

"But aren't all romance books like that—make you fall in love with the hero in the story and wish you had someone like him? It's just the fantasy, and that's what we enjoy about it," Mom added.

Lisa nodded. "True. But what adds to the fantasy is that this story didn't come from a woman's mind, it came from a man. That fact alone increases the swoon factor by ten. While the author is using his imagination, there has to be some part of him in the character. So you have to wonder if there are men out there like Malaki and/or the author who exist in real life."

Her mom continued, "On some level, I think so. But you have to remember that this Justin Love is out here to make money, and he wrote what we want to read. No doubt he's been studying some woman or has some really good experience. The writing is too authentic to be otherwise."

Ginger lifted her glass. "Here, here. Aunt Wanda, you're mighty quiet. What's up?"

She shook her head, wide-eyed, looking at each of them like they'd grown a second pair of lips. "I'm just bewildered. How can y'all not see Lisa and Jayden in this book?" She dug through her bag sitting at her feet and pulled out the book, waving it around in the air.

The group erupted in laughter.

She flipped open the book to a page she'd bookmarked. It was clear she'd been waiting for this moment. With her palm up, she silenced them and read the highlighted text. *"Malaki would go to the ends of the earth for Jasmine. Nothing was off limits. Whatever she asked or anticipated, he had to be the man to meet her needs."*

Lisa interrupted her. "That doesn't mean anything."

Aunt Wanda pursed her lips and hiked her eyebrows. 'Ends of the earth?' Now ordinarily, that wouldn't give me pause, but the author overused the phrase. And hasn't Jayden always said he'd go to the ends of the earth for you?"

"I mean, that's a common phrase, so I wouldn't think too much about it," Lisa said as she considered the possibility.

Aunt Wanda nodded, "Okay, so you need more proof. Remember the scene where Malaki confessed that he was the reason her prom date cancelled on her back in high school?"

"That never happened. Jayden and I always had plans to go to prom together."

"Yeah, because he talked some other guy—Calvin, Craig…"

"Cody?"

Aunt Wanda snapped her fingers. "That's the one. He talked Cody out of asking you because he wanted to be," she finished with air quotes, "'the one.'"

Lisa stood and reached to remove her wineglass. "I think that's enough for you, young lady."

"Well…" Ginger cocked her head to the side and shifted her gaze to the ceiling as though pulling her thoughts from the air. "Now that I think about it, that could be why the heroine felt so familiar. She's you. And if she's you, then Jayden is Malaki." Her eyes welled as she sucked in a chest full of air. "Oh my goodness. Jayden wrote this book," she screamed and leaped out of her seat. "Lisa, did you know?"

Lisa reached over and removed Ginger's glass from her hand. "Looks like you've already had too much as well. Momma Wanda, why did you start this? Jayden didn't write this book or any book. There's no way he wouldn't share something like this with me," Lisa said to convince herself. She couldn't count on her fingers and toes the number of times the thought crossed her mind as she read Justin Love's book. But surely, Jayden wouldn't write, publish, and have so much success with a book and not share that with her— his best friend and girlfriend. Plus, he was always busy with work— not counting the stress of determining where to take his career. All thoughts she used to rationalize that Jayden would not and could not be Justin Love.

"You're right. We'll meet the real Justin when he does the book signing at your store, right?" Momma Wanda asked.

Lisa gave a slow nod. "Right." Was she dropping the subject that easily? That couldn't be right. Did she know something Lisa and the rest of the group didn't know?

"Good. I'll just take this back." Momma Wanda reached for her glass and refilled it with another pour of wine. "Who has the next question or comment?"

Lisa didn't believe Jayden would go off and have a whole author career without her knowing, but Wanda was his mother. If anyone knew Jayden better than Lisa, it was his mom.

Her mom asked a question to the group, but Lisa missed it, completely engaged in her own thoughts. Was this the secret he'd been keeping from her? Because there was obviously something off between the two of them. And hadn't she asked him about his writing? What if this was his book? On one hand, she was excited because he'd finally written that book, but on the other hand, she had so many questions, starting with why he'd keep this from her, and were they as close as she thought?

Chapter Sixteen

The time on Jayden's laptop screen read twenty minutes after six p.m. Ordinarily, that wouldn't be an issue for him, even on a Saturday. But now, he had even more of a reason to wrap up work at an earlier time: Lisa. Tonight was her book club meeting, which meant she was unavailable, but the idea of sitting behind his desk in the office no longer appealed to him. And for the life of him, he couldn't figure out how this could have ever been appealing to him.

His client promised him their working trial balances and uncertain tax position workpapers six hours ago. And this wasn't just any client, this was *the client.* It was his work on this project that he'd like to think tipped things in his favor to get the partnership offer. Even though he hadn't quite made up his mind about his next steps, he wouldn't screw up the relationship he'd built over the years. He also had to show up for his team. Jayden never liked the idea of a partner or senior manager asking him to stay late or come into the office on the weekend and the boss not showing up. While his superiors didn't seem to work much or at all, the idea of them showing up meant something to him.

Jayden pushed away from his desk and strolled through the corridor to the conference room. Their offices were generally quiet but the after-hour level of quiet had always seemed eerie. This evening was no exception. It was as if there was no life in the building—and that was true to an extent because no one wanted to be at work on the weekend without the extra pay. This was one instance where being salaried sucked. He'd even said as much when attending college recruiting events. That fact didn't stop most hungry-eyed college students with a thirst to race to the top of the corporate ladder who wanted the cred of having worked for a prestigious accounting firm inked on their résumé. Some things were worth the sacrifice, he supposed.

Two associates and one senior associate sat around the mahogany table with enough chairs to seat three more people. They were talking and laughing about something, but when he walked into the room, communication ceased. No sense in telling them they didn't have to stop on his account because he'd been in their seats, always wanting to put his best face forward.

"Mr. Reynolds, any word from the tax manager on the UTPs yet?" the senior associate Matt asked. He adjusted his posture and smoothed his hands along the front of his polo shirt—yet another thing Jayden would have done, dress nice on the weekend after being told countless times that Saturdays were casual days.

Jeff and Camille stared at him with wide eyes and weak smiles as if they'd been caught cheating off each other's work product.

He shook his head. "First, it is completely fine to call me Jayden. I prefer that. Second, no word on the UTPs or trial balances yet, so you all can pack up and go home. Enjoy the rest of your weekend. I don't want you to wait around here any longer."

The three of them hesitated, so Jayden smiled. "I'm serious, guys. Go home, or you'll be here by yourselves. I'm headed out, too. See you on Monday."

Jayden turned on his heel and headed back toward his office. Mumbled voices and bag zippers reached his ears—a sound he felt good about. When he started his own accounting firm, there had to be a no-coming-into-the-office-on-the-weekend rule among other things he would do differently to show his employees and his family that he valued family time.

He stopped short when he arrived back in his office. Where'd that thought come from? More like, why did that thought continue to occur? Could he really leave all that he'd known and built here to start over? While he and Lisa hadn't discussed how they were going about their relationship before they'd made it official, he'd bet she wouldn't be willing to go back to a holding pattern while he rebuilt his career. However, the more he considered the idea of starting out on his own, the more he liked the sound of it. But what would that mean for him and Lisa?

And Justin Love?

∞

Book club meetings turned girls' night out sessions always ran past their allotted time of two hours, yet the group always put a time frame on their meetings. Lisa argued that they needed to establish some type of order. To oblige her, they'd set the time from five-thirty to seven-thirty every second Saturday each month.

At half past nine, Ginger collected the dessert tray, glasses, and charcuterie board. "Anything else you need me to do before I leave, Lis? I promised Brock I'd be back by ten so that we could catch a late movie."

Lisa stood and wrapped her arms around Ginger in a tight squeeze. "No, ma'am. I can take care of the rest."

"Alrighty. Call you later."

Lisa walked Ginger to the door and waited until she'd pulled out of her driveway.

Back in the living room, Mom and Momma Wanda stood.

"I'm going to run to the ladies' room, and I'll be ready to go as well," Momma Wanda announced.

"Honey, are you sure you don't want us to help you put anything away?" Mom asked.

Lisa glanced around. "No. Ginger did the bulk of it. I'll just toss the dishes in the dishwasher and relax on the couch for a while before bed."

Mom pulled her into her arms, but held on to her shoulders after their embrace instead of releasing her. She stared into her eyes for a moment and squinted with that knowing mother's look. "Sure you're okay? You're not letting Wanda's comments about Jayden and that book get to you, are you?"

Lisa shook her head and waved off the comment. "Nah. I know how she is. I'm good." Lisa hesitated several seconds before asking, "But do you think Jayden would write an entire book, publish it, and not tell me?"

Okay, so maybe she did let Momma Wanda get to her. With the likelihood that Jayden could be Justin Love and successfully publish his first book, she should be half ecstatic, but instead, her belly sank lower each time she considered the idea.

Mom cocked her head to the side and thought for a moment. "I don't know. He seems to tell you everything, and if by some farfetched chance, he is Justin Love—that doesn't even sound right coming out of my mouth—he must have his reasons for not telling you. Why don't you just ask him?"

"You're right."

Or was she? Hadn't Lisa asked him before? Well, maybe not specifically, but she'd brought up the idea of him writing his book, and he'd dismissed it. Could that be why he didn't want to talk about the book? He'd already written it? Lisa had to stop her thoughts. She was spiraling.

Mom squeezed her once more and turned as Momma Wanda waltzed back into the living room. "Barb, are you ready?"

"Just waiting for you, old lady."

"Good because this old lady isn't driving back." She dug inside her purse and handed Lisa's mom the keys.

Lisa hugged Momma Wanda tight. "I'll walk y'all to the door."

She leaned into the doorjamb and watched as they drove away. Her house was once again quiet, leaving her to her thoughts. Before she created a story in her head, she trekked into the kitchen, picked up her phone off the counter and called Jayden.

"Hey. How'd you know I needed to hear your voice?"

In that instant, her concerns faded, replaced by that swooning newly-in-love feeling.

"Hey, Jay," she heard herself say. She sounded different to her own ears. Light and flirty. She could hear the smile in her voice. "How was work this evening?"

"Not as productive as it should have been. Couldn't concentrate for thinking of you anyway."

"Stop. You know you don't have to feed me any lines." She didn't mind hearing the sentiments coming from him, though.

"Never. Only the truth. How was book club?"

Thoughts of Justin Love resurfaced, and she considered whether to ask him about writing once more. Lisa decided against it. Whenever she broached the subject again, she wanted to look in his eyes.

"Good. Everyone just left. About to curl up on the couch and search for a movie to watch."

"In the mood for company?"

"How soon can you get here?"

"I'm not far from you now. Fifteen minutes."

"Alright. See you in fifteen."

∞

194

Lisa sunk into the security of Jayden's arms. This man always felt like home. For a solid two minutes, they stood in her foyer enveloped in their own little world.

His head rested securely on top of hers.

His biceps squeezed her gently.

His heart beat steady, and the scent of his cologne—notes of cedarwood, vanilla, and masculinity—teased her senses.

Jayden loosened his hold. One hand glided behind her head, and the other lifted her chin. In one slow, smooth motion, his warm lips caressed hers until he needed air.

Jayden released a guttural moan. "*Ummm.* This is what I've been missing today."

His baritone voice snapped her out of the trance he'd just put her in. A heavy breath fell from her lips. She didn't respond right away, led him to her sofa. She needed the distraction of the movie. Fast. Her first choice had been a romance movie, but she decided against that, especially after the way he'd just kissed her. A Marvel superhero movie would have to do.

Jayden sat, and Lisa snuggled up next to him with her head on his shoulder. She echoed his earlier sentiments. "This is what I've been missing today."

Jayden kissed the top of her hair and slipped an arm around her shoulder. "Looks like we're both getting what we want."

Lisa scrolled through their choices. "*Thor* or *Avengers*?"

"Honestly, it doesn't matter. I just want to be here with you."

She looked up at him and smiled. "I told you. You don't have to feed me any lines. I've already said yes to being with you."

Jayden tossed his head back and chuckled. "Do you want the truth or not?"

"Always the truth." This was her chance to get the answers she needed. Did he or did he not write that book? Ask him about Justin Love and get it over with. Why this thing mattered to her, she didn't know. But, again, she put off asking because she didn't want to risk losing the moment.

Jayden rubbed his hand along her arm. "Good."

They settled on Thor's second movie, which they'd seen at least seven times together. Nevertheless, they watched in silence for the first thirty minutes.

"I always thought Thor would somehow end up with Lady Sif," Lisa said.

"That would have been too easy for the plot. Giving him a love interest with someone who isn't from his world makes the plot more interesting," Jayden said.

"So what I'm hearing is that you don't like easy relationships?"

Jayden laughed. "We can always count on you to make any conversation personal, but to answer your question, I prefer non-complicated relationships, like what we have. In full transparency, you were all I ever wanted, Lis. I just wanted to be ready for you, to be the man you need."

Lisa paused for a moment. *Be the man you need* sounded a lot like a line from Justin Love's book, but she couldn't overthink. Not right now. She readjusted herself so that her legs dangled over his. "Now, who's making it personal?"

Jayden shrugged and smiled. "Well, we both knew where the conversation was headed."

"So, I take it you're ready now?"

He nodded and squeezed her knee.

"Not quite the answer I expected."

Jayden took a deep breath. "Yes, I'm ready to be the man you need. It's just that my life may get a little more complicated workwise."

Lisa's heart pounded, and her belly cinched, unsure of what Jayden was getting at. His work-life balance or non-balance was already an area of contention between them. Her body stiffened. "Okay," she spoke slowly. "What does that mean?"

He held her gaze, and she blinked, determined not to get caught up in the eyes that stirred her heart.

"It means that I'm considering turning down the partnership offer and starting my own firm." He paused, seemingly gauging her reaction, but she didn't flinch or speak, giving him room to continue. "That's not quite the plan I had for my life, and I know we hadn't talked about our future, but I want you to be my wife, Lisa. And I don't know how things are going to turn out with me stepping out on my own. But what I do know is that I don't want to stall our relationship or move backward. I want to move forward. As my wife, I don't want you worrying about finances or our future."

Dang it. Jayden was serious. How did they go from superheroes to talking about marriage? It's crazy how marriage was something neither of them had ever discussed, and yet, they'd always been each other's person. Hearing him speak the words terrified her but also provided somewhat of a relief.

Lisa enclosed one of his hands in both of hers. "First of all, the idea of you starting your own firm is exciting, Jay, and I'm here for it every step of the way."

"I know you mean that, but I'm not sure you understand the commitment I'll have to make to get the business up and running. At the start, it'll only be me, so the long work hours aren't going away."

"Yeah, but weekends and mandatory eleven-hour days won't be the norm. Eventually, you'll have staff, and you have the autonomy to work how you want and make time for us."

Jayden leaned forward, his posture more erect. "You're serious, aren't you?"

"Yes. Weren't you?"

He massaged his forehead. "Yes, of course, I guess I'd run the scenario in my mind and didn't think you'd respond like this. And speaking the plan—well, idea—out loud sounds crazy. Giving up a three-hundred-thousand-dollar-a-year gig to start my own business is insane, right?"

Lisa rubbed his back, her palm making continuous circles. "While the money is great, think about everything else—the real reason behind why you'd want to build your own business because we know this isn't about the money. What will you gain by working for yourself?"

"Everything."

"No matter what you choose, I'm here, Jay. And in the words of Momma Wanda, if I haven't gone anywhere in almost forty years, I'm probably not going anywhere."

Jayden hiked an eyebrow. "Wait. Momma Wanda?"

Lisa laughed. "Yep. One of the developments from book club tonight. Since we're official now, Aunt is too weird. I'm part of the family now."

Lisa smiled and parked her hand on his shoulder, her chin resting against it.

Jayden leaned over and kissed her lips. "Always have been. I love you."

And he was right. She couldn't recall a moment when she hadn't felt like part of his family or vice versa. The only difference now was that she'd officially chosen him. Lisa had come to realize that she'd fought against what she'd always known to be true. Just as he'd strived to be the man she needed, subconsciously she'd done the same for him.

They were destined to end up together, and after all this time, there was nothing that could tear them apart.

Nothing.

Chapter Seventeen

Jayden and Lisa strolled across the jet bridge to board their aircraft. By the time they made it on the plane, familiar eyes looked back at them. The first six to seven rows were filled with family and friends of the bride and groom. His and Lisa's seats were in between in row three. Jayden placed his laptop bag and Lisa's carryon in the overhead bin while she slid into the window seat.

Kenneth Evans, Ginger's dad, stood to greet him. "Nice to see you, Jayden. Thought I'd have to tell the pilot to leave you and Lisa behind. Can't be messing around. I've got a wedding to get to."

Jayden laughed.

Lisa stuffed her purse under the seat and half-stood, one knee pressed into the seat. "C'mon now, Mr. Evans. Don't do me like that. We just had a misunderstanding with the luggage check-in."

Both Jayden and Kenneth quirked an eyebrow at her.

"Okay, fine. I may have overpacked a little."

Kenneth laughed. "I somehow figured that was the case."

"We got it taken care of." And by *we,* Jayden meant that he paid the oversized luggage fee, although Lisa insisted she move items from her bag to his. They simply didn't have the time for that, nor did Jayden have the patience. When he pulled up at her house and saw that suitcase the size of her powder room, he knew it was too big and would cause problems. He'd said as much, but she claimed she was well aware of what fifty pounds felt like, and her bag was closer to forty. Short on time, Jayden didn't argue. Now, here they were.

"All that matters is that we're here to support my girl," Lisa said.

Kenneth looked between the two of them. "I'm surprised you all didn't get out of here two days ago when Ginger and Brock left."

"I wish. The more days in paradise, the better, but duty calls. I had to solidify a few things for the bookstore's grand reopening. Hope you'll be there."

"Yes. Ginger mentioned the store's event. I'll be there, dragging along a few guys from my bowling league."

Lisa's smile widened. "Sounds like a plan."

"Well, I don't want to be the one holding us up, so let me grab my seat. The flight attendant is giving me eyes." He chuckled before adding, "I'm glad to see the two of you together." Kenneth glanced at Lisa and slapped Jayden's shoulder. "Enjoy the ride."

Jayden was ninety-nine percent sure Kenneth was not referring to their travel plans. He took his seat next to Lisa and released a heavy breath. For a moment, he didn't think he would make this trip—not because of Lisa's tardiness, though that was a factor, but because of work. Of all the time he'd put in at the firm, some of the partners still gave him slack for taking the time off during busy season—which was a no-no in general. However, Jayden had done his time—more than his fair share—and he'd notified them months in advance. Either way, he still brought his laptop along to pacify his boss.

But Lisa, on the other hand, was probably close to a heart attack when she saw his laptop bag. She didn't verbally mention it, but she'd bucked her eyes and sucked in a breath heavy enough to fill the expanse of her chest. At any moment, he expected her feet to lift from the ground and to see her floating to Jamaica. His love pouted all the way to the airport.

Lisa linked her fingers through his, causing a sudden bout of warmth to creep up his arm. "Sorry about my attitude earlier. I want us to have fun. This is our first trip out of the country together and our first trip as a couple, so let's have a good time, okay?"

And that meant that she'd better not see him looking at his laptop screen or responding to work calls or texts.

Jayden lifted her knuckles to his lips and planted a soft kiss. "Okay. And I promise not to let work interfere with everything we have planned." He shouldn't have made that promise, given that work had interfered with their plans numerous times in the past. But today, he'd like to think that he was a different person on a different, less workaholic path. At least, that's who he wanted to be right now.

She leaned closer to him and presented her lips. Without hesitation, he accepted. "Is that all a brother needs to say?"

Lisa tossed her head back and chuckled, creating a new melody in his mind and heart every time she did so. He loved to hear it. She hiked one eyebrow when she recovered. "I guess we'll just have to wait and see."

The voice of the pilot, Captain Rick Crandell, came across the plane's intercom. He announced that they were ready for takeoff and instructed the flight attendants to do their final checks. Minutes later, the plane pushed back from the gate while the flight attendants stood in the aisle demonstrating safety procedures. But Jayden didn't pay them any attention. And not because he'd heard the spiel a hundred times before, but because his thoughts were preoccupied with the upcoming events of the weekend.

While the festivities were not about him and Lisa, he needed everything to go well and work in his favor. He'd use the time to make a decision about the partnership and starting his own firm. But if he were being honest with himself, that decision had already been made when he talked to Lisa about it a week ago. He'd made other decisions that night too when he overshared that he wanted Lisa to be his wife. That wasn't a conversation that he'd planned to have that evening, but it was one worth having. She needed to know and understand how serious he was about her and their relationship. How he'd always been meticulous in his choices because they all led to this moment—this weekend.

∞

At ten thousand feet in the air, Lisa looped an arm around the crook of Jayden's elbow and nestled her head into his shoulder.

Exhausted could not even begin to describe the way she felt. For the past week, she had to make sure everything was in place for next weekend's grand reopening. She'd confirmed her favorite male author—Sebastian—would attend. That confirmation alone got her excited. Not to mention Justin Love had agreed to attend. Although a new author, he didn't have any digital footprint, and this would be his first event. She was thrilled to be the bookstore to host both male authors—an accomplishment that meant the world to her as the new owner of the bookstore. She'd also confirmed three local poets, and an additional twenty-five authors and vendors; Among them was her favorite Cajun food truck vendor, Carter's Trinity, and her favorite sweet treats—Ginger's Goodies.

Solidifying that she had everything in place for the bookstore's event wasn't the only reason she couldn't sleep. Jayden contributed to her sleepless nights and earlier-than-normal awakenings. She kept replaying his words in her mind like a broken toy in need of a fresh set of batteries. Like the fly wheel on her indoor spin bike, there was no end to her mind spinning.

I want you to be my wife.

As my wife, I don't want you to worry about finances or our future.

His words had her in a chokehold.

They hadn't even been official for an entire month yet, and he'd entertained the idea of marriage. But she'd be in denial if she didn't acknowledge where their relationship was headed. This was the road they'd always traveled—*unofficially*. And the idea of being with him forever excited and terrified her at once. Her, a wife? Jayden's wife? Her best friend's wife?

Crazy.

Jayden kissed the top of her head, sending a bout of heat down to the soles of her feet. "I thought you'd be reading a book, not taking a nap."

"I really need the rest. I haven't slept much this week with getting things ready for the grand reopening next weekend."

"Speaking of that, I'm sorry I haven't been much help. Is there anything you need me to do?"

"No. You're good. I suppose I won't push my luck what with this being a busy time of the year for you at work. I'd just like you to stop by for a while, that's all. Everything else has been handled, and Momma Wanda is a Godsend."

"Stop by? I'm going to be there all day for you. You should know that by now."

She lifted her head away from his shoulder and squinted up at him. "Two weekends in a row away from work? What gives?"

"Let's just say that I want to give my attention to the people who are most important to me. I meant what I said the other night, Lis. This is me turning my words into action."

Seconds later, before she could respond, she noticed Momma Wanda out of her seat with a huge smile plastered across her face. She wiggled her eyebrows and lifted praise hands in the air. However, she remained silent for once. Lisa took her actions to mean that she'd heard what Jayden had just said. Two rows ahead in the opposite aisle, and the woman acted like she was the third passenger on their row.

"Well, be there by eight."

"Maybe a half hour earlier with breakfast. I'll have to coax you into eating since you tend to ignore your hunger when you're nervous."

"Thanks, Jay," was all she could muster before she settled back into the comfort of him.

Typical Jayden. Consistent with his actions. He'd always been there for her in the past, but now she felt more like she could relax and settle into the fact that he wanted to cater to her every need. Although the feeling was surreal, she'd allow herself to bask in her new normal. Her best friend was now her love.

Chapter Eighteen

From the time it took Lisa, Jayden, and the rest of the group who had traveled on the same plane to get through customs, secure their luggage, and travel from the Montego Bay airport to the all-inclusive resort in Negril, Jamaica, two hours had passed. Maybe more than two. But Lisa had to stop herself from ticking off the minutes. There she was in paradise, and it seemed to be taking forever to get to her final destination. Yes, she was probably acting, or at least feeling like a spoiled child, but she wanted to get to the fun and experience the Caribbean vibes as soon as possible and for as long as possible. The local musicians in and outside of the airport singing Bob Marley's "One Love" and other songs that sounded similar quenched her anxiety a tad.

In their private transport, she wiggled to the driver's music and cast smiles and glances at Jayden, who kept checking his phone.

He pulled her close and whispered so that the driver couldn't hear, "You will enjoy yourself this weekend, my love. Be patient. We're almost there." He held his phone in her line of vision where he showed a map on his screen. He'd punched in the resort's address to follow along with the driver's route. True Jayden fashion.

"I can't help myself. I'm way too excited. The music. The culture. *Oooh,* the food that I can't wait to try."

The driver, a short, pudgy man who was dressed in all black with a matching hat trimmed in green and gold, butted in. "Be sure you try the jerk chicken, mon. Not like what you have in the States, I'm sure."

Lisa grinned. "Sure will. Any other food you suggest we try?"

He gave a wide, white smile where he was missing one of his teeth on the top row. "Callaloo. Your resort may serve it for breakfast. Green vegetable similar to spinach."

Lisa rubbed her palms together. "Got it."

Jayden pointed toward the window. "We're pulling up now."

"Let me be the first to officially welcome you lovebirds to paradise. Enjoy your time in our country."

The driver climbed out of the car, removed their bags from the trunk, and opened the door for them. He held out his hand for Lisa. That's when she saw his gold name tag. Zidane. He may have introduced himself when he picked them up from the airport, but she'd been too distracted by how much time everything seemed to take.

Jayden climbed out after her and handed Zidane a tip. "Thank you, sir."

"You're welcome. And thank you. Enjoy your time here." He handed Jayden a card. "Please give us a call the day before your departure to schedule your transport back to the airport."

"Will do."

Jayden pulled her close and squeezed her to his chest. "I love you. I'm already digging the vibes, and I've been standing here a minute."

The hotel concierge greeted them with two cold towels. Lisa took one and patted it against her face and neck. "*Ooh,* this feels good."

Jayden hardly used the towel before handing it back.

"Is that my girl?"

Lisa jerked her head at the sound of Ginger's voice. She spotted her friend waltzing toward them in a white maxi dress with sun-kissed skin. The Jamaican sun favored Ginger because her skin glowed brighter than headlights on high beam. She screamed and jumped into Ginger's open arms.

"You look fabulous, Gin. This sun is showing you favor. Look at you. Shining bright. Goodness, I'm so happy for you."

Ginger squeezed tighter before letting go. "Thanks, but I'm happy for you. If you get your act together, we'll be back again next year for your wedding," Ginger said, releasing a deep belly laugh.

"See, you're starting already. Let's just focus on you this weekend."

Ginger squealed, all thirty-two of her teeth sparkling. "I cannot believe this is happening."

"Well, you'd better believe it because we have to get you down the aisle in forty-eight hours."

"I see you, bro. How's it going, man?" Jayden said to Brock and gave him a one-armed hug and handshake.

Lisa released Ginger. "Sorry, Brock. You know I'm not being rude. How are you?" She gave Brock a quick hug and stepped back to Jayden's side.

Brock pulled Ginger closer and kissed her neck. "I'm about to marry the most amazing woman in the world, I'm great. How was the flight? How are you?"

"Look around. Palm trees. Sunny skies. Concierge waiting to take care of my needs." One of them walked by and handed her a glass of champagne, which she accepted. "What more can I ask for? I am great. My swimsuit is tucked in here," she said and patted the beach bag slung across her shoulder.

Brock and Jayden chuckled.

"Ginger was the same when we arrived a couple of days ago."

Ginger shrugged and smiled. "How could I not? This place is amazing! Let's go get you checked in." She turned to kiss Brock. "Babe, mind if I spend a few moments with Lisa?"

"Nah. Have fun. I'll catch up with Jayden." He flipped his wrist. "Let's meet in an hour on the beach."

Ginger's lips curved into a smile, and she hiked a brow. "Our favorite spot?"

Brock pulled her into his arms and whispered something in her ear. She giggled like the woman in love that she was. "'Kay. One hour."

"Okay, Jay. I hate to burn out on you when we just got here—"

He held up his palm. "No worries. We're here to have fun. We'll have plenty of time together." He pulled her closer. "Probably so much time together that you'll be ready to get rid of me."

Lisa softened in his arms and inhaled his masculine scent. "*Hmmm.* Never. I haven't gotten rid of you in all this time, so that should tell you something."

"Yeah. Everything I need to know." He planted a soft kiss on her lips. "Now go on. Ginger is giving me the side eye."

The group chuckled.

Ginger looped her arm through Lisa's and led her to check-in. "Am not, but we're on the clock. We said one hour." She lowered her voice since they weren't quite out of earshot of the guys. "How are you? This is you and Jayden's first official trip as a couple, and this isn't just any old trip. You're in Jamaica at this beautiful resort. In freaking paradise. How will you even deal after all of this?"

Lisa chuckled. "The same way I've been dealing. You know things aren't like that with me and Jayden. We're easy. Known each other forever. And there's no need to try to impress one another. So this," she said, waving her hand in the air, careful not to spill her glass of champagne, "is just another experience we get to share."

Ginger smiled big like she knew something Lisa didn't know, but she wouldn't press her on it. This was her weekend after all so, there were a number of things that could be behind it.

"I'm so freaking happy for you, Lis."

Lisa approached the check-in desk and handed over her passport and credit card and greeted the woman whose smile was just as wide as Ginger's. She turned to her friend. "Oh, really? Why is that? That's my line."

"Finally allowing yourself to be free and accept what is—the love that's been in front of you your entire life. And I've gotta say that I like this look on you." She wagged her finger up and down in front of her.

"This is your weekend, so I won't fight against anything you just said. I'll simply say thank you."

"Are you also getting married soon, Miss?" the woman behind the desk with a gold name plate that read Debra asked.

"Not quite." She glanced at Ginger. That huge grin on her face returned. "For now, I'm here on maid-of-honor duties."

Debra handed Lisa her key card, gave instructions on how to locate her room, and indicated that her bags were already inside. "It is a requirement for each of our guests to present their passports at check-in. When can we expect your companion?"

"He was right behind me. He'll be in shortly."

"Thank you, Miss. Enjoy your stay at our resort. And I do hope you'll also consider us for your nuptials as well."

"Thanks."

Ginger looped her arm through Lisa's again, and they turned away from the desk, but stopped short when Brock and Jayden entered. She pointed at Jayden. "Miss Debra, this is her companion and the man you'll need to talk to about those future nuptials."

"Huh?" Jayden scrunched his brows. Both he and Brock looked confused.

Lisa tugged her away. "Miss Debra, ignore her." She held up her champagne glass. "She may have had one too many glasses of this already." She stopped short before the exit and handed Jayden his room key. "She'll need to verify your identity using your passport and you should be all good after that."

"Forty-five minutes," Brock called to their retreating frames.

∞

Jayden looked at Brock. "Part of me doesn't even want to know what that was all about."

"Trust me. You don't. I don't either," Brock said.

Jayden strolled to the front desk to check in. Debra smiled big at him. "Welcome. How may I serve you today?"

He handed over his passport. "Lisa just checked into our suite, but it's my understanding that you need to see both of our passports."

"Correct. It's policy for all of our international guests." Debra reviewed his travel document and clicked around on her computer for several seconds. She handed it back and gave him instructions on how to find his room and information regarding excursions. "As I told your companion, your bags should have been delivered to your room."

"Thank you."

"There's a QR code beside the telephone. Scan it, and it'll provide you with more than enough information about our resort. In the building to your left, there's an associate available to schedule any tours or excursions you may be interested in."

"Appreciate it. Thank you, ma'am."

"Enjoy your stay, and let me know if you have any questions."

Jayden returned his passport to his blazer pocket along with his room key. Meanwhile, Brock stood nearby, quiet, with a funny look on his face.

"What's up with you, man?"

They walked out of the building, with Jayden on his way to his and Lisa's suite.

"Not to get in your business or anything…"

"The exact thing someone says right before they get in your business." Jayden knew where the conversation was headed before Brock said anything, but he'd give Brock a chance to get his concerns off his chest.

Brock chuckled. "Yeah, you're right. But Ginger would kill me if I let something like this slip by me without mentioning it."

Jayden kept stride. "I'm listening."

"What's the deal with the room-sharing situation?"

"You're right. You do sound like your bride." Jayden shrugged. "Our relationship status doesn't change the fact that we were always going to share a suite. It's no big deal. But to answer your question, we're on this trip together, so why put two rooms on our credit card? We're all good."

"Our credit card? As in a shared card? I'm getting married this weekend and I don't even share a credit card account with my future wife."

"We've had the same card since college or something like that—been a long time."

Brock stopped and stared at him like another head had popped out on his shoulder causing Jayden to break his stride. He shook his head. "Wait a minute. Seriously? I'm not even going to get into details about that. All I will say is you two are the strangest people I've ever known."

Jayden laughed. "Not the most common situation, I know. Had a woman break up with me once when she found out that Lisa and I shared a credit card."

Brock doubled over in laughter. "The fact that you believed any woman would go for any mess like that is crazy. I don't know why you and Lisa have been playing around this long."

They reached the set of elevators that would take Jayden to his suite. "Timing is everything, man."

"Yeah, keep telling yourself that." Brock glanced over his shoulder as if making sure the coast was clear before he continued speaking. "Everything still all good for this weekend? Who am I kidding? You should have done this long before me."

Jayden didn't need to feel his inside jacket pocket again to ensure the box was where he'd last placed it. In fact, he'd ensured it was secure when he returned his passport "Yeah. This has been a long time coming."

Brock tapped his shoulder. "We're both happy for y'all. Ginger may be more excited than all of us."

"You don't think her excitement will spoil things for Lisa, do you?"

"Nah. She lives for stuff like this, especially when it comes to Lisa. She won't say anything, even though I'm sure it's probably killing her not to."

"Right, but just to be on the safe side, let me change real quick to get to the beach. The longer they're alone together, the more tempted Ginger will be. You may trust her not to say anything, but I don't."

Brock chuckled, dapped and fist bumped him. "I'm going to change and grab sunscreen. See you shortly."

Jayden entered the suite. The sky-blue waters floating in small waves called to him through the glass French doors. He noted his and Lisa's bags parked against the wall and strolled past the en suite, master bed, and a sitting area decorated with two chairs and a pull-out sofa—his bed for the next few nights if he wanted to resist temptation. Stepping outside the French doors, Jayden inhaled and took in his serene surroundings. The water gently splashing near his feet and skies that knew no clouds that afternoon greeted him. Jayden removed the tiny velvet box from his inside jacket pocket and flipped it open. The contents sparkled in the afternoon sun—a sparkle that reminded him every bit of the woman he'd ask to wear it.

Yes, this weekend would be a long time coming.

Chapter Nineteen

Lisa and Ginger had found a couple of lounge chairs on the beach facing the ocean. They'd both adorned large sunhats and settled into their seats. The waves crashing against the sand relaxed Lisa enough to bring about all kinds of thoughts about her present and future with Jayden and the bookstore and just life in general.

"Gin, twenty years ago, could you have imagined we'd be lying here in Jamaica, sunbathing, drinking champagne, and getting ready for you and Brock's wedding?"

She chuckled and turned over on her side to face Lisa. "Absolutely not. If you recall, twenty years ago, Brock and I were done. You couldn't even speak his name to me."

Lisa laughed and faced her as well. "Yeah, I remember when you told me about him. That was the first time you'd ever shared anything so personal. We'd gone from discussing books, baking, sororities, and parties to the love of your life. Probably the turning point in our relationship that made us besties. The look in your eyes and the way you talked about him made me think you would probably always love that man. And here we are."

Ginger lifted the brim of her hat and quirked a brow. "Really? Why didn't you say anything?"

"And lose maid-of-honor status? I think not."

Ginger burst into laughter. "Yeah, you're probably right."

"Plus, you were hurting. What I thought didn't matter."

"All things happen when they're supposed to, which is why I'm so happy for you and Jayden. I know I joke around a lot about you guys, but I really am. There are no two people more deserving of each other than you two."

"Thanks. I appreciate that."

"I also don't know anyone else who's been together without being together for so long. Maybe Justin Love can use your story as material for his next book. Folks won't even believe that it's based on a true story."

Lisa howled in laughter. "If sand didn't burn the eyes, I'd grab some and toss it at you right now."

"You must learn to take responsibility and have some self-control. The truth is the truth. But after this weekend," she said, holding out her pinky finger, "I promise to not bring up how long it took you and Jayden to get your acts together again—well, at least for a long while."

Lisa hooked her pinky finger into Ginger's and shook. "I don't know why I'm even going through this with you because you can't help yourself, especially now that you're getting married."

"I'm serious. Can't be losing my matron-of-honor privileges." Ginger wiggled her eyebrows for effect.

"Hey now. No one told me it was girl time already." Momma Wanda's voice carried across the beach. She had to be about twenty-five feet away. Mom walked alongside her. Both of them with swimsuits, floral coverups, beach hats, and glasses of champagne. Or at least that's what Lisa suspected was in their glasses.

Lisa and Ginger stood to greet them. Lisa hugged her mom first, then Momma Wanda. "We're just hanging out waiting for Jayden and Brock to meet us."

Mom took a deep breath and smiled. "So this is paradise. Ginger, I saw your Dad on our flight. Have Brock's parents made it yet?"

She wrapped Mom in her arms. "Yes. They're all around here somewhere. I think everyone is just taking it all in. It's beautiful here, isn't it?"

"Yes, honey. I don't think I want to go home," Momma Wanda answered.

The group laughed.

Lisa smiled and reclaimed her seat. "I think you speak for all of us. This scenery is like an image from a magazine, TV, or a movie. Unbelievable."

"Amen." Momma Wanda huffed and grunted as she squatted to take the second beach chair. Mom sat between Wanda and Lisa.

Lisa focused on the water dancing before them. The clear blue skies were like a kiss from heaven—the perfect picture of what the weekend should be. Not that she wasn't already enjoying herself, but thoughts of vacationing alone with Jayden on an island filled her thoughts. They wouldn't have to give of their time to anyone else. They could just be.

"What are you grinning about?" her mom asked.

Whisking her head toward her, Lisa hadn't realized that the thought and images that filled her mind had brought a smile to her face.

"Nothing. Just enjoying the relaxation. No worries or cares right now."

Mom gave one of those knowing smiles. "*Ummm-hmmm.* I bet."

Thank goodness she didn't bring too much attention to her. Momma Wanda would love to hop on the train and ride it around the beach. She'd probably already planned her and Jayden's wedding in the same location, and they weren't even engaged.

Caribbean music played in the distance, reaching their ears by the second, as if the music were coming to them. The next thing Lisa knew, Tina, Ginger's future sister-in-law, and Della, her future mother-in-law, were sashaying toward them to the beat of the music.

"Hey now. There's plenty of time to chill. Right now, it's party time," Tina announced and pulled Ginger to her feet to dance alongside her. "I love this song."

Ginger didn't seem to protest much. She moved her hips from side to side for a few moments before pulling Lisa to her feet to join them.

Lisa didn't know the song, but found herself shaking her body to the beat. She didn't consider herself much of a dancer, but there was something about the atmosphere and the music and the freedom she felt that made her go along with it—no thoughts about the bookstore's tax issues, her future with Jayden, or what he may be hiding from her filled her mind. Only good old-fashioned carefree fun. Della grabbed Mom and Momma Wanda. They danced until a new melody began to play.

"Are we not invited to the party?" Derek, Ginger's future father-in-law, asked.

Lisa looked up to see him along with Jayden, Kenneth, Brock, and Bryce, Tina's husband, strolling up to their area looking like a group of handsome black kings.

Della stepped into his arms and answered him, but Lisa didn't hear what she said.

Jayden took her by the hands and pulled her close. "Hey, don't sit down yet. Dance with me."

The island vibes must have gotten hold of him, too. She couldn't recall any moment in her life when Jayden walked up to her and asked her to an impromptu dance. The musical melody playing in the nearby distance was just as beautiful as the first, so she swayed her hips much like she'd seen in other Caribbean dances on the internet. At least that's what she hoped she looked like. She'd sway in front of him a few times before he spun her around and pulled her close. They'd move their hips in sync to the beat. Caught up in Jayden and the dance moves she didn't know he had, she didn't realize that all eyes were on them. Neither did she care. Any time with Jayden just felt good—and right.

The song ended, and he spun her around to face him. He wrapped her in a hug and whispered in her ear, his scent mixing with the salt water from the ocean. "If I haven't told you today, know that I love you."

She pressed her lips into his and lingered for a moment. The heat from the sun and Jayden's lips traveled up her spine. She stepped away. "I love you back."

Jayden's hand slid down to connect with hers and they rejoined their group.

"Now that the show is over," Ginger announced, and the group laughed, "Brock and I would like to take a moment to thank you all for saying yes and agreeing to vacation here with us while we exchange vows. While you're all here for the wedding, this is your vacation, too, as Jayden and Lisa just showed us."

"The jabs…" Jayden winced and grabbed his torso.

Brock picked up where she left off. "Right. We want you all to enjoy yourselves. Gin has posted all of the information in the GroupMe chat. The welcome reception is tonight at…" His words dangled in the air for Ginger to catch.

"Six p.m. Our ladies pampering session will follow. Outside of the rehearsal dinner tomorrow at four, , you all are free to do what you wish. This is your vacation, enjoy it."

Brock added, "Guys, we'll meet up afterward as well. Until then, enjoy paradise."

As if their speeches were planned—and maybe they were, she couldn't be sure because she'd been caught up in Jayden—a waiter dressed in a sea-blue collared shirt and black shorts appeared with a serving tray of champagne flutes.

Bryce, who looked like he could be Brock's twin except that he wore short dreads, lifted his glass. "Let's toast to Brock and Ginger." When the group lifted their glasses, he said, "Bro, I'm proud of you and the strides you're making. It's a blessing that the two of you have found and reconnected with each other. No doubt that Ginger will keep you in line."

Brock burst into laughter.

Echoing Bryce's sentiments, a round of "Cheers" came from the group. Indeed, the two of them had found their happily ever after. Lisa couldn't imagine anything that would make the weekend more perfect.

∞

Jayden couldn't recall a time in his life when he'd experienced such lightheartedness. Life had always been about work and striving to climb to the next rung on his career ladder. But this evening, walking across the resort sands with Lisa by his side and their friends surrounding him, he relished in this feeling—the feeling that made him want to stop and dance along the shore of the beach.

He dressed in light blue linen shorts with a matching buttoned-down shirt, compliments of Lisa, who wore a matching linen blue dress that fit her perfectly well. He found it hard to look away from her and fought the urge to tell her how beautiful she looked for the third time. After a while, he was certain his words wouldn't have the same effect, not that he hoped to gain anything from letting her know how stunning she was in his eyes—and those of the men they'd passed as they strolled to the restaurant for Brock and Ginger's welcome reception. She didn't seem to notice, but he did, and he didn't like it. Instinct, and maybe a slight tinge of jealousy, made him pull her a little closer.

A huge sign strung on the outside of the building in pink and gold letters read, *Congratulations Brock & Ginger*. The patio area was lined with a row of tables filled with silver warming trays. String lights were looped from one end of the patio to the other, all through surrounding greenery and light posts. As the sun began its descent, the cascading hues of warm orange and yellow provided the perfect backdrop.

Lisa gasped. "This is gorgeous, isn't it?"

"It is. Would you want to come back some other time?"

"Are you kidding me? In a heartbeat. I was actually going to suggest we come back—just the two of us. Here or any resort, really. Can't believe we haven't taken a trip like this before now."

He could only imagine how that conversation would have gone with him asking her to go with him to a couples-only resort. She'd have blown him off as if he were joking, and he'd have tucked his feelings away and pretended she hadn't stabbed him in the heart. Jayden couldn't count on his fingers and toes the number of times he'd wanted to ask Lisa out but didn't for fear that they'd ruin their friendship or for fear of her rejection. But there was no reason to go down that road. They were here now.

"I can't believe it, either."

Lisa swayed her hips much like she'd done earlier that afternoon. "And why haven't I been listening to this music before now? I can't stop dancing."

Jayden laughed. "New playlist coming soon, I guess."

Lisa chuckled. "Now you know I've already started one."

They caught the attention of Ginger, who waved them over. She said something to Brock who lifted his head and waved as well.

Jayden and Lisa were greeted by the aroma of fried seafood and the open arms of their friends.

After a round of hugs, Ginger said, "Looking good. Whose idea was the matching outfits?"

Jayden cocked his head to the side as if she should know the answer to her own question.

"Just kidding. This has Lisa written all over it. We're just hanging out. Feel free to grab some light bites and drinks."

He'd spotted his mom across the patio in conversation with Barbara and Brock's parents and had planned to speak to her after grabbing an appetizer of jumbo shrimp. But the next thing he knew, she'd scurried up next to him with that sneaky grin on her face.

"Hey, beautiful."

"Hey, son. How are you?"

"Good. Enjoying the island life."

She shimmied her shoulders. He knew he should have never shared his plans with her. She wouldn't let him rest until the deed was done.

He mouthed, "Don't start."

She shrugged and lifted her palms. "What? I didn't say anything?" She kept her voice low, surprisingly, looking over her shoulder at Lisa whose back faced the two of them as she was caught up in conversation with Brock and Ginger. She turned back to him. "Just don't mess this up. I want to come back here next year."

Jayden threw his head back, and a hearty laugh escaped. He should have known she'd already come up with some sort of plan. "Relax, Mom. Everything will be fine."

She danced away, and Lisa joined his side. "What was that about?"

"Just my mom being herself."

Lisa smiled in understanding. "Say less."

Two hours of eating, dancing, and celebrating passed. Ginger and the rest of the ladies went on to do their pampering stuff, while Jayden joined Kenneth, Brock, his brother, and Dad for the rest of the evening in the billiards room.

Brock handed each of them a pool stick. "Sorry to disappoint you guys, but there won't be any manicures, pedicures, or massages this evening."

The group broke out in laughter.

"We forgive you this time," Kenneth slapped his shoulder.

"Maybe Jayden will pick up the slack," Bryce added.

Jayden shot Brock a look.

"Hey, you know I didn't say anything. Ginger pretty much told them."

"Nah, it's cool. As long as no one says anything to her before I do."

Derek took the break. "You've got a lot going for you, son—the engagement, and I hear you're about to be partner."

Jayden took the first shot. "Red. Corner pocket. Not sure about the partner thing yet. Might step out and start my own firm."

Kenneth leaned against the pool stick. "What does Lisa think about that?"

"Says she's on board, which I appreciate. Just didn't think I'd be starting over at the point when I'd be asking her to marry me."

Derek scrunched his eyebrows and rubbed his chin. Brock, Kenneth, and Bryce had taken their shots. It was now Derek's turn again. "Yellow. Right center pocket." The ball sank, followed by the next two. A waiter came by and offered them drinks. Jayden and Brock took bottled water while Derek and Bryce declined beverages for the moment. Kenneth requested a shot of Bourbon.

"What if you didn't have to start from the ground up? Our tax law practice could use a CPA to help us branch out to build an accounting arm."

Jayden looked from Derek to Brock and Bryce. "Seriously?"

"Yeah. We've already talked about it. We think you'd be a great fit if it's something you're interested in," Brock added.

"And we heard you were hesitant about signing on the dotted line. I won't presume to know what's holding you back, but I think the Pearson Group can offer you what your firm can't," Bryce said.

The Pearson men had Jayden's attention, especially considering he'd been holding on to the unsigned agreement for almost a month. "And what's that?"

"The opportunity to build something you can be proud of and the flexibility to spend time with your new wife," Brock said. "Take that from someone who has been in a similar struggle."

Jayden couldn't lie. They were speaking his language. And Jayden remembered the way Brock worked hard to get the head position in Decadent Dough's mergers and acquisitions department. He'd been willing to do whatever he had to do, almost losing Ginger and his dignity in the process. Before he left for this trip, Jayden had asked God for clarity and had promised himself that he'd make his mind up by the time he landed back in Houston.

"Mr. Pearson, your offer sounds like an answered prayer, but I'd need some time to make sure I'm making the right decision."

"No problem. I wouldn't expect anything less from you. Besides, this is a big weekend. Let's talk things over when we return home."

"Thank you, sir."

"I've been watching you for a long time, and you've done well for yourself. No doubt that a Pearson & Reynolds partnership could go far. It'll be my last major move before I retire."

Jayden took his shot and allowed Derek's offer to sink in. "Pearson & Reynolds does have a nice ring to it."

Derek slapped his shoulder. "It does, doesn't it? But no pressure." He dropped his hand from Jayden's shoulder. "Pray about it, and talk it over with the future Mrs."

They played several more rounds of billiards, though Jayden lost count of the number of games—could have been three or ten? Derek and Kenneth gave marriage advice and some life advice, too, but Jayden couldn't recall anything they'd said. His thoughts were consumed with discussing the possibility of a Pearson & Reynolds partnership with Lisa. He would build the tax accounting practice. Because their firm practiced tax law, convincing their clients to hire them for their return preparation and tax accounting needs shouldn't be a hard sell. He could do that. And considering he'd be restricted from pursuing his current clients and he'd have to sign a three-year non-compete agreement with his firm when he left, Jayden could spend his energy winning over The Pearson Group's current clients.

When, not if.

Had he already made his decision?

Chapter Twenty

What a magical weekend. And Lisa hadn't even seen to it that her best friend made it down the aisle yet. The vibes in Negril, Jamaica were everything. To top off the evening with a luxurious spa treatment alongside the women she loved most set her above the proverbial cloud nine. Soft skin, beautiful nails, and a body so relaxed that all she wanted to do was crash on top of her plush mattress.

She glided out of the spa with her arm hooked around Ginger's. They maneuvered around a group of three women with the same smiles plastered across their faces—smiles of bliss and relaxation.

"Why don't I always treat myself this well? I think I might be in heaven."

Ginger laughed. "You and me both. Let's make it a plan to try Spa World Houston when we get home. We've always talked about it, but being here just reminds me that we need these little moments for ourselves."

"You're right about that. We'll go when Brock can stand to be away from his new wife."

Ginger quirked a brow. "You do have a point there. It's a date."

Tina piped in, "I hope y'all don't think you're leaving me behind. Bryce will have to be on daddy duty while I break free for a while. Geez this feels good, especially when you have a baby latched on to you all the time. Now, don't get me wrong, I love my little honey bunchie, but Momma needs a break. I didn't know how to feel when my parents volunteered as tribute to stay behind and keep an eye on Baby Carissa."

Lisa and Ginger burst into laughter. Tina and Bryce's baby was seven months old and the cutest little baby that Lisa had laid eyes on in quite some time. "*Awww.* Carissa is so precious."

"Want her? Just kidding." Tina laughed off her comment. "She is amazing, but this momma is tired. You're welcome to babysit for practice."

"Practice? Jayden and I haven't talked about having any children just yet." The conversation had come up in the distant past, but not a subject they'd broached lately. She knew he wanted children, and so did she, but they weren't even engaged yet. Plus, he'd just mentioned wanting to have things on track with his career. With the possible changes of him starting his own business, marriage and a baby would have to wait.

Ginger squeezed her arm. "But, you still want kids, right?"

"Yes, of course."

Ginger grabbed her chest with her free hand. "*Whew.* Thought you were about to destroy my dream of our girls growing up together as besties."

Lisa and Tina chuckled followed by Momma Wanda and Mom. They were walking several steps behind, so Lisa didn't think they heard the conversation. She should have known better.

"One step at a time. Let's get you down the aisle this weekend first. We can talk baby logistics later. It may take me a while, and I'm pretty sure Brock will not hear of you waiting for me."

Ginger pursed her lips. "While you do have a point, this is my weekend and my dream, so don't spoil it for me."

"*Haha.* I won't." They'd walked through the courtyard and made it to the building where their suites were located. "I'm this way." Lisa pointed. "Go get your rest, honey, and I'll see you tomorrow."

Lisa issued a round of hugs to Ginger, Tina, Momma Wanda, Della, and Mom. "Good night, ladies."

About a minute later, she stood in front of her door. Her belly danced to the beats stuck in her mind from earlier that evening. She and Jayden had shared sleeping spaces before, but not as a couple. He'd already agreed to take the sleeping sofa, which removed a bit of her nervousness, but not all. She inhaled, filling her belly, expanding her ribs, and then her chest, slowly releasing the breath in reverse order.

It's all good.

She glanced down the hall to her left and right as if she were about to do something she had no business doing.

Okay. Get it together. It's just Jayden. And he could still be out with Brock and the guys or even asleep. She unlocked the door and eased it open in case of the latter. However, her belly went back into that rhythmic dance when she caught sight of what Jayden had done.

Chapter Twenty-one

*B*reathe, Lisa. Breathe.

She removed her sandals and stepped inside the room, allowing the door to close behind her. With each step, she crushed a cool, soft, red rose petal under her feet.

The French doors leading to their private pool were open. There, Jayden stood facing the water, his head tilted down. He turned to face her at the sound of the door closing. His smile reached his eyes as he inched toward her dressed in a different linen outfit than the one he'd worn to the welcome reception earlier. This one was similar but khaki. His feet were bare, and he looked more handsome than she remembered. She was unsure why. She'd seen Jayden thousands of times in her life, but there was something different about him in that moment.

Lisa crossed the room, still crushing rose petals beneath her feet. She drew closer to him, noticing the candles lit around the room.

She wanted to ask what was happening but figured this was one of those moments where she should allow him to do the talking—or at least speak first.

"Welcome back." He pulled her into his arms and squeezed. She wouldn't dare complain, but his cologne smelled different. Sexier. And even the way he held her felt different. Or was her imagination playing tricks on her because of the candles and rose petals? Or was it the champagne she had earlier?

"Thanks. How was your evening?" She leaned away but stayed in his arms, looking up into his eyes.

"Nice actually. Want to come outside with me so we can talk about it? The sky is beautiful tonight."

"Sure."

Lisa allowed him to lead her outside when she really wanted to stay inside and enjoy the candles and rose petals and learn the meaning behind all of that. Surely he didn't do all of it to take her outside to talk. But she'd do her best to be patient.

Deep breath.

Jayden helped her down, easing her onto his lap so that both of her feet dangled into the water.

"Sure this is comfortable for you?"

He gave a slight nervous chuckle. "Yes, it's okay. Allow yourself to relax and just be with me, Lis."

The simplest words sent electricity to her belly, causing the dancing to cease, but her heart rate kicked up as the alternative. "'Kay. I'm chill, and I'm listening."

He pushed a stray hair behind her ear and rested the hand on her thigh. His eyes never left hers. Whatever he was about to say was serious. Lisa paid attention.

"First, I kind of hate to bring up work since I promised I'd focus on the trip, but Mr. Pearson offered me partnership in his firm to build the tax practice."

Lisa covered her nose and mouth with her hands. "Seriously?" she said through her fingers.

"Seriously."

"That sounds like a great opportunity for you. So many choices. What did you say?"

"I didn't give him an answer. He suggested I think and pray on it and talk with you about it."

She turned in his lap and hugged his neck. "You are amazing. I am so proud of you, Jayden. You're all outside of the country getting job offers."

Jayden chuckled. "Thanks, babe. I think it's the best of both worlds. I wouldn't have to start from the ground up, but I would have the opportunity to build the practice as I would if I were doing it solo. They already have clients, which gives me a little leverage since my firm will have me sign a non-compete. And I'll be partner. We'll be Pearson & Reynolds."

"All I can say is *wow*. Your face tells me that this makes you happy. And by the way you were trying to convince me, sounds like you've thought it through already."

"Because my decision affects you. I love you, Lisa, and I want you to be a part of every area of my life."

She couldn't help but wonder if the rose petals and candles were leading to this conversation, or if there was something else.

"Thanks for including me, babe. We should celebrate this new beginning for you. Let's not wait."

Lisa moved to stand, but Jayden held her tighter to keep her from moving out of his lap.

"I agree, but there's something else I need to tell you, too. It's been weighing on me for some time, and I don't think we can move forward the way we need to if I don't share this with you."

This sounded like preparation for one of those conversations that could blow everything up between them. She rubbed the knot forming in her chest and took a heavy breath. Was this the reason he'd thrown rose petals on the ground—to soften her up for what was to come out of his mouth next?

"Okay. What is it?"

"I am Justin Love."

And there it was—the thing she knew he'd been hiding from her. Not that she was one hundred percent certain that Jayden and Justin were one and the same, but that she knew he'd been keeping something from her. Part of her wanted to be upset with him for not sharing this news before now. She was his person and he was hers. Big moments were meant to be shared together.

"First, congratulations on taking the leap. I'm really proud of you, Jay. Second," she said, swatting his shoulder, "why didn't you say anything before now? Writing a book has always been a dream of yours. You had to know I would have done whatever you needed me to do to help make it possible. I kind of feel cheated that I didn't get the opportunity to share this moment with you. I could have asked you to be the headliner for the grand opening. That could have been your big signing."

So many could-haves had Jayden shared this before now. Heck, she probably wouldn't have gushed so much over Sebastian at the reader event back in San Antonio. Probably.

"I know. Please forgive me for keeping that from you. Trust that the guilt weighed heavily on my heart. I was a little nervous about the whole thing, not knowing how it would turn out. I'd rationalized that if the book didn't do well, no one would know, not even you. It's important to me to be successful in your eyes, Lisa. Can you understand that?"

Malaki wanted to be everything Jasmine needed just like Jayden's need to be the same for her.

Lisa's heart softened. "Yes, I understand, but you must know that I support all your dreams. And as with everything you do, God is with you and has given you success. I love you regardless of the outcome of whatever you set out to do."

She hadn't realized it until now, but Jayden had been that way since his dad died when he was twelve—that desire to be the best at whatever he did and prove himself successful.

"Thank you, Lisa. Will you please forgive me?"

She twisted her lips and tilted her head to one side. "I might need a little convincing."

Jayden leaned in and pulled her closer until their lips met. Not that she needed his kisses to convince her because she'd forgiven him anyway. The way she fell into a half-trance the moment their lips touched didn't hurt matters.

"*Mmmm.* Forgiven. I think we should celebrate now."

"I've got just the thing, but it's inside."

Lisa stood. "Where is it? I can grab it."

"In the fridge. Chocolate and fruit tray."

Lisa went inside the suite to grab the tray, but Jayden stood and followed. Inside the refrigerator was a plate filled with strawberries arranged in the shape of a heart with the milk chocolate in the center.

Jayden picked up a piece of chocolate and fed it to her.

"*Mmmm.* This is so good. You have to try one." She fed him a piece as well.

He chewed, but while he did so, he removed the plate from her hand and knelt on one knee. She thought her knees would buckle and send her crashing to the ground.

∞

Jayden wanted to make this moment romantic and memorable, which was why he'd planned to propose at Brock and Ginger's wedding reception—an arrangement they happily supported, suggested, and agreed to. He didn't want to take the spotlight away from them this weekend, so he'd planned to wait until after they were married. However, this needed to be private. Their friends and family would be happy for them and would have loved to witness this occasion, but he didn't want their excitement bleeding into this moment. In the years to come, when they looked back on this evening, he needed Lisa to remember that this evening was about him seeking her hand and nothing else.

He took her left hand in his. In an instant, his heart slid across his chest like a volleyball player's feet in the sand. Never mind the fact that he'd been in her presence his entire life, and they'd made things official between them. Fear of her rejection still surfaced within him, but he quenched his nerves because another day of not knowing was too much to bear. "Lisa Renee Atkinson, first, let me apologize for taking so long to get to this moment. I just want to be everything you need me to be. But know that there has never been any other woman I've wanted in my life besides you."

She frowned, and he felt the need to explain.

"Yes, I've dated other women, but that was only because I thought I'd never have a chance with you—you friend zoned me in elementary."

Lisa laughed through the tears pooling in her eyes.

Her tears did something to him.

Made his heart crack.

Made his heart expand.

Made his heart want to envelope hers time and time again.

Not a woman on this earth had made him experience the plethora of emotions that Lisa had made him feel. And to be honest, he didn't want any other woman to touch him in the way that she had. Forever and always, he only wanted her.

"No woman has or can compete with the love I have for you." He kissed the back of her hand. "You're my best friend, the love of my life, and the woman I want to celebrate every high and work through ever low with. And if you'll allow me, I want to spend the rest of my life showing you how much I love you." He cracked open the red velvet box. "Lisa Renee Atkinson, will you do me the honor of being my wife?"

She fanned her eyes with her free hand. "Jayden, are you sure? Are you serious?"

"There's nothing else I want more."

"Yes," she squealed and jumped a few times.

Jayden slid the sparkling diamond on her finger and pulled her down so that she sat on his knee. His lips captured hers, and he took the opportunity to explore her mouth. A mountainous thunder erupted in his chest followed by his abdomen. This woman made him happy and crazy at the same time. He broke the kiss and rested his forehead against hers.

"Lisa, I love you."

"I love you, too. Forever and a day."

They stood and she rested her head against his chest, flexing the fingers on her left hand. The diamond sparkled in the candlelight. "I cannot believe I'm about to marry my best friend."

Jayden kissed her forehead. "And I wouldn't have it any other way."

Chapter Twenty-two

Lisa stood in front of the bathroom mirror and assessed her eyes. Were they noticeably puffy? Were there any dark circles? No dark circles or puffiness, but to her, lack of sleep was obvious. After their engagement, she and Jayden had stayed up several more hours talking and planning their future. Yesterday was no different. They spent a lazy day on the beach before and after the rehearsal dinner, soaking in the beautiful space they were in. Their night ended the same as their engagement night—hours and hours of talking and planning their future until they fell asleep. And as opposed to him sleeping on the sofa per their original plan, he slept in the bed next to her, cuddling her through the night. In theory, that was cute, but in reality, the positioning was uncomfortable. She hoped he didn't think she'd be able to spend many more nights like that. As a person accustomed to sleeping on her back, she didn't get any restful sleep last night lying on her side.

Bryce had stopped by to grab Jayden to help with something—an intrusion she didn't mind. Lisa needed a few extra moments to process what she'd agreed to: marriage. The idea sounded great and was an institution she always cheered for on behalf of others in life and in the romance novels she read, but was she ready? Would she be a good wife to Jayden?

She fixed her makeup in the mirror and donned her bridesmaid dress to meet Ginger in the bridal suite. Lisa and Jayden had decided they would save the news until after Brock and Ginger's wedding. She managed to conceal her ring during the rehearsal dinner since she held a bouquet of flowers almost the entire time, in addition to her turning the ring around so that the diamond faced her palm. That was the best she could do, because the ring Jayden bought for her—all three carats—was not coming off. That thing looked amazing on her hand. Dang it, she might need to do curls to strengthen her fingers in order to hold that baby in place. Laughing at her silly thoughts, she tucked away her makeup and dashed out of the room to be on time.

Minutes later, she waltzed into the bridal suite where Ginger; Della, Ginger's mother-in-law; Mom; Momma Wanda—definitely Momma now—and Tina were already huddled.

"Today's the big day," Lisa announced when she entered. She beelined to the side of Ginger who faced the mirror and assessed her makeup.

Ginger spun on the stool to face her, her smile bright and wide like that of a bride ready to walk down the aisle. "I thought I would have to send a search party looking for you."

"No drama today, missy." Lisa flipped her wrist. "I'm on time."

"No you're not. Didn't you check that MeGroup?" Mom interrupted and advanced toward her. She sized her up like she was seconds away from using her belt on her behind. Lisa had to wonder what she'd done wrong.

"GroupMe? I didn't. Slept a little late this morning, and I didn't think to check it. I thought the schedule was solid."

Mom eyed her for several long, excruciating seconds. It took everything within her not to reveal that she and Jayden had gotten engaged. Whose idea was it to keep their engagement a secret anyway? She thought for a moment. Oh, hers.

Perhaps Lisa had used the wrong language because all eyes were now on her. She shrugged and offered a smile. "What? I'm here and ready to perform my maid-of-honor duties."

Ginger eyed her and pushed up from her seat. Focused on her like a lion toward its prey. If Lisa didn't know any better, she'd think they could smell and see the change in her. Was she not acting as natural as she thought?

Be cool. You can tell them in a few hours.

Lisa avoided eye contact with Ginger and moved past her to pick up her headpiece. "C'mon. Let's check your dress and veil."

Ginger grabbed her shoulders and spun her around. "We're best friends, right?"

"Right."

"And you love me, right?"

"Right."

"And you want this to be the happiest day of my life, right?"

Lisa had no idea where Ginger's line of questioning was going, but discomfort settled in the pit of her belly. "Right," she answered, her response slow and uncertain.

Ginger lifted Lisa's left hand. "Then why would you think this wouldn't make my day?" She screamed and gripped Lisa in a hug so tight, she saw tiny sparkles in the air. Never mind the fact that Lisa also thought she'd lost an eardrum forever.

Mom and Momma Wanda's theatrics followed. Mom screamed and jumped. Momma Wanda screamed and gripped her chest, pretending to fall backward and pass out.

"Oh my father in heaven, you've answered my prayers, and these children have finally gathered some sense. I thank you in advance for the grandchildren that are on the way."

The ladies erupted into laughter. They could count on Momma Wanda being over-the-top. As always, Mom was there to catch Momma Wanda as if they'd been rehearsing this moment their entire lives.

Mom pulled Momma Wanda into a hug. "We finally did it."

Momma Wanda high-fived Mom. "Amen. Now, five dollars that the first kid is a boy."

Lisa interrupted their shenanigans. "How about we get Ginger down the aisle and pregnant before we get to me?"

Tina, Ginger's future sister-in-law, bubbled over in laughter. "This is pure entertainment. I can't get this on TV, so thank y'all."

Lisa chuckled and shook her head. "You sound like Ginger. Please don't encourage these shenanigans."

Ginger squeezed her again. "Lis, I'm so excited for you. Jayden was supposed to propose at the reception this evening."

"Wait a minute. You knew?"

"We all did," Mom added. "But good for him not making a show of things and asking you when the time was right."

"Right. I'm proud of that young man," Della said. Her smile was like that of a proud aunt.

"Shoot, the time was right five, ten years ago," Momma Wanda mumbled, "but nevertheless, it has finally happened, and I can officially call you Daughter. Congratulations, sweetheart. I carry on a lot, but I only want what's best for you and my son. And I've known for a very long time that was you for him and him for you." She winked.

"Congratulations, Lisa. Jayden is one of the good ones." Tina lifted a champagne glass, which Lisa hadn't even realized she had. "Here, here. To all the love your heart can handle."

"Thank you, Tina." Lisa took a heavy breath. "Feels good to get that secret off my chest."

"Actually, you didn't get it off your chest. I got it off my chest. Brock texted me and told me. Apparently your boo thang can't hold water. I can't believe you were going to walk in here and not share the good news. Because today is a happy occasion, I'm going to forgive you."

The group erupted into laughter. Lisa was certain that the conversation didn't happen quite like Ginger alluded to, but none of that mattered. Everything was out in the open, so now she could breathe.

A knock on the door quieted their antics. Seconds passed before the resort's wedding planner poked her head inside. "Is my bride ready?"

Ginger puffed her chest and grinned. "Yes, ma'am. I am."

Della waltzed forward. "Well, let's not keep my son waiting."

Lisa gave Ginger a side hug. "Agreed. Let's get you married."

∞

The late-afternoon sky made the perfect backdrop for the occasion, with the waves gently crashing against the sand adding a nice touch. Lisa followed Tina down the aisle runner covering the sand, gliding to the tune of a jazz saxophonist, a bouquet of white lilies in one hand and the other looped around Jayden's arm. With all that had transpired within the last forty-eight hours, she couldn't believe that she'd be walking down the aisle again—this time, her getting married—probably within the next year. Jayden's firm bicep steadied her as she walked to her assigned spot to the left of the officiant, a handsome older gentleman with a bald head and teeth that had obviously been through a few whitening procedures. A green and gold stole hung around his black linen robe, which was surprising to Lisa. She assumed everyone would be in something cool and island-like. She nodded to Brock and his brother and best man, Bryce. Jayden kissed her hand and joined their side while she stood next to the officiant.

A gorgeous little girl, Destiny— Brock's third cousin— followed Lisa and tossed rose petals from her woven basket. Missing one tooth in the front, she smiled proudly while she danced and tossed the flowers. She found encouragement from the chuckles and sighs of adoration from the crowd, causing her to shake and move more intentionally to the saxophonist's tunes. By the time she made it to Lisa's side, she'd dumped the remaining flowers in the spot where Ginger would stand, bowed, and stood in front of Lisa and Tina.

The saxophonist's tune changed to that of the traditional wedding processional, and the audience of about forty stood. Della was on the front row, groom's side with a smile as wide as the ocean before them. She dabbed at the tears in the corners of her eyes. Lisa turned her attention to Ginger, escorted down the aisle by her father, Kenneth Evans. Her friend was gorgeous with her smile competing with that of the setting sun. The train of her dress dragged behind her as she glided to meet her groom. Mr. Evans spoke something only her ears could hear, but Ginger's eyes were locked on Brock's, and Lisa glanced at him to see that the glow in his eyes matched Ginger's. And with that, her heart was satisfied knowing that the two of them only had eyes for each other.

At the end of the aisle, Mr. Evans placed Ginger's hand in Brock's and hugged him before taking his seat on the front row.

Brock led Ginger before the officiant. She turned to Lisa and handed her the bouquet. "Thank you."

With Ginger's back turned to her, all Lisa could focus on was Brock. The love in his eyes for her friend was immeasurable. She recalled the moment he'd begged her to help him win Ginger's heart back after they broke up in Austin while at a baking competition. Lisa refused. As much as she believed that Brock was the man for Ginger, she couldn't interfere. Brock and Ginger standing before her proved what she believed to be true: Things, relationships, situations that are meant to be will come to pass in Kairos—God's perfect timing—not Chronos—man's timing. Whatever God has planned, no devil in hell can prevent. While the enemy worked hard to tear families apart, Lisa was proud to witness Ginger and Brock persevere.

She glanced up at Jayden because she could feel his stare. When their eyes connected, he mouthed, "I love you."

"I love you back. Forever and always," she mouthed in return. They held each other's gaze so long that the officiant had to clear his throat to get her attention to hand over the rings.

"Oh, sorry." Lisa removed the ring, which she'd looped into a string in her bouquet, and handed it to the officiant.

Ginger and Brock recited vows they'd written for each other, bringing tears to Lisa's eyes. She dabbed at her eyes so many times, unbelieving that she was so emotional.

After the sand ritual, the officiant pronounced them husband and wife. Without waiting, Brock kissed his bride. The crowd encouraged him with shouts and whistles. Lisa was pretty sure Ginger was dizzy after the way Brock kissed her. He gripped her back to keep her from falling backward, Lisa was certain of that fact.

The bride and groom led the wedding party down the aisle, posing for pictures with every step. A walk that took less than a minute on Jayden's arm at the beginning of the ceremony took thirty minutes to ease back down afterward, but Lisa didn't mind, fixing Ginger's veil and train here and there. This evening was a long time coming, and her heart swelled knowing she'd had the opportunity to see her friend get her happily ever after. Or beginning. However one chose to look at the situation.

Chapter Twenty-three

The wedding reception was hosted on a secluded island away from the resort. Jayden and the rest of the guests had taken a boat to the location while the bride and groom traveled in a private boat. There were two separate areas set up. One with a dance floor, bar-height tables, and a bar on either end of the area. Guests mingled and nursed champagne flutes. The second area contained dinner tables, tables encircling the area topped with serving dishes, and servers ensuring everything was in order.

"Come with me," Jayden said to Lisa. He guided her to a secluded picturesque part of the island where they could watch the setting sun and the ocean waves gently crashing against the shore. She stood in front of him while he wrapped his arms around her waist and inhaled the fresh scent of her hair.

"This is so beautiful. I know I've said this a thousand times since we've been here, but it's worth repeating."

"For sure."

"And speaking of repeating," she said, turning in his arms, "I thought we weren't going to say anything about our engagement."

Jayden flashed what he hoped was his best smile. "Well, I said we wouldn't tell Ginger. What had happened was Brock asked if I was all set for the reception, and I had to come clean."

Lisa tossed her head back in laughter. Her curls danced in the gentle breeze. He couldn't help but run his hand through her hair to smooth the strands away from her face.

"Be honest. You wanted to gossip anyway."

It was Jayden's turn to release a guttural laugh. "Can you blame me? How could I not want to shout the good news for the entire island to hear? But just so you know, I did want to respect your wishes and not interfere with Ginger and Brock's festivities. They're happy for us, though."

"Don't I know it? I thought your mom would have a full-blown heart attack."

Jayden laughed harder. "Leave it up to hear to be dramatic. Everyone knew already, except you. It's not much of a surprise or an interference."

"So I heard."

He lifted her chin so that their eyes met and held her securely in his arms. "But I did want the moment to be special for you. Our first night here just felt right. I didn't want to wait until tonight's reception."

Lisa tiptoed and kissed his lips. "I'm glad you didn't wait. And just so you know, I'm looking forward to becoming Mrs. Jayden Reynolds."

"Don't kiss me like that again, or you'll become Mrs. Jayden Reynolds tonight."

And in true Lisa fashion, she kissed him in a passionate way again, but broke free of his embrace and took off running, forcing him to chase her until he caught up with her and crashed into the sand with her in his arms. Jayden's back was flat into the ground with her on his lap.

She laughed. Hard. When her chuckles subsided, she said, "I always want to be this way with you—fun and free. I love you and what we have."

Jayden pulled her close and held her securely so that their lips met. She'd come up for air, putting about two inches of space between them. He could still feel her breath on his face. "Then, let's be this way. I love you."

The deejay's tunes from the early 2000s echoed in the atmosphere, and Jayden knew it was time for them to rejoin the group. In fact, he was playing one of Lisa's favorite songs. She'd jumped off his lap, and Jayden stood, dusting sand off their clothes. "C'mon. Let's get you to the dance floor."

"As long as you promise to save me a dance or two."

Hand-in-hand, they retraced their steps through the sand to rejoin the wedding party. The group danced and swayed to the deejay's beats. Lisa dropped his hand and maneuvered through the crowd, moving her hips in a way that made him crazy. He needed water—and lots of it. When the waiter came around with a tray of champagne, he requested a cold bottled water.

For at least an hour, the wedding guests entertained themselves on the dance floor before the bride and groom arrived. They greeted their guests, hugging and kissing each one until they made their way to the center of the dance floor for their first dance.

The DJ's voice cut through the music. "Introducing, for the first time in eternity, Mr. and Mrs. Brock Pearson."

The crowd howled and cheered as Brock and Ginger danced to Luther Vandross. As with every traditional wedding ceremony he'd attended, after their first dance, the best man stood to give his congratulatory speech.

"May I have everyone's attention please?" Bryce stood with a glass of champagne in his hand. His wife, Tina, stood by his side with her hand wrapped around his waist. The crowd quieted and gave Bryce their attention.

"My brother has been doing his thing over the past year—joined the family's firm, and most importantly, reconnected with the love of his life. When I saw the sixtieth birthday cake Ginger made for Mom, I knew this was the road we were headed on."

Brock laughed.

"But to see my brother happy and in love and experiencing all the good things life has to offer, I couldn't be more proud. And I know Ginger has your back. I have no doubts that she's the beauty who can tame the beast."

The crowd burst into laughter. No way Bryce came up with that on his own. Those words were straight from Tina's mouth. Jayden would bet money on it.

Bryce handed the microphone to Lisa. As the maid of honor, it was her turn to toast the happy couple. Her ring and smile sparkled in the early evening sky. Jayden had to force himself to listen to her speech. Sure, she'd rehearsed it for him, but now all he could think about was how she'd agreed to marry him, not the fact that she was there to congratulate and send well wishes to Brock and Ginger.

She grinned, all of her teeth showing. "I don't think they want me to share their reconnecting story."

Giggles came from the crowd, and Lisa took a deep breath.

"But," she paused and looked around at the crowd until her gaze landed on the bride and groom, "I will say that I am so happy to see my friend get what she's always desired—companionship and a fierce love that will last throughout eternity. That's what the two of you have, and I'm honored to witness the beauty and evolution of your relationship. May God bless you more than you can think or imagine. I love you both. Cheers to a happily ever after."

Ginger ran over to Lisa, hugged her, and took the mic away from her. "Thanks, boo. And fam! Save ya coins!" She grabbed Lisa's left hand and held it for everyone to see. "Lisa and Jayden are next."

Their friends and family cheered and whistled. Next thing Jayden knew, he was bombarded with a plethora of well wishes and congratulations. Lisa had been shoved to his side. Camera phones were jammed in their faces with Brock and Ginger on either side of them in several shots.

Honestly, the attention was overwhelming—the gist of what he wanted to avoid when he proposed in private.

He held Lisa to his side. "Thank you all for your well wishes. We haven't made any arrangements yet, but when we do, you all will be the first to know."

The remainder of the evening was filled with dancing and celebrating the bride and groom. While Jayden didn't consider himself much of a dancer, he found himself on the dance floor more than he'd been in his entire life, and he enjoyed it with Lisa as a dance partner. He was certain they'd received as many congratulatory remarks as Brock and Ginger, which he would expect given they were all close friends and family.

By the end of the night, something had unlocked inside of him. He was ready to move on to the next phase of his life, and that meant leaving his old career and life behind. His future with Lisa and this new partnership with The Pearson Group took front and center in his mind. Time to take things to the next level—and he hoped it wasn't just the vibes of the Caribbean talking.

Chapter Twenty-four

The incessant bird chirping outside the bookstore's walls matched the erratic rhythm of Lisa's heart. After all the moments of relaxation she'd experienced last weekend in Jamaica, she'd think she would have been somewhat calmer. Life was good. Her best friend had tied the knot, she and Jayden were now engaged, he'd made up his mind about his career, and she had a feeling that the grand reopening of the bookstore would go well today. True, she wouldn't earn twenty thousand dollars, but the tax office would take five thousand and a payment plan. That, she could do. She had twenty-five hundred dollars already. But, now that they were to be married, Jayden would not accept her no. He would pay the balance, and that was final—his words, not hers. How could she argue?

So, everything was good, wasn't it? And she believed that with all her heart, so why was the anxiety coursing through her body as prevalent as the blood pumping through her veins? She had that nagging pit-in-the-belly feeling that told her something was off. It was one she couldn't shake whenever it came about.

Never.

And the feeling always proved to be right.

Always.

The door chimes jingled, and Jayden came inside. Dressed in basketball shorts and a white tee, he promised to change once he finished bringing out the tables and helping her get everything in place. Not that she complained about how he looked. In her eyes, he was always handsome, but a change of clothes would be much more suitable for the occasion.

"Got all the vendor and author tables set up. Brock is setting up the tent for Sebastian."

She clapped and did a little shuffle. "Yes. I'm so excited Sebastian agreed to attend."

"You're making your fiancé jealous with the way you're grinning and dancing about seeing another man."

Lisa chuckled. Rounding the counter, she met him in the doorway and wrapped her arms around his waist. "You have no reason to be jealous. I only love him a little bit. You, I love lots."

Jayden laughed. "He's about to get cancelled."

"This could have been avoided if you had told me sooner you were Justin Love, but we're not going to go there." She stepped out of his arms and winked.

"Point taken. What else do you need me to do?"

"Help Brock with the tents and then hang the event sign. I want it out front, but not blocking any of the tables. You may have to hang it on the side of the building. I'll let you figure it out." She gave her best I-trust-you-to-bring-my-vision-to-life smile.

"Understood. I've got you. Where is it?"

"In the trunk of my car. I accidentally had it shipped to my house instead of the store. It arrived the day before our trip, and I hadn't thought about taking it out."

"You haven't inspected the sign? What if the printer messed something up?"

"Let's just pray that didn't happen. How about you check it for me? If it's messed up, come up with an excuse about why you can't hang the signage."

Jayden laughed on his way out the door. "I'll just tell you I couldn't find it. Or maybe I'll get sucked into some kind of warp zone in the trunk of your car, and we won't have to worry about it at all."

Facts. Her trunk was where things went to die. But in this case, she knew Jayden would take care of it. He'd seen the inside of her trunk more than she had. Old shoes and clothing bags that never made it to the donation shop took up most of the space. Maybe. But she didn't concern herself much with the contents because Jayden did trunk sweeps every now and then. Once he announced he'd cleaned it out for her, the thing magically became full again.

She went back to the counter to grab her clipboard, which housed her checklist for today. Yes, she could have used her electronic tablet, but writing things down gave her comfort, and she loved checkmarks. Lisa added one next to tents and tables. Momma Wanda should be on her way as she'd agreed to be the author liaison, with the exception of Sebastian. Lisa would take care of him herself as her personal guest. Outside, she scanned the area and smiled. The tables were lined neatly in the parking lot with the tents properly shielding them from the sun. Although it was fall, the weather didn't seem to get the message. Her authors would need the covering in the afternoon sun.

Ginger rounded the side of the building wheeling a cart of pastries, which she'd agreed to donate for the authors and vendors. Check. Lisa was doubly thankful that Ginger and Brock jumped into action after arriving back in town yesterday from their honeymoon.

Lisa placed her clipboard on a nearby table and advanced to Ginger's side. "I can help you with this. The refreshments will be set up inside with the water station."

"Thanks. You're on it. I have a few more things in the car to grab." She hugged Lisa and kissed her cheek. "Be right back."

Her nerves eased. Things were coming together. Now, she only needed Mom and Momma Wanda's presence to go over logistics for the day. Her thoughts must have summoned them because seconds later, they waltzed inside, each greeting her with a tight squeeze followed by a kiss on the cheek.

"Good morning. Tell us what you need us to do," Mom said, straight to business. She stood at attention before her with clasped hands and eager eyes.

Lisa peered at the clock that hung above the entry door. The authors and vendors should start arriving in thirty minutes to decorate their tables.

"Momma Wanda, remember you'll be working with the authors, showing them to their tables and helping them get settled.

Mom, I need you to be in charge of customers. We have a reader bingo event to encourage participation. I'll go over the rules with you and grab the cards from the counter."

"You do know that I almost invented bingo. Complete the task on the squares and get a mark. Right?"

"Right. But they'll also have an opportunity to win the grand prize of a gift basket filled with ten autographed books from authors across several genres. Ginger also donated a Ginger's Goodies gift card. Just make sure they sign up for our email list."

"Got it. I wasn't as fancy as you, but your mother knows a little something about bringing readers and authors together. Did it for more than thirty-five years."

Momma Wanda chimed in. "Right. Not our first rodeo."

"Yeah, you're right. Sorry about that, Mom. Just a little nervous since this is my first big event."

Mom hugged her. "Trust me. Everything will be fine. You're bringing readers and authors together. The rest will take care of itself. Try to relax."

Lisa nodded. Mom had valid points. "You're right. I think what we need now is music while we wait for the deejay to arrive." She whipped out her phone and opened the playlist she'd created with her most recently added Caribbean tunes and pressed play. When the music seeped through her Bluetooth speaker, she was mentally transported back to the previous weekend in a healthy and relaxed mental space.

Nothing or no one could kill the vibe today.

∞

Two Saturdays in a row, Jayden skipped out on weekend office work. If he hadn't announced his engagement to the partners when he'd returned to the office, they might have thought he'd lost his mind. One weekend off during busy season simply wasn't heard of, but two weekends in a row was career suicide. To his surprise, no one asked him about signing the partnership agreement or where he stood on the matter. Perhaps they knew his time at the firm was close to an end. That could be all in his mind because the idea of leadership knowing he'd decided to quit would make the discussion easier. While the path that awaited him was much more aligned with his personal goals and better for his life in general, he would be forever grateful for the knowledge and opportunities he'd had while at the firm.

He planned to hold off on the talk until after he finalized his arrangements with Derek. That meeting was scheduled for Monday. Meanwhile, he'd spend the weekend supporting his fiancée. He could only thank God that she took the news well about him being Justin Love. One of the many reasons he loved her—she gave him so much grace, and she loved him despite his shortcomings.

Jayden removed the box that contained the signage from her trunk. He knew because that was the only box in her trunk amid the three garbage bags filled with clothes, a few shoeboxes, and a spare gym bag that housed a gym outfit with the tags still attached for emergencies.

"What's next?" Brock called to him.

Jayden slammed the trunk shut. He hoisted the box. "Need to check this sign and figure out where to hang it."

"Let's see it."

He opened the box and unrolled the vinyl. About five feet wide, the white sign read, *Between the Lines Grand Reopening Celebration* in pink letters. "Well, there are no misspellings, so that's good. I guess we could secure it to the front of one of the tents. If anything, it'll provide shade to whoever sits there."

Brock stood before him with his fists pressed into his sides, like he was positioning himself for Jayden to toss him a basketball. "Sounds good to me." In a matter of seconds, Brock's attention was elsewhere.

Jayden followed his line of vision to see he'd locked eyes with his wife. "I'll take care of this," he said, but he wasn't sure Brock heard him, so he left him standing there while he finished his task.

Fifteen minutes later, Jayden positioned the sign on one of the tents, but not to where it would interfere with the author or vendor. He stepped back to assess his work—tables, tents, signs. The deejay had arrived and started his setup. In a few hours, the bookstore would be swarming with readers who wanted to connect with local authors and him—Justin Love. Seldom did he find himself nervous about anything, but the reality of the situation settled in. He was a published author about to have his first book signing.

Wow.

Jayden trekked inside the building to see if Lisa needed him to do anything else before he cleaned himself up. Caribbean beats greeted him when he walked in the bookstore. Lisa, her mom, Ginger, and his mom swayed to the music. "Y'all are having too much fun in here."

Lisa wiggled her eyebrows and stretched out her hands. "I know. Come dance with me."

At first, he refused, but then the first song they'd danced to in Jamaica played through the speaker, and he couldn't resist. He pulled her into his arms and spun her around so that her back faced him. From there, he led her in a sway from side to side to the beat of the music.

She looked over her shoulder. Happy eyes and a huge grin greeted him. "Look at you," she cooed.

"Anytime I can get you in my arms, I'm for it."

Halfway through the song, she stopped, turned to face him, and released a heavy breath. Her palms rested on his chest and sent his thoughts in a completely different direction. "Okay. We need to focus. I know you didn't come in here to dance."

Jayden took her hands in his, removed them from his chest, and brought them down by her side. There was no way she realized what her touch did to him. "Just came to see if you needed anything else before I cleaned myself up and changed."

She looked around. "Nope. I think we're good."

"Cool. I love you. I'll be around, so just let me know if you need me."

He went to his car to retrieve his duffle bag filled with his toiletries and change of clothes. Many years ago when he thought about this moment—his first book signing—he'd been prepared to wear a nice suit. But this was Texas, and they'd be outside. So today, he chose a red polo shirt and a pair of jeans—a choice he might regret later if the Texas sun did its job.

Attire was the least of his worries, however.

He couldn't help but regret not telling Lisa sooner, because this could have been his moment, not Sebastian's. And just how would his mom and friends react to knowing he and Justin Love were one?

Chapter Twenty-five

For a moment, Lisa stood outside the door of Between the Lines and assessed the crowd. Her heart bubbled with gratitude, filling the expanse of her chest. The grand reopening had become a celebration—a mashup between a family reunion and her college annual homecoming festivities. Even though the authors and readers weren't close friends of hers, they felt like family, all coming together for a singular purpose—books. The crowd exceeded her expectations. At one point, she'd counted five readers at each local author's table, plus a few lingering around her vendors who sold scented candles, costume jewelry, and handmade soaps.

Dewana, one of the owners of LitJava, an indie bookstore in Pearland, Texas, approached her with a side hug. "Congratulations, Lisa. Your event is amazing."

Lisa snapped out of her reverie and returned the hug with both arms. She squeezed Dewana tight. "Oh my gosh, thank you so much for coming out. I know the drive was no joke, so I appreciate the extra effort."

Standing shoulder-to-shoulder with Lisa, Dewana's bright eyes beamed, and her mouth spread into a wide smile, showcasing a set of braces. "No problem at all. You know we have to support each other. Plus, Angie and I know what it's like in this business. We just wanted you to know that we're here for you."

"Much appreciated. Now tell the truth: You want to meet Sebastian, don't you?"

Dewana burst into laughter. "Yeah, that, too. Who wouldn't?"

"Tell me about it. I met him in San Antonio at the reader festival. He was too kind."

"So I've heard, but I also want to meet Justin Love. First book. First appearance. The suspense is killing us all."

A twinge of jealousy tickled her belly. And it shouldn't because she was engaged to Justin Love.

Lisa's gaze darted left and right, checking the grounds for Sebastian. His signing was scheduled to start in thirty minutes, and he still hadn't made an appearance. She'd be lying if she said she wasn't worried. Those tiny knots in her belly became larger by the minute. If Sebastian didn't show up, she'd have some kind of panic attack. True, the present authors and readers were having a great time, but most of them were there to meet her headliner.

And Justin Love.

Be calm.

She looped an arm through Dewana's. "Let me introduce you to my best friend, Ginger, while I go check on something for a bit."

Yes, Dewana could have found her own way around or even visited with other authors, but part of Lisa felt like introducing Dewana to her friends was good hosting.

Lisa craned her neck and spotted Ginger among the crowd talking to her sister-in-law, Tina, and two attendees.

"Hey, Gin and Tina." She turned to the guests and extended her palm. "I'm Lisa, the owner of Between the Lines. I hope you two are having a good time."

"We are," said the shorter friend with a silky jet-black bob.

Her friend's eyes darted to her phone, checking the time, no doubt wondering the same thing as Lisa: Where was Sebastian? "Yes, this is so nice. We need more events like this."

"Maybe we can work something out. Dewana co-owns LitJava in Pearland. Maybe we can co-host a similar event in the future."

Ginger piped in. "I've heard a lot about your bookstore, but haven't been able to make it to that side of town to visit you just yet."

Tina joined the conversation. "I had a chance to swing by when you had the grand opening. The Brown Sugar Shaken Espresso is everything."

Dewana chuckled. "Thank you. It's one of my favorites as well."

"Excuse me, ladies. I'll be back." Lisa took the opportunity to duck away, checking emails to ensure Sebastian would still show, or at least hadn't backed out. And that's when she saw the message in her spam folder. Sebastian had cancelled two days ago. Lisa could have passed out on the spot.

She shuffled toward the entrance of the bookstore, but Jayden appeared in her path seemingly out of thin air, catching her stride.

"Hey. Everything okay? You look worried."

Oh. She thought she'd managed to hide her impending anxiety. "Really? I'm not that worried. Everything is fine. The event is a success." She added a smile for good measure.

"I agree. You've gotten a ton of support from the community, and you know you don't have to worry about the tax situation anymore. We're going to take care of it."

Lisa nodded but continued inside the store. "Yeah, you're right. Come with me."

While it was true that she didn't have to be concerned about the tax situation, she did have to be concerned about Sebastian not showing up. Why? Everyone would remember if she wasn't able to keep her promise. And yes, her event was a success, but him not sitting behind that beautiful table, accented with balloons and a comfortable leather chair in the next twenty minutes could change that. Would his absence prevent other well-known authors from attending her events in the future?

She would not be concerned about Sebastian any longer when she had Jayden—the answer to her problem—in front of her.

"Change of plans, Jay. Today is your big day. That nice table you set up for Sebastian is for you. This is your signing."

Jayden frowned. "Wait. What? Not that I'm complaining, but what happened to Sebastian?"

She held her phone to his face to show him the cancelation email.

"I'm so sorry, Lisa."

"I am, too, but everything happens for a reason. Maybe this was meant to be your time to shine all along. Let's get your books on the table, and I'll make the announcement."

∞

Jayden blew a heavy stream of air and strolled toward his signing chair. Like one of those movie scenes where everything fell into place instantly, all eyes were trained on him the moment he sat, almost as if they knew Justin Love was his pseudonym. His chest expanded from the excitement spiraling through his veins. This was a moment he'd dreamed about for years.

Ginger rushed to the front of the line, followed by his mom and Momma Barbara. "Oh my gosh, I knew it was you." Ginger lowered her voice. "The characters in the book are you and Lisa," she said and jammed her finger in his direction. Her eyes darted around the area. "Where's Lisa? Does she know?" Before he could answer the question, Ginger disappeared.

His Mom piggybacked off Ginger's comment. "I told the book club it was you when we read your book."

Jayden laughed. "How did you know?"

"Son, you were too obvious. To the woman who raised you, it wasn't difficult to figure out. Regardless, I'm proud of you."

"We both are," Momma Barbara added. "Congratulations. We will all have to get together and celebrate later."

Jayden beamed. "For sure."

They snapped pictures of him with his book and hopped out of the line.

"Justin Love, you are amazing," the first reader in his line said. The young woman stood about five feet tall and sported braids that hung to her waist. She flipped a few dangling strands over her shoulder and hugged her copy of his book to her chest. "Will you please sign my book?"

He reached for the book and smiled. "Of course I will. Who should I sign it to?"

"Veronica."

Jayden signed her copy: *To Veronica, Thank you for your support. Justin Love.*

He handed the book back to her.

"Oh, and can you sign this one for my mom and this one for my best friend?" She handed him two additional copies, which he signed in the same manner.

"I appreciate your support, Veronica."

"You're welcome. I fell in love with Malaki. You wouldn't happen to have any friends who inspired the character, would you?" she asked and then burst into a hearty chuckle.

Jayden laughed. "No, I don't. Sorry."

"Darn. Can I have a selfie?"

He didn't get a chance to respond before she rounded the table, crouched beside him, and angled her phone in the air to snap their photo.

"So nice to meet you, Justin. I hope we'll be getting a sequel soon."

"Thank you, Veronica."

A sequel? He'd thought about writing a second book, but at this juncture, his focus would have to be on building the tax accounting practice of this new partnership with The Pearson Group, plus becoming a husband to Lisa. He had no idea where he would find the time to write again. But this wasn't the moment to be concerned with sequels. He had to enjoy his current space.

He smiled and welcomed the next group of ladies in line—four friends who had their own book club, no name. They simply enjoyed reading and discussing books. When they heard that he would be there today, attending the grand reopening became a must-do activity. Jayden signed their books the same as he'd done before. *Thank you for your support. Justin Love.* Before today, he thought he'd write something more personal for each person, but when he saw the line wrapped around the grounds, he knew that wasn't happening, so he stuck to gratitude. *Thank you* had to suffice.

The group giggled among themselves as he signed each of their books, plus one for each of them to gift to someone else. After he signed the last copy, they asked for selfies. First, as a group, then individually, to which he obliged.

"Okay, so I just have to ask because closed mouths don't get fed. Are you single? You aren't wearing a wedding band, but these days, that doesn't mean anything," the last friend said after her selfie with him. She peered up at him with piercing deep brown eyes. Stunning, really, but unmatched against Lisa's beautiful hazel orbs. Her lips stretched across her face in a huge smile, showing all of her teeth. She wiggled her brows.

"Engaged."

"Dang it. Your story might be fiction, but we all know those words have to come from somewhere deep inside. I hope she knows how blessed she is."

Jayden could feel her eyes on him before he saw her. Lisa stood across the grounds recording or taking pictures with her phone, he couldn't be sure. But her illuminated eyes were an expression of warmth. She waved one hand and smiled, melting away the buildup of nerves. He nodded toward her and said to the young woman in front of him. "She's right there. We're both blessed, if you ask me."

"Okay, sis," she shouted toward Lisa and snapped her fingers to emphasize her point.

"Thank you, ladies, for your support," he said.

"You're welcome. Keep writing. And make sure you love that woman the way Malaki did in this book," the one inquiring of his relationship status said and waved her book in the air.

Jayden nodded. "Will do."

He turned his attention to the next person in line. For the next hour or so, he held similar conversations about his relationship status and a sequel while autographing copies of his book. When the line dissipated, he shook his wrist and stretched and flexed his fingers. *What an amazing experience.* His heart and soul were now satisfied.

Conversations about him, revelations about his love life, and his book surrounded him. Good things, but none of which he wanted to engage in at the moment. He needed to talk to Lisa. Although he'd only received the spotlight because Sebastian didn't show, he needed to thank her for the opportunity.

He rose from his table and scoured the crowd for her. She smiled and accepted congratulatory wishes on her engagement and served as the perfect event host.

"Excuse me. Can I steal her away for a minute?" he said to a group of readers she stood among and guided her away from the tents and through the crushed gravel to her parked car.

"What's up, babe?" she asked sweetly.

"I can't tell you how much this moment means to me. Although it came about as a result of Sebastian not being here, I still want to thank you for your support."

"You're welcome. I'm glad it worked out this way. You deserve to have this opportunity to celebrate your accomplishment."

They shared a lengthy embrace. The sweet sounds of the jazz saxophonist Anthony Rejiv could still be heard in the distance.

Jayden released her. There was enough heat coming from the afternoon sun. Lisa close to him only increased his temperature. He gave her a quick peck on her lips. "There's something else I wanted to show you."

"What's that?"

Jayden unlocked her trunk. He still held on to her keys since he'd removed the banner earlier.

"Check your trunk."

She frowned. "What? The mess that's inside or the fact that you cleaned it again?"

Jayden reached inside and handed her a copy of his book, *At Last.*

"I already have a copy."

"Open it to the title page and read it."

She huffed. "To Lisa. I dedicate this book to you as you are my inspiration and the reason I can write about love. Before I even understood my feelings for you, I was in love—completely enamored with you. For the rest of my days, I will be *Just In Love* with you. This is dated three months ago," she said with a hint of awe in her choked voice. Tears glistened her eyes.

Jayden nodded. "Yeah. You've been riding around with your autographed copy for that long. True, I could have handed it to you, but a part of me hoped you'd find it. The idea sounded interesting at the time."

She half-chuckled and swatted him with the book. "You're so wrong for this, knowing that it's a mess back here."

"That's what kind of makes it funny." He pulled her into his embrace. "You know I love you, woman. Thanks for adding joy to this moment."

She pulled away, but not out of his arms, and peered up at him. "So, does this mean we get another story?"

Jayden laughed. "Not you, too."

"Hey, we readers want to know."

He shrugged and pulled her back into his embrace. "I'm not sure yet. Maybe at some point, but I have to focus on a few other things right now—this new business and my new wife."

"The future wife in me understands, but the reader in me says to just get it done."

Jayden tossed his head back and released a hearty laugh. "Of course."

Lisa brushed his jawline with her fingertip. "I'm proud of you, Jay. No one is more proud of you than me. I love you."

He wrote a seventy-thousand-word book, but could not adequately express how those three words from her lips made him feel.

"Want to hear some more good news?"

He nodded.

"We've raised the other half of the money to pay the down payment for the tax debt."

"I had no doubt. Congrats, babe."

They sealed their conversation with one last kiss before returning to the tent. Monday morning, they'd go to the tax office and pay the entire bill, because Jayden promised to pay the balance. Now they could move on with their lives and fully enjoy the present while preparing for their future together—with nothing else in their way.

Chapter Twenty-six

Between the Lines didn't operate on Sundays—usually. But today was different. And while she didn't expect many customers because they were normally closed, she still changed the sign from closed to open and posted her impromptu operating hours on social media. Lisa was excited about the new beginning. She had the money for the taxes and was now prepared for a fresh start. To commemorate the new, she made a slight change to name of the bookstore—Between the Pages—a nod to new ownership and new beginnings.

She busied herself organizing display shelves for new releases until the door chimed. The steady, determined steps reached her ears before she saw the person. Her belly fluttered like the pages in a book when she saw him. And not in a good way.

Melvin.

He had a smirk on his face that told her she wouldn't like what he was about to say or do. Melvin glanced around the store. "Saw your little post on social media about you being open today so decided to pay you a visit. Love what you've done around here.

Sofas are a nice touch." He shrugged. "Just feels new. Too bad this won't last because I paid the taxes, so the building is mine."

He handed her an envelope, spun on his heels, and retreated out the door.

She ripped open the envelope, containing a "thank you for your payment letter" and receipt. Sure enough, he'd paid the taxes. But that didn't mean anything, did it? Her hands trembled as she folded the paper. With wobbly legs, she hobbled to the checkout counter and rested her forehead against it.

Deep breaths. Slow and forced releases of air pushed through her lips.

How dare he attempt to bully her and take her store.

Her store.

Lisa gathered her composure, called Jayden, and relayed to him the events concerning Melvin.

"Nothing sounds right about any of this. I'm pretty sure there are rules in Texas that prevent him from owning the store simply because he paid the taxes. If anything, he did you a favor and corrected a wrong. Try not to stress about this. I'll take care of it."

She found solace in Jayden's promise to handle the situation, but she'd be lying if she said she wouldn't worry. Melvin had practically kicked her off cloud nine with his tax receipt and announcement.

"Okay. What do you need me to do?"

"As hard as it may be, right now, nothing. Give me a day or two to handle this."

She nodded her agreement, not that he could see her. "Thanks, babe. I'll try not to worry and will give my attention to these boxes of books that need to be organized and shelved."

"Good. Call me if you need me."

"I will. Love you. Bye."

On her knees in front of the romance section, she twisted the symbol of love and promise of forever hugging her left ring finger. In the deep recesses of her mind, she trusted Jayden, but not taking any action was the hardest thing in the world right now. She had to focus on the books before her—the future once Melvin was completely out of her family's life—or her upcoming nuptials. Anything to not get stuck in a mental rut.

An hour or so had passed when the door chimes jingled. She couldn't be sure about the time because she'd allowed herself to be consumed with her task of tagging, scanning, and shelving books. Lisa pushed herself up from the floor and walked to the front of the store to greet the person who had entered—as long as the person wasn't Melvin. Her belly recoiled at the thought. She'd had enough of him.

Ginger came inside, followed by a young woman and her boyfriend, Lisa assumed. She had a possessive grip on the guy's bicep as they walked through the door, her smile bright.

"I saw your post on social media," the young woman said. She dropped her hand from around the guy and rubbed her hands together. "I'm glad you're open because I missed the event yesterday and was hoping to grab a few books by the local authors you hosted."

"Welcome. I'm usually not opened on Sundays, but had a few things to take care of. Let me show you to our local authors section." She called over her shoulder to Ginger, "I'll be with you in a moment, Gin."

She waved her off and sat on the sofa. "Take your time. I'll be here."

Lisa pushed all of the crazy to the back of her mind and focused on the good, her blessings—family, friends, and a business she adored. She tended to her customer and chatted with her about yesterday's event while ringing up her purchase—of course, a copy of Justin Love's book, along with five books by local authors. With promises to return again and bring friends, the young woman, who introduced herself as Rylie, left with her boyfriend holding her bag.

"What's up, Gin? I'm surprised to see you here today."

"You shouldn't be surprised, not one bit. We were supposed to go out for brunch today. When you didn't answer my calls, I had to track your location. It's not like you to skip out on brunch." Ginger patted the sofa cushion.

"I'm so sorry. We were supposed to go out today, and it was my idea. I completely forgot."

Lisa plopped down on the sofa with her arms spread wide and released a hard breath. With one eyebrow lifted, she glanced over at Ginger. "I'm freaking out about the tax situation again."

Her skin crawled every time she replayed Melvin's words in her mind. Common sense would say to stop doing so, but she couldn't help it.

Ginger nodded. "Brock told me about Melvin's shenanigans. I understand how his li'l stunt may have made you feel, but make no mistake, Jayden and Brock are going to handle this."

Lisa frowned. "Brock?"

"Yep. Jayden called Brock after he talked with you. Sidebar: It's nice seeing them work together. This partnership is good for them," she gushed. "Anyway, Jayden doesn't think this is the first time the old guy has pulled something like this, so they're going to bring him down. Jayden, of course, is handling the tax part, and Brock is researching his past business dealings. They're bringing a whole case against him. I don't think you should worry."

A wave of relief washed over her after hearing Ginger's summation of things.

"So, were you on the phone as well or…?"

Ginger chuckled and readjusted herself on the sofa so that she faced Lisa with one leg tucked under her bottom. "Nope, but I may as well have been. They were discussing my friend's business, how could I not ear hustle? I had to take what I could get because Brock didn't want to share any details with me—said he didn't want me to worry or get facts twisted and have you worrying. I imagine this situation will be cleared up soon. They talked twice before I left to come see you."

Jayden moved fast, and she appreciated that. Ginger's report sent a stream of relief coursing through her veins. She ran her palms along her thighs. "Honestly, that makes me feel a lot better. Thanks for ear hustling."

They shared a laugh, which was interrupted by the door chimes. Lisa got up to tend to her customer, a young woman she remembered from yesterday's grand reopening. She'd stopped by to purchase another copy of Justin Love's book for a friend, along with two copies of local authors books that she'd missed yesterday. Lisa rejoined Ginger on the sofa when she left.

"Okay, so now can we talk about the juicy stuff?"

Lisa chuckled. "You are the most. What juicy stuff?"

"Your wedding and the fact that your fiancé is *the* Justin Love.*"*

"Crazy, right? He told me before he proposed. I can't believe he went through the entire publishing process alone. But, things worked out in his favor when Sebastian canceled."

Ginger twisted her lips and tapped her chin. "I wonder if he pulled a Malaki and did something to prevent Sebastian from coming."

"Oh goodness. Like what?"

"I don't know. Reached out to Sebastian and told him the event was canceled and then created an email address posing as Sebastian to cancel with you. You had to know Jayden was jealous about how excited you were when Sebastian agreed to sign at the re-grand opening."

Lisa cackled. "I don't think Jayden would go that far. That is a bit much."

"I guess my imagination can get a little wild. Ignore me." Ginger waved off her comment. "But how does it feel to be engaged to the Justin Love—the man who wrote a book about his love for you? That's next level."

"First of all, he never said the book was about his feelings for me. And secondly, he's still Jayden to me. But I'm proud that he stepped out and did the one thing he'd always wanted to do. Just wish he would have allowed me to part of his journey."

"Literally, you were, Jasmine." Ginger leaned in and raised her voice a bit to emphasize the idea that Lisa inspired the character. Well, in Ginger's mind, she was the character.

"Whatever."

"If we can't admit that, at least we can agree on two things."

"What's that?"

"One, Jayden is an amazing writer. And two, we have a wedding to plan." Ginger showed all her teeth and clapped.

Lisa whipped out her phone. "Wanna see some of my dress options?"

Ginger slid closer to her. "You know you didn't even need to ask. I guess we can call Judy from the bridal shop to make an appointment for your dress fitting and to let her know that Jayden is off limits."

Lisa chuckled at the memory of Judy asking if she could give Jayden a call since Lisa didn't want him. Not in this life or the next would she have allowed that to happen. While Ginger's intent may have been to come over to check in on her, she'd given her so much more.

Hope.

One of her favorite scriptures came to mind—Romans 8:28 which says, *And we know that in all things God works for the good of those who love Him, who have been called according to His purpose.*

And if she didn't believe anything else, she believed that she'd been called to run Between the Pages—that the bookstore would be a beacon of light in Katy, Texas, filled with books that uplifted His people and gave them hope.

∞

Although Jayden was settled in his spirit about the pending conversation with his mentor, Joe, that didn't make what he had to say any easier. His path forward did not include the firm, Dallas & Smith, LLP, and he was okay with that. What bothered him was how Joe would take the news, though he sensed Joe knew this talk was coming, given Jayden had hesitated to sign the partnership agreement. This was the path that they'd discussed during his and Jayden's first meeting more than seventeen years ago. Receiving those papers should have been a moment of celebration, which it was, but Jayden couldn't have imagined just what he'd be celebrating—his exit.

Jayden made reservations for him and Joe at McCormick & Schmick's. Before he formally declined the partnership offer, he wanted Joe to be the first to know. While he waited for him to arrive, Jayden perused the lunch menu. The waitress had already brought two glasses of water to the table. He sipped from his glass, draining it half-empty in the first two minutes.

"Sorry I'm late. My meeting with Mitch ran long."

Jayden stood to greet him and gave his hand a firm shake. "No worries."

Joe unbuttoned his suit jacket and joined him at the table for two. He eyed Jayden for a moment. "Time sure does fly, doesn't it? I don't know if you recall, but I brought you here for lunch on your first day—our first official mentor-mentee meeting."

Jayden released a soft chuckle. The memory flooded his mind. Joe had affirmed that every conversation they had would be confidential and that he'd do everything within his power to encourage him, support him, and root for his success. He remained true to his word, and because of that, he'd become more than a mentor, but a friend.

"I do remember. We both had the steak for lunch."

Joe leaned forward and rested his linked fingers on the table. "Right. And do you remember what I shared with you that day?"

Jayden mirrored his movement. "I've never forgotten."

"So, you do know that you don't have to prep me with your goodbye speech, right?"

The waitress stopped by to take their orders, giving Jayden a moment to collect his thoughts. As Joe mentioned, he had prepared a bit of a farewell speech, at least where his position at the firm was concerned. The two of them ordered steaks with vegetables, and Jayden waited for the waitress to leave their table before he addressed his mentor.

"I wouldn't call it a goodbye speech."

"You may not, but I would. When you hesitated to accept the position you've been working toward your entire career here, I knew you'd turn it down. And that's your prerogative. Never allow anyone to make you feel bad or uncomfortable about your choices."

While Jayden had yet to confirm, he said, "Yeah, I know, but I'm sure the partners and a few others will think I'm crazy for walking away from this opportunity."

"And let them think and feel how they want. Only you know what's right for you. Besides, you must live according to your own convictions, not anyone else's. While I was hoping to call you friend and partner, congratulations on making the tough choice. I'm glad you've come to terms with your way forward. You look lighter."

Jayden released a breath of relief. The anchored weight had been lifted from his chest. "Thanks."

"Now that we've gotten that out of the way, I still want to hear the farewell speech."

They shared a laugh.

"If I've never said it before now, know that I appreciate you and everything you've done for me over the years. I couldn't have asked for a better mentor."

Joe lifted his glass of water in salute. "Hear! Hear! You're one hardworking young man. It has been my honor to walk alongside you in your journey, Jayden."

They clinked glasses.

"So, what's next for you?"

He replaced his glass on the table. "Joining a friend and his family to start a new partnership."

Joe squinted and wagged his finger. "Wait. Don't tell me." He bucked his eyes when it came to him. "Pearson?"

"Yes. The partnership gives me the opportunity to create a legacy, more autonomy of my schedule, and time with my bride."

Joe lifted his glass again. "Congratulations are in order. I hope I'm still invited to the wedding."

Jayden clinked his glass. "Of course."

"Not to take away from your moment, but I have a bit of news of my own to share."

He gave Jayden a look, which prompted him to guess before Joe continued.

"You're retiring?"

Joe nodded. A huge smile spread across his face. Come to think of it, he appeared lighter these days himself.

"Congratulations, man. Well deserved. When is your last day?"

"Two weeks. Enough time to transfer my clients and prep the partner and senior managers taking over in my stead. Pam has already booked a cruise for the day following my retirement, so there's no backing out now."

They shared a laugh.

"Oh, sounds like she's been waiting for this day. I'm happy for you two."

"You better believe it."

The server approached their table with their entrees. Jayden blessed the food and took a bite. "Just as good as it was seventeen years ago."

Joe lifted his fork. "Agreed."

Their extended lunch lasted two hours as they reminisced over the past seventeen years.

Back in the office, Jayden whispered a prayer before he emailed his formal rejection and resignation. His spirit and conscience were settled within him. Fifteen minutes later, he received the three-year non-compete agreement in his inbox. That was fast—almost as if they were waiting for his resignation. He signed without hesitation.

Three taps on his open office door drew his attention. Ephraim, one of his associates, stood there with sagging shoulders and crinkled eyebrows, clearly upset or confused about something.

"Come on in."

He came in and took the seat across from Jayden's desk. "Mr. Reynolds, you're leaving?"

Word traveled fast. With Ephraim being one of the best associates on his team, he would have preferred to talk to him personally before he found out through someone else.

"Yes, I am. I'm building a new partnership with a friend of mine." That was all he was at liberty to say. He didn't want anyone to think his plan was to poach the firm for employees.

"Oh. Well, it was nice working with you. Can we stay in touch?"

"Sure." Jayden took a business card from the holder near his computer, wrote his personal email address and phone number on it, and slid the card across the desk. "I'll still be around town. Contact me anytime."

Ephraim scooped the card off the desk. He looked at the contents before shoving the card into his wallet. "Take care of yourself. I need to get back to work."

Three more associates stopped by his office in the same manner. For a moment, Jayden felt a tinge of emotion swell in his chest. He would miss his coworkers, but the time had come for him to take his life and career in a different direction.

Chapter Twenty-seven

Lisa flipped the sign from open to closed and paced in front of the door for ten minutes while she waited for Jayden and Brock to arrive with news of her tax situation with Melvin. She'd tried her hardest to get Jayden to just tell her everything over the phone, but he refused, stating that the discussion would be best held in person with the information both he and Brock had gathered. *Ugh.* She hated it when he made her wait.

With each slow step across the floor, she heard a small creak underfoot. Where had that noise been all this time? Perhaps it was always there, but now it was the only thing that drew her attention other than watching the clock that hung above the door frame.

The door chime signaled Jayden's entrance. Lisa spun on her heels and threw herself into his arms. She hugged him tight, receiving the security and warmth his arms tended to provide in every moment.

She kissed his lips and pulled out of his embrace. "Hey. Good to see you."

"With a greeting like that, it's good to be seen." He tugged her back in his arms and planted a firm kiss on her lips—a kiss so firm that she almost forgot the reason he showed up—before he released her.

Instinctively, her fingers touched her lips. Dang. Where had this man been all her adult life with his soul-snatching kisses?

Seconds later, Brock entered. Good. Now she could redirect her thoughts to the matter at hand. He greeted Jayden with a fist bump and gave her a hug. "Hey, Lisa. Ready to get started?"

She cocked her head to one side with a lifted eyebrow. "I think we all know the answer to that. C'mon. Let's sit."

She and Jayden sat on the orange sofa while Brock sat in one of the adjacent orange chairs. He lifted his satchel over his shoulder and removed his laptop. Jayden had done the same—the two of them looking like men on a mission, which she could appreciate when it came to Between the Pages.

"Okay, so what do we have?" Lisa asked.

Jayden spoke first. "As I suspected, but just needed to confirm, Melvin cannot assume ownership of the bookstore just because he paid the delinquent taxes. In Texas, he has to have a clear title—"

"Which he does not have," Lisa added.

"Right."

"So the taxes are now paid. What does that mean for me and the store?"

"In the eyes of Fort Bend County, all that matters is that the taxes were paid. And although there was a tax lien on the property,

Texas does not recognize tax lien certificates. There is nothing he can do. So basically, he did you a favor."

Lisa clutched her chest and breathed a sigh of relief. "Oh, good."

"However, we have to make sure that he doesn't try anything underhanded," Jayden added.

Brock jumped in. "Right. He's attempted to do this to other small businesses before. You'd think he'd know by now that this foolishness won't fly. His endgame is to assume ownership and sell to an investor for a profit. We're going to make sure he doesn't try this mess again by filing a lawsuit against him on your behalf for stealing the funds and attempting to steal your property."

Lisa just wanted this entire dilemma behind her. "Is going through the motions of a lawsuit worth it?"

"To stop him from trying this crap again? Yes."

"And to get you punitive damages as well," Jayden added. "We're not going to let him get away with this."

Lisa released another heavy breath, one that pushed her worries away. This felt like the end of her nightmare. "Okay, then. So tell me what you need from me."

"We've got everything we need. Sitting down with you to explain things was your fiancé's idea. I'll file the suit first thing tomorrow and have him served."

She threw herself into Jayden's arms once more. "Thanks so much for everything. I love you, Babe. This whole deal has been driving me crazy."

Brock cleared his throat. Lisa laughed and pulled herself away from Jayden.

"I'm not expecting a declaration of love, but a thank you would be all good."

"C'mon here, dude. I appreciate you as well." She hugged Brock. "I can agree with Ginger. The two of you make a great team, and I'm looking forward to how far this Pearson & Reynolds partnership will go."

"You're welcome, Lisa. We've got your back." He fist bumped Jayden. "Later, man. I need to get home to my wife."

The door chimes signaled Brock's exit, and Lisa took the opportunity to snuggle into Jayden's waiting arms again. "Have I ever told you how amazing you are?"

He tilted his chin and looked toward the ceiling. "Nope. Never. But, that's not something I need to hear. The only words I'm interested in are *I do*. So, can we decide on a date?"

"Nothing would make me happier."

Jayden lifted her chin with his forefinger. His lips descended onto hers, forever linking their hearts and souls. Her heart seized in her chest while her belly danced a rhythm that matched her racing pulse. The whirlwind of emotions she experienced from one simple action was beyond her. This moment had to be akin to what the characters in her favorite novels described. With her best friend and love of her life, she now got to live her own happily ever after.

Epilogue

Patience was a virtue Lisa lacked. At least twenty times over the last six months, she'd suggested that she and Jayden forget about the whole destination-wedding ordeal and stand before the justice of the peace. However, he'd reminded her that they'd waited for more than forty years to officially spend the rest of their lives together, so a few short months would be nothing in comparison.

She disagreed.

Especially after the trips to bridal shops to find the perfect dress. The endless search online for the perfect hairstyle. Their arguments—well, disagreements—over destinations. Nassau, Bahamas; Montego Bay, Jamaica; Los Cabos, Mexico; or Cancun, Mexico.

Cancun won.

Their day had finally come. As much as she wanted and should have been mentally present, focusing on this moment, Lisa couldn't help but reminisce about how far they'd come and how much their lives had changed when her mom transferred ownership of the bookstore to her. That event seemed to have unlocked something between her and her husband-to-be. But, the more she thought about their relationship, the more she'd come to terms with the truth: She'd been in love with Jayden for years, and she never could have married anyone else. It was crazy to think about how much longer they'd be dancing around each other if he'd never said anything. Because she would have allowed fear or the crutch of him being her friend to stand in the way of her saying anything to him.

Ginger's cold hands gripped her shoulders, snapping her out of her reverie. "You ready?" Bright eyes and a huge grin set her already glowing face. At least that was the term older women used to describe pregnant women. And her seven-week-pregnant friend fit the bill.

"Of course I am."

Giddy, Ginger did a little jig. "I'm so happy for you, friend. You and Jayden deserve each other." She wrapped her arms around Lisa's bare shoulders, exposed by her strapless wedding dress.

"Thanks, Gin. Honey, I'm just glad the day is finally here. Seems like it took forever. But there's also a part of me that can't believe this is really happening."

Ginger air-kissed her cheek. "Well, believe it, and there's no backing out now." She glanced down at her small mound. "You have to catch up."

The friends shared a laugh as Ginger stepped out of the way, and Mom and Momma Wanda stood before her.

"I am so proud of you and the woman you've become. I have no doubt that God has blessed you and Jayden's union," Mom said and wrapped her in a tight squeeze. "No matter what, I'm still your mom and here for you whenever you need me." Lisa caught the flinch in Mom's jaw. No doubt, she held back tears.

Momma Wanda waved praise hands in the air and shuffled to the right and the left in a little dance. "Hallelujah to the Lord on High! There were times that I didn't think I'd live to see this day."

All four ladies burst into laughter.

"I know I joke around a lot, but life should be fun. No need to be so serious all the doggone time. Here's my advice: When things get tough between you and my son, remember the good times. Remember God's promises, and seek Him in all things."

"That's right, dear. God is the light that will guide you through. Never forget that," Mom added.

"I appreciate you all and the support you've given us over the past few months. If I haven't said so before now, let me go on record to say thank you."

"We love you, Lisa, and want nothing but the best for you and Jayden," Ginger said.

The four of them joined hands and stood in a circle while Mom, Ginger, and Momma Wanda prayed over her and spoke blessings into her life and her womb. Seconds later, the wedding coordinator, Sasha, entered the room. Her floor-length orange wrap dress matched her lipstick and the flower pinned in her hair.

"How's my bride?" she asked in a lovely Spanish accent.

"Great. Ready to get this show on the road."

"Good. Good. That's what I like to hear." Standing about two inches taller, she circled Lisa before adding, "You look beautiful, *señiorita*. Let's get you married."

Sasha ushered Ginger and the mothers of the bride and groom out of the holding room and spoke into her walkie-talkie. "We have the ladies on the move."

Ten minutes later, Sasha gave the prompt for Lisa to ready herself to leave the holding room. Outside the door, stood her father waiting to escort her down the aisle. One thing she was grateful for was that God allowed him to live long enough to experience this moment with her. His health challenges over the past few years had scared Lisa, but today was a happy occasion. He'd made it.

Dad lifted his arm. "Ready, my dear?"

Lisa hooked her arm into his. "I am."

Her dress dragged behind her onto the runner and partly in the sand. A myriad of emotions plowed through her mind, but the overwhelming feeling above all was happiness. She couldn't control the sides of her mouth when she locked eyes with Jayden standing next to the preacher.

Finally.

Their moment.

"You know, I always had a feeling you two would end up together."

Lisa squinted and looked up at her father. "Really?"

He nodded. "Yeah. If I have to give you away to anyone, I'm glad that it's him. He has always adored you." He leaned in and kissed her forehead at the front of the aisle before the preacher and wedding party.

"Who gives this woman to this man?"

Mom stood. Together, she and Dad said, "We do."

Dad placed Lisa's hand in Jayden's. "She's the only daughter I have. I'm counting on you to take care of her."

"You have my word, sir."

Together, Lisa and Jayden stood before the preacher with whispers of *I love you* during the ceremony. She locked eyes with the man she'd spend her forever with—eyes she'd stared into on thousands of occasions, but nothing could have prepared her for this moment. The moment that confirmed that whatever lay ahead of them—relationship, careers, or otherwise—they could overcome the obstacles together. And together sounded pretty good—she wouldn't have it any other way.

∞

"You may kiss your wife."

Jayden had told himself that when this moment in the ceremony came, he wouldn't go overboard.

He lied to himself.

Lisa was now his wife, and whoever didn't want to witness the moment could close their eyes. The second his lips touched hers, he couldn't help himself—or at least he didn't want to. What started out as a gentle peck grew into a passionate, lingering kiss that lasted far longer than he'd witnessed at any wedding ceremony he attended. And he probably wouldn't have stopped kissing her if the preacher didn't clear his throat. He wanted to whisk her back into their suite and catch up with the guests later, but he showed restraint he didn't think he had.

"God knows I love you with everything in me," he said, breathless when he broke the kiss.

"And I love you. Can't wait to show you how much later."

"Don't tempt me."

The preacher cleared his throat again, and they all laughed.

"I present to you, for the first time in eternity, Mr. and Mrs. Jayden Reynolds."

Jayden and Lisa waltzed down the aisle, hand-in-hand, posing for pictures here and there. The wedding guests sailed ahead of them to a private island for the reception while they stayed behind to take professional wedding photos with the sunset as the backdrop.

After the last photo, he held her close and kissed her again. "Mrs. Lisa Reynolds. I love the sound of that."

"It does have a nice ring to it, doesn't it? You've made me the happiest woman alive today."

"We've added to each other's happiness. I can't wait to show you over and over and over…" He nuzzled her neck.

"We could just skip the reception. Our guests will understand."

Jayden threw his head back and laughed. "Don't tempt me because I would carry you straight to our room right now. Say the word. You know I'd do anything for you."

Her face grew serious. She circled her hand behind his neck and pulled him close, massaging his lips with her own. "I know. Just another reason why I love you."

He'd just proven he'd do anything for her when he went after Melvin for trying to take her bookstore. After the lawsuit Pearson & Reynolds filed against him, they sought and retrieved punitive damages for fifty thousand dollars. The judge also ordered Melvin to five years of community service. In Jayden's eyes, a light sentence. Melvin deserved jail time, but the decision wasn't his to make. Ultimately, what mattered was Lisa's contentment.

"I love you, too, but now is not the time for sweet talk. You're seconds away from missing your wedding reception. If we don't leave now, we aren't going."

Lisa released a hearty chuckle. "Yeah, you're probably right."

Although it took him years to conjure the courage to tell Lisa how he felt about her, he wouldn't change anything about their journey. He'd loved her and she'd loved him for a long time, they'd seen each other at their highest and lowest, and they'd been the constant in each other's lives. The best part about waiting was that they had a lot of making up to do—and that part he couldn't wait to get to.

###

Dear reader,

What did you think of Lisa and Jayden's journey? This was a fun story for me to write. My favorite character was Jayden's mom, Wanda Reynolds, because she often brought humor to the story. I hope she put a smile on your face while reading.

Lisa and Jayden had difficulty seeing what was right in front of them all along—each other. As a person who enjoys romance novels, I'm happy she got to experience her own love story.

I am often asked if there are parts of me in my stories. For this one, the answer is yes. I'm a little bit of Jayden and a little bit of Lisa. You may not know this, but I am a CPA and like Jayden, worked in public accounting right out of grad school. According to my word weavers group, we don't often see people who enjoy math and reading, but I'm one of them.

One of my favorite things about both Lisa and Jayden was their drive to go after what they wanted in their careers. If you're struggling about your next steps whether in a relationship or career, my encouragement to you is this: Have a little faith. Take the step. The answer is always no if you don't move forward. And above all else, trust God in the process.

I hope you enjoyed *Love Between The Pages*. Please take a moment to let me know what you think by leaving a review on Amazon/Goodreads/Bookbub.

Until next time,

Natasha

About the Author

Natasha fell in love with love around the age of twelve because of artists like Babyface, Boys II Men, Whitney Houston, and New Edition. Around sixteen when her mother purchased a romance novel and left it lying around the house untouched, Natasha read it and a spark for the written word had been ignited.

Natasha believes that writing is one of her purposes and contributions to the world. She feels accomplished when she can get a few words written and like blah when life gets in the way. Her hope is that at the end of every novel, readers will feel like they've been wrapped in a cozy blanket with a mug of their favorite coffee/tea/warm drink.

When she isn't reading or writing, she is likely working out or watching movies with her family. Natasha resides in Richmond, TX with her husband, Eddie Frazier, Jr. and their three children, Eden, Ethan, and Emilyn. Her greatest joy and commitment is to her family who she hopes to inspire above all else. One of her many mottos in life is: Faith removes limitations. Natasha and her family attend Parkway Fellowship in Richmond, TX, where she volunteers as an Usher. Natasha is also a member of the Houston Area Alumni Chapter of Jackson State University and Alpha Kappa Alpha Sorority, Inc.

Connect with Natasha online:

Bookbub @NatashaDFrazier

Instagram @author_natashafrazier

Twitter or X @author_natashaf

TikTok @author_natashafrazier

Facebook @craves.2012

Website: www.natashafrazier.com

Also by Natasha D. Frazier

Devotionals

The Life Your Spirit Craves

Not Without You

Not Without You Prayer Journal

The Life Your Spirit Craves for Mommies

Pursuit

Fiction

Love, Lies & Consequences

Through Thick & Thin: Love, Lies & Consequences Book 2

Shattered Vows: Love, Lies & Consequences Book 3

Out of the Shadows: Love, Lies & Consequences Book 4

Kairos: The Perfect Time for Love

Fate (The Perfect Time for Love series)

With Every Breath (The McCall Family Series, book 1)

With Every Step (The McCall Family Series, book 2)

With Every Moment (The McCall Family Series, book 3)

The Reunion (Langston Sisters, book1)

The Wrong Seat (Langston Sisters, book 2)

The Missing Link (Langston Sisters, book 3)

Batch of Love

Non-Fiction
How Long Are You Going to Wait?